Someone
for Me

A **SOMEONE TO LOVE** BOOK

Someone for Me

ADDISON MOORE

SKYSCAPE

SKYSCAPE

Text copyright © 2014 Addison Moore

Published by Skyscape, New York

www.apub.com

Amazon, the Amazon logo, and Skyscape are trademarks of Amazon.com, Inc., or its affiliates.

ISBN-13: 9781477847121
ISBN-10: 147784712X

Book design by Girl Friday Productions

Library of Congress Cataloging-in-Publication Data available upon request.
Printed in the United States of America

Also by Addison Moore

New Adult Romance:

Someone to Love (Someone to Love Book 1)
Someone Like You (Someone to Love Book 2)
3:AM Kisses (3:AM Kisses Book 1)
Winter Kisses (3:AM Kisses Book 2)
Sugar Kisses (3:AM Kisses Book 3)
Beautiful Oblivion
The Solitude of Passion
Perfect Love (Celestra Short)

Young Adult Romance:

Ethereal (Celestra Series Book 1)
Tremble (Celestra Series Book 2)
Burn (Celestra Series Book 3)
Wicked (Celestra Series Book 4)
Vex (Celestra Series Book 5)
Expel (Celestra Series Book 6)
Toxic Part One (Celestra Series Book 7)
Toxic Part Two (Celestra Series Book 7.5)
Elysian (Celestra Series Book 8)
Ephemeral (The Countenance Trilogy Book 1)
Evanescent (The Countenance Trilogy Book 2)
Entropy (The Countenance Trilogy Book 3)
Ethereal Knights (Celestra Knights)

PROLOGUE

Kendall

They say the day you fall in love is the most magical day of your life. They say that moment sears itself over your soul for eternity. You never forget true love's first kiss; it plays again in your heart forever.

For me true love's kiss came on a snowy winter morning. We wrote forever over our hearts with our lips. It was a miracle. It was magic.

And now, here we are just about a year later, already poised to move on to the next big step in our relationship and seal our fate as husband and wife. But are we really ready? Will we ever be?

The door rattles, and I snap up the cuffs and paddle and spin around to find Cruise standing there with not a stitch of clothing on—holding out a round, gloriously *huge* cake.

"For the love of all things chocolate." My mouth falls open, and I don't know what to drool at first.

He steps in and shuts the door, glancing behind me at the plethora of kinky equipment displayed, and—swear to God—Cruise Elton just *blushed*. He sets down the cake on the nightstand and presses his hands together like he's about to get to work.

"Now"—Cruise snatches the blackout blindfold and quickly straps it over my eyes—"about cheating on those exams." He pulls me into his bare chest and rides his lips slowly over my neck. "How far are you willing to go with this?"

I slip the blindfold up an inch and inspect him for a moment. "All the way."

And we do.

1

OUT OF THE CLOSET

Kendall

Bedroom or bathroom?" Cruise asks with his lids hooded low, his enthusiasm for all things coital tucked hard against my thigh. He's holding back that wicked grin he's been liberal with all night, while an entire swarm of bodies swim around us.

I glance over at Lauren and Ally cackling away on the sofa. Lauren thought it would be a great idea to throw Morgan and Ally a surprise housewarming party at their new apartment, only Morgan wasn't that impressed once dozens of people flooded his living room while he was still in his boxers. My brother never was an exhibitionist.

"Bedroom or bathroom? I don't know." I tighten my arms around my fiancé's waist. Cruise Elton is a god in training. No, wait—he's already a god who is large and in charge of his domain. By *domain* I don't just mean our bedroom, as most of our private exchanges take place outside of those four walls. And by *large* I mean, well, you know what I mean.

He has his dress shirt on and a slick tie that is the exact robin's-egg blue of his eyes. Of course he's wearing jeans, because he likes to keep his sense of style down to earth. This is pretty much his everyday attire now that he's running his mother's bed-and-breakfast full-time. She's out of town taking care of her own bedridden mother, so Cruise is flying solo

"Sounds like you need a little convincing." Cruise dips his mouth over my neck and gives a searing kiss that trails all the way to the hollow spot just above my chest. I let out a guttural moan, perhaps a little too enthusiastic for a public gathering, but the room is buzzing with noise, and I doubt anyone really cares about our quasi-carnal exchange.

"Hey, cool it, would you?" a male voice barks out.

My eyes spring open to find my brother glaring at the two of us. His black hair and cobalt-blue eyes are twins to mine, but I'd bet good money his dimples are a million times more adorable than the ones digging into my cheeks right now. Needless to say, I love my big bro to infinity and back. That's how we used to say it when we were kids. We practically raised each other once our father ran out on us. Our poor mother was too busy trying to find a replacement daddy, so we were all we had.

"Come here." I slip out of Cruise's grasp and pull Morgan into a nice tight hug. "I'm so proud of you." Morgan made Garrison University's baseball team because he's the best damn college player in the country.

"Would you stop with that?" His cheeks darken a shade. "I know you're proud. And I'm proud of *you*, too." He gives my shoulders a quick squeeze. "Don't be a fool, stay in school, and all that cool stuff."

"You ready for your first day tomorrow?" I ask while he scans the crowd behind my shoulder. Morgan can't stand to be away from Ally for more than fifteen seconds, and I think it's the cutest thing on the planet. Cruise and I are sort of the same way, I realize, as he reels me back into him and secures his arms around me like a seat belt.

"I'm ready." Morgan scowls at some guy who's busy hauling in a keg. "But I'm not really used to hosting wild parties the night before a new semester starts. I want all these people out of here at a decent hour."

Considering it's almost midnight, I'd say he might need to redefine *decent*.

He nods to the couch where Ally and Lauren are motioning us over. Lauren's main squeeze, Cal, is there, trying to impress a group of jocks with his overblown muscles. He's tan to the point of shoe leather, and his veins bulge under his skin like an entire network of cables. He's beyond intimidating, until you get to know him. Cal owns the only gym in Carrington, and rumor has it he's redesigning the one at school.

"Great party," I say, landing on the couch next to Ally. Cruise takes a seat on the armrest and glides his hand over my shoulder.

"Thanks." Ally pushes into me playfully. "Speaking of parties, we were just talking about Lauren's next big bash—her megawedding."

Both Ally and I are bridesmaids in Lauren's wedding. Lauren's wedding is going to be so big it'll eat other, far more anemic weddings for breakfast. Namely mine.

"Oh no." Lauren wags a finger, emphatically. "I'm going the sweet and simple route. Once the guest list is manageable, everything else will just fall into place."

"So have you picked a date?" A burst of adrenaline fills me. I love talking all things matrimonial, especially since Cruise and I are getting hitched on Christmas Eve.

"New Year's Eve." Lauren flips back a curtain of dark hair. She has always reminded me a little of a sexy librarian, with her hair cut blunt just below the shoulders and the designer power suits she sports 24-7. Okay, well, an extremely wealthy librarian. It's no secret Lauren comes from money—lots and lots of money. In fact, I think if you inspected her DNA sequence carefully enough, you'd see the access code to her trust fund.

And then it hits me. "Wait"—I lean in because obviously I didn't hear her right the first time—"did you say New Year's Eve? As in *this* New Year's Eve?" That can't be. It would be just a week away from *my* wedding.

Lauren gives a casual nod, and my stomach does a cartwheel.

"She booked the chapel at Garrison!" Ally looks amazed by this seemingly trivial detail.

"Really?" My nerves bounce like a bucket of Ping-Pong balls that Lauren accidentally knocked over. The chapel at Garrison is the exact place where Cruise and I are planning to tie the knot. It's amazingly beautiful and Gothic, plus it just so happens to be located at the university we both attended when we met. I still do—he sort of got kicked out on his rear. "I was going to run by after class tomorrow and book the chapel myself."

Why do I suddenly feel as though Lauren is stealing the spotlight? I know for a fact she wouldn't think to do it on purpose, but honestly, I'm feeling a little uneasy about Lauren's wedding jockeying alongside mine—and moving faster at that.

Lauren and Ally glance at one another before breaking out into cackles.

"What's so funny?"

"*You.*" Lauren can barely get the word out. "You're joking, right?" She wipes the tears from the corners of her eyes.

"No, I'm not joking." I glance back at Cruise as if he could explain their strange behavior, but he offers nothing more than a simple, sexier-than-hell shrug.

"Kendall." Ally shakes her head at me like I'm a child. "The chapel is highly sought after. You need to book three full years in advance. Every Garrison graduate wants to get married in that hallowed hall."

"Three years?" A spike of alarm fills me. Usually I'm pretty easygoing, but when it comes to my wedding day everything has to be perfect, starting with that damn chapel. When I was young, there was an entire decade when my mother got hitched at least once every other year, and I swore up and down I would never do that. It's one and done, and for sure Cruise Elton is the one for me. I pull his arm tighter around my chest. "So how did you manage to get in?" I look at Lauren accusingly, because I have a feeling I know which financial district this conversation is headed toward.

"Let's just say it cost a small fortune for my father to get the other bride and groom to host their nuptials elsewhere." She chortles as if it was the greatest coup, probably because it was. "Anyway, it's water under the bridge, and the happy couple who generously gifted me their wedding slot now have their very first house."

Crap. First of all, my father hasn't seen me *in* a house for the past twenty years, let alone bought one for total strangers just to make my special day happen at the locale of my dreams. It's no wonder everyone envies Lauren. It's because they should.

"Well, I'll run by tomorrow and see what happens." I glance up at Cruise, unsure how much of that he actually heard, and judging by the bored look on his face, I'd guess none.

"Have you chosen a good couples counselor yet?" Lauren doesn't give me a chance to answer. "You should definitely try to see the one we are." She flicks her wrist in Cal's direction. "He specializes in curing with tears."

"Couples counseling?" It's probably another adorable quirk the wealthy like to engage in right after paying off other people's mortgages to procure their wedding venue. Besides, the last thing

I want to do is make Cruise cry. The entire idea sounds like an emotional pain in the ass.

Ally perks up and threads her fingers with Morgan's. "We should totally go, too! I bet we can iron out all kinds of crazy things we never even knew about."

"We should totally *not* go." Morgan gives Cal a hard look that says, *Call off your psycho girlfriend.* "The only thing we need to be ironing out is a budget."

"Yes," Cruise rumbles from behind me, and I jump a little because who the hell knew he was listening? Obviously, it was selective listening. "I one hundred percent agree. I've been trying to get Kenny to sit down with me these past few months and crunch some numbers. We're only harming ourselves by guessing how much we have to spend."

Gah! I practically shake him off my person. He *so* is paying attention to the conversation. I knew he wasn't avoiding *all* talk about the wedding. A *budget*, really? I hate that word and I hate focusing on the fact we're always broke. I'm well aware of how much money we don't have—thank you very much, Morgan. I shoot him the stink eye for landing me in this financial quicksand of a conversation.

Morgan nods to Cruise. "How do you control your spending if you don't know what's coming in and going out?" He looks to me. "Unless there's some magical ATM you're not telling him about, you'd better figure things out before it's too late."

Really? Does he honestly think I enjoy the fact I've landed in a pile of currency-deficient crap? Clearly he has no idea what a sparkling party conversation consists of. I'll have to school him later in the fine art of couples' gab that won't effectively end the relationship of every couple in a fifty-foot radius. Come to think of it, he's mighty lucky Ally isn't drilling him a new one right now.

Ally narrows her gaze at him with a look that could freeze his balls off.

Atta girl. God knows I can't control my brother.

"That's what I've been telling her." Cruise leans over and high-fives Morgan. That act alone sets off all kinds of sirens and alarms. Cruise and Morgan haven't exactly gotten along since my brother came into town earlier this summer. It would figure they would bond over the greatest division between our respective relationships, namely our serious lack of bank. Legal tender and I haven't traditionally gotten along. I don't really hate it—I just don't own enough of it for me to love.

"You know what I think I need?" I cut Cruise a sly look.

"A money management system?" He looks serious as shit, and this simultaneously alarms and pisses me off.

"No." My eyes saucer out, incredulous he would even go there. "I need to go to the *bathroom*." I bat my lashes in the event he needs a reminder of his earlier proposition.

"Go ahead." He pats me on the shoulder before leaning back toward Morgan. "I've got this software you should see. It actually categorizes spending into his and hers categories."

"And that's where you'll see where the real damage is being done." Morgan offers up a knuckle bump, and I roll my eyes at Ally. I hope she freezes him out for an entire week for even insinu ating that either of us was capable of single-handedly inducing a fiscal catastrophe.

Cruise nods at my brother's lunacy, obviously agreeing. I should probably freeze Cruise out for a week, but he's a tall, lean, mean sex machine and I'm pretty sure depriving Cruise of his testosterone release is illegal in at least forty-eight different states—Massachusetts being one of them. In fact, I'd better haul him off and have my way with him before I get arrested for the greatest felony of all, fornication deprivation. It's been at least six hours since our last meet and treat.

I give a firm tug to Cruise's tie. "Maybe *you* can show me where the bathroom is?"

"You know where it is." He looks genuinely puzzled for a moment before leaning farther toward my brother. Cruise opens his mouth and closes it. "On second thought, I'd better walk you there myself." He takes up my hand and glides me past the enthusiastic crowd engaging in a riotous game of beer pong at the kitchen table.

The warm scent of his cologne wafts over me like an erotic dream. Just holding his hand like this, feeling his hot skin next to mine, still has the power to make my panties fall off on command. I can't help but feel like the luckiest girl on the planet to have Cruise Elton by my side. Even though, in truth, he might have slept with half the coeds in this room. Cruise was quite the playboy before I stepped into the scene. But now, right after the girls drill into him with that lust-driven gaze, the next thing they do is look to me and frown because Cruise Elton is very much taken. He is taken as taken can get, and I've got his grandmother's wedding ring on my finger to prove it.

I lean in close until my lips brush against his cheek. "It took you a minute to catch on," I tease, licking the rim of his ear. I know for a fact that drives him insane, because he told me so himself— not to mention his back shudders and he rewards me with a groan each time I do it.

His eyes close for a moment as he takes in the sensation. "Took *you* a while to change the subject." His lips broaden.

"You!" I smack him across the chest and pull him in by the tie. Cruise knows I'm allergic to all things monetary. No wonder he rode that financial pony. He knew it'd be his quickest ticket off that sofa—and most likely his ticket away from all things bridal.

We head toward the bathroom and smack into a wall of bodies lined up clear to the kitchen.

I shake my head at Cruise and point over to the bedroom, where there's a note taped to the door.

"What's this?" Cruise leans in over my shoulder, and we inspect it together.

Keep the fuck out. I've got a baseball bat, and I'm not afraid to use it.

I sigh. "That's Morgy for you."

Cruise reaches past me, twists the knob, and whisks us inside, encapsulating us in the quiet reserve of Morgan and Ally's bedroom without regard to Morgan's quasi death threat.

A light floral scent mixed with Morgan's signature Polo permeates the air. The bed is neatly made with a pink sateen comforter, and a giant stuffed bear holding a heart sits crookedly in the center.

"Aw, isn't that cute?" I lean into Cruise while staring dreamily at the scruffy little beast.

"Yes." Cruise spins into me with a smile tugging at his lips. "I think it's adorable the way Ally chooses to emasculate your brother."

"That's not funny." I tickle his ribs. "You know my brother loves Ally just as much as you love *me*. And if I wanted a pink frilly comforter and a boatload of stuffed bears, I hardly believe you'd deny me."

He picks up my hand and presses it to his lips. "I'd give you every damn real or imagined animal on the planet if I could." That sexually deranged look I love takes over his features as he walks me back toward the mattress. His eyes gloss over with lust, and he's flirting with his lids hooded low.

"I know you would." I lean in and run my tongue along his jawline, enjoying the roughness of his five-o'clock shadow. "And that's why I know you'll understand I can't possibly do anything with you in this bedroom." I shrink a little when I say it.

"What?" His head inches back a notch, and his cutting good looks set my insides on fire.

"This is Morgan and Ally's special place." I wave my hand over the neatly made bed. "It's practically sacred."

Cruise lets out a low moan before glancing around.

"I got it." He presses out a dull grin and kisses both my eyelids in turn. "Close your eyes."

I do as I'm told, and Cruise leads me carefully by the shoulders less than ten feet away. I hear a door creak open. It smells like shoes and leather, and instinctually I know we're in the closet.

"Open," he says, shutting the door behind him.

The lights are on, and, as I suspected, we're surrounded by sneakers and heels, jackets, and . . . feathered boas?

"Kinky." I pull out a bright-red one, and a few loose feathers fly around the small walk-in. "You think this comes in my size?"

"There's only one way to find out." Cruise gently lifts the sundress right off my body, and I don't protest the effort. There's not a whole lot of protesting that goes on in our private lives. Mostly it's *Yes, oh God, yes, faster, right there!* followed by a cataclysmic scream on my part—and believe you me, neither one of us is about to complain.

Cruise ties me at the wrists with the overgrown string of feathers before securing my hands to a pole near the ceiling.

"Well, looky here"—he brushes his lips across mine, rough and determined, and a soft moan escapes my throat—"it does fit after all." He steps back and brazenly examines me, with that lewd grin I love twitching on his lips. I'm laid bare in my lace bra and matching panties, my spiked FMs that are just about to live up to their name.

I can totally tell he doesn't mind one bit that an alarming amount of our "budget" gets portioned out to Victoria's Secret.

"Taking off my clothes? Tying me up?" It comes from me breathy, and I know for a fact it drives Cruise insane when I do that. "Why, if I could, I'd take that belt right off your body and teach you a lesson, Professor Elton."

His lips twitch with a grin as he reaches down and unhooks his buckle. He pulls his belt off nice and slow, like a snake charmer luring a cobra out of a basket, all the while keeping those stealth-blue eyes locked on mine.

"Maybe I'll use this on *you*." He slips the length of it from his body and gently fashions it around my waist, pulling me in. "Look here, princess, I've got a really hard problem brewing in my Levis, and you're going to help me out with it whether you like it or not."

A string of giggles escape my throat. I lean in, aching for his lips to find mine, but Cruise tucks his head back a notch and winces as if he's about to say something.

The door crashes open, and Morgan wields a bat in our direction, with Ally looking terrified behind him.

I let out a scream and spin into Ally's dresses to avoid exposing my lacy boobs to my brother any longer than necessary before I realize I've just given him a full view of my G-string-clad ass, so I spin again—this time taking down the entire pole, clothing and all.

"You little shit." Morgan yanks Cruise out by the back of the shirt like he's about to beat him senseless, before they both start in on a brawl in the bedroom.

Ally jumps into the closet and does her best to untie me.

"Aren't you the lucky little slut?" She gives a sly wink.

"It takes one to know one," I tease, waving the boa in her face.

She helps throw my dress back on and we hightail it into the bedroom to find the two of them rolling around on the floor like a pair of bear cubs. Bodies fly, and the pink comforter is ripped right off the bed, exposing a set of black satin sheets. As soon as this whole nightmare is over, I'll have to ask Al where she got them. The thought of slipping and sliding all through the night with Cruise gets all of my erogenous zones ticking at once. The poor stuffed bear goes airborne, and the lamp at the side of the bed tumbles to the ground.

I lean into Ally and sigh. "You think they'll ever get along?"

"Not as long as Cruise is trying to have his way with you in your brother's closet."

"Touché."

I wrap my arms around Ally and watch as Cruise and Morgan come to final blows before each rolls over to nurse his respective family jewels.

"Looks like there are a lot of boo-boos to kiss," she whispers.

"Aren't we lucky."

Cruise

kick Morgan in the thigh one more time for the hell of it before getting up.

"Oh my God!" Kenny comes over and pulls me away from her moronic brother. "Are you okay?"

"I'm fine." I press the back of my hand to my lips and check for blood, and sure enough, a seam of crimson drips over my skin.

"See you tomorrow, Kendall." Ally gives a slight wave before we leave the room. I'm glad Ally found someone, but at the same time I'm a little stymied by what she or anyone else finds so amazing about Morgan Jordan. I guess at the end of the day he's a good guy. He just got his feathers a little ruffled seeing me hang his sister in his closet by way of a bright-red boa.

A slight chuckle bucks through me as we head down the hall. Hell, if I saw someone doing that to my sister, I'd shove his dick down his throat so fast he wouldn't know what hit him. Come to think of it, that's exactly what Morgan was doing. In that respect, I commend him as a brother.

Kenny wraps her slender arms around my waist, and I press a kiss just below her ear. Kenny is a goddess, with her long midnight-colored hair, velvet-blue eyes. You could write a poem on her lips with just one kiss, and I try to do just that every single night.

I moan into her. "Let's blow this joint and pick up where we left off. I'm ready to help you celebrate the last night of summer in the most memorable way possible." I run my hand around her ribs and touch the soft underside of her breast.

"Memorable, huh?" She blinks at me with those long, thick lashes, and my balls whimper for attention. "Have you been saving some of those mattress moves of yours for a special occasion?"

"Mmm." I warm her arm with my hand. "I was thinking of hitting the beach one last time. That way we can give summer a proper farewell on its own turf."

"I like the way you think, Elton." She curls a finger under my chin, and I playfully bite it.

We head into the living room, and Molly catches my attention as some muscled-up linebacker twirls her in the air. Her blonde hair flies around her face while he manhandles her like a rag doll.

"Hey! *Dude.*" I start to head off in Moll's direction, but Kenny holds me back.

"Whoa, cowboy." She secures her arms around my waist as if she's holding me back for real. "That's one rodeo you're not invited to."

The jock holding my sister hostage proceeds to tickle her mercilessly before bending her over the couch and offering a nice firm slap to her bottom.

"Sometimes you don't need an invitation." I head over and push the asswipe clear across the room before helping Molly back to her feet.

"What the hell are you doing?" She smacks me hard in the chest and takes off after the dick.

"What the hell?" I hold my hands out, confused as fuck as to what just happened. "That guy just publicly humiliated her, and it's *me* she's mad at?"

"They were playing," Kenny purrs into my ear like a kitten ready and willing to seduce me. "He's obviously into her." Kenny's clean-scented perfume wraps around me like a smooth pair of arms, and suddenly I want nothing more than to run my lips over every square inch of her body.

"I don't like him being 'into her,'" I growl as I watch Molly cling to the bloated pile of biceps as if he were her new best friend.

"Now you know how Morgan feels."

"Sounds like I owe your brother an apology." I wrap my arm around Kenny and lead us toward the exit "And I suppose this is as good a time as any to let you know you may never be an aunt." I hide the shit-eating grin wanting to spread a mile wide.

"I wouldn't brag. Once he recovers he'll be exacting his revenge and our own children's lives will be in peril."

"I'm all about revenge." I take a playful bite out of her neck. And I love the idea of having kids with Kenny one day. I picture a dozen little girls with her perfect hair and dimples, and then the thought of paying their college tuition—paying for their *weddings*—has me blinking them right back out of my mind.

"Geez." Cal slaps me on the back. "Can't you two keep your mitts off each other for five minutes? I saw Jordan head back there, swearing to rip you a new one if he found you fornicating in his closet one more time."

I pat my lip with the back of my hand, and a tiny crimson stain turns up on my skin. "I hardly call that ripping me a new one."

"You up for talking about that home gym sometime this week?"

"Yeah, sure." I had mentioned to Cal a few weeks back that the B and B could use a boost, and he mentioned a workout room might up the value. I hate to break it to him, but I'm pretty sure I can't afford thousands of dollars' worth of new gym equipment. I'll have him check the place out anyway. The worst that can happen is that I'll owe him a six-pack.

"Hey"—he leans in—"I've been meaning to tell you my cousin is coming into town from Connecticut. She's old fucking money, dude. She needs a place to stay, and she wants to rent out the B and B."

"The whole thing?" Kenny's eyes expand to the size of silver dollars.

"Yeah." Cal holds up his hands to attest to the fact. "Her friend's got a band. They're pushing through town, and she mentioned they needed a place to crash."

"What about a hotel?" A frown comes and goes. I'm pretty much resigned to the fact that if it seems too good to be true, it is. And the thought of someone breezing into town and renting the entire B and B is for damn sure too good to be true.

"She says they hate hotels. Anyway, I gave her your number, so expect a call." He pats me on the back before popping the collar on his polo and taking off.

"Hey, keep an eye on Moll for me!" I shout after him, but he's already lost in the crowd.

"Doesn't look like Morgan is going to get much sleep tonight." Kenny chews on the side of her cherry-red lip.

I lean in to kiss her gently. "Mmm." Kenny tastes like sugared strawberries, and my dick starts knocking at my jeans. "If I get my way, you're not going to get a lot of sleep tonight, either."

───

Kenny opted for the cabin instead of the beach, citing the sand that might actually work against us. Plus it's close to one in the morning and she's got a class tomorrow at ten. I'm the last person who would want to sabotage Kenny's college education. I know how shitty it feels—my ex-girlfriend sabotaged mine.

"Go ahead and get your pj's on." I give her shoulders a slight massage as soon as we walk through the door, and she gives a grateful moan.

"What pj's?" She glances back. A strand of her jet-black hair gets caught between her lips and she looks sexy as hell.

"Don't you have pj's?" I move my massaging efforts down her back, and she melts into me in a puddle of groans.

"I sleep naked, remember? You're mostly responsible for that."

"And believe me, I'm grateful." I take a gentle bite out of her ear, and she lets a cry rip from her throat like she's about to lose it right here in the living room. "I thought you might want to get some sleep—you know, first day of school and all."

"Oh, you're right." Her left brow does its impression of a fish-hook. "I'd hate to have any bags under my eyes in the event I've got a hot professor I'd like to impress."

"Whoa." I spin her into me while guiding us back toward the bedroom. "I knew you were only using me for my scholastic standing."

"Oh hush, you." She loosens my tie and slips it from around my neck before unbuttoning my shirt. "That was a mean trick you pulled last semester by not telling me you were taking over my class."

"I've got a few more mean tricks I'm ready and willing to pull on you." I track my hand up her thigh and run my fingers down the back of her G-string.

We hit the end of the hall and enter the bedroom. I flick the lights on, and Kenny is quick to shut them off again.

"You can pull all the tricks on me you like." Kenny trails her hot lips down my neck, my chest, until she's kneeling before me and freeing me from my Levis. "I'll let just about anything happen in the dark."

Kenny isn't a fan of having a white-hot spotlight over her in the bedroom, but every now and again she gives in, and damn, it's hotter than a brushfire watching Kenny Jordan work me over with that heavenly bod.

"Now, if the rest of Garrison isn't getting much sleep tonight"—she tugs my jeans down to my thighs—"I'd hate to be the exception." Kenny strokes my dick with her tongue, and I let out a groan that puts any wild animals hanging out around the cabin on a three-mile alert. "You like that?" she teases. Kenny grazes over the tip before plunging her mouth over me, eager and willing, and I can feel myself growing to capacity in her.

"Damn, Kenny." The words hiss out of me like a train sputtering into the station. I run my fingers through her long, glossy hair until I've tangled myself in her mane, and I hang on while she rides me slow and even. "Yes." I can hardly catch my breath as I start to tremble over her. Kenny reaches up and gives my balls a gentle massage *"Fuck*, yes."

Kenny plunges down again and this time sucks in her cheeks, holding my cock hostage in the best way possible.

"Oh shit," I whisper. "Where the hell did you learn to do that?" On second thought, I don't want to know. Kenny doesn't bother to answer the stupid question. Instead, she brilliantly brings me to a climax that has me groaning and moaning at the top of my lungs. I try to pull out but she digs her nails into my ass, imprisoning me in her mouth while I indulge in one of the best happy endings Kendall Jordan has ever treated me to.

She pulls back and spits out the reserves over her shoulder.

"Sorry." The moonlight sweeps over her as she wipes her mouth with the back of her arm.

"Don't be." I flick off my shoes and free myself from my boxers and jeans. I pull Kenny up to the bed with me. "I'll have my dick write you a thank-you note in the morning."

She belts out a laugh, and her teeth shine like a row of stars.

"I'm so damn in love with you, you know that?"

"Then come here and kiss me." She pulls me in but I resist the invite.

"I will kiss you." I pull her up until she's sitting.

"On the *lips*."

"That's exactly where I plan on kissing you." I reach down and run my fingers soft and light over her inner thigh and she lets out a whimper. "You didn't think I was going to let you go to sleep without returning the favor, did you?" I gently lift her dress off. Kendall leaves her arms in the air for a few extra seconds, and I admire her that way. "I can't believe in a few short months you're going to be my wife," I whisper, mostly to myself. Kenny's had me under a trance since that first night we met at a frat party last December, and I never want to break free from the beautiful hold she's got on me.

"You *are* excited about the wedding!" She scratches playfully at my chest.

"Of course I am." I pull her hand in and kiss it. "But, truth be told, I'm pretty damn excited about the wedding night, too." I kiss her other hand as well because I don't play favorites. "And every other night that follows."

"I especially like the sound of that." Kenny starts in on a series of kisses up the side of my neck, working her way to my ear until my skin tingles with goose bumps. It drives me insane when she—I suck in a breath through my teeth—dives her mouth over my ear.

I lay her gently back down and glide my hands around her until I manage to unhook her bra.

"In fact"—I pluck off the lace number and toss it in the corner, taking in the view with her back arched over the mattress—"I'll make sure we have one hell of a creative honeymoon. How's that?" Kendall's got the body of a goddess-in-waiting—those round perfect nipples call to me like candy. I bend over and graze one with my lips and she starts to pant as if she's halfway there.

"I think that sounds perfect. But it doesn't have to be anything fancy. As long as we're together, that's all I need. I swear to you, the cabin is fine."

I know Kendall will want to be back for Lauren's big day, but that still gives us plenty of time to do something memorable.

"It won't be the cabin. You deserve something way more exciting."

"But we're just going to be doing this." She lowers me to her chest and I kiss her soft quivering flesh before burying my face between her blooming mounds. Kenny Jordan has perfect tits. And she's right. We will very much just be doing this.

"This is my favorite." I dot each of her nipples with a kiss. "But I want you to have a dream honeymoon."

"You're my dream honeymoon."

I trail my lips down her midsection and her stomach cinches beneath my mouth. I gurgle a laugh into her heated skin before rotating my tongue in her belly button for a moment.

"Think about it," I whisper. "I want to make all of your dreams come true."

I sink lower, gently parting her knees and burying my face in the curls just below her panty line before biting her G-string off with my teeth.

"Are you wet for me?" I run my fingers over her folds and confirm that, yes indeed, Kenny is more than a little wet for me.

She lets out a satisfying groan, and I bury a string of kisses in her moist slick until she's screaming my name at the top of her lungs.

I press her thighs back and ride my tongue over her quick and steady until Kenny's panting hits an all-time high. I graze my teeth over her and she bucks into me hard, losing it in a fit of spasming quivers.

"Cruise." She moans it out while clasping her knees over the top of my head in a vise grip.

I sit up and pull her legs over my shoulders with my hard-on ready to rock and roll again.

Kenny bites down over her lip. Her hair is heaped over itself and she looks dangerously sexy.

"My, *my*, Professor Elton." She gravels it out low and sultry. "Aren't you insatiable?"

"With you in my bed, who could blame me?" I plunge into her warm, tight body and her neck arches back as she gives a heated cry.

Neither one of us gets much sleep.

2

THE CHAPEL GRAPPLE

Kendall

Fall swoops in on Garrison University like an eagle carrying off a poor, unsuspecting summer in its icy talons, leaving dozens of defenseless coeds shivering in their skimpy first-day-of-school attire, me included.

The air is heavily scented from the evergreens, and the sky is marbled with swirls of dark-gray and steel-blue clouds as I venture into this, the final class of the day, Creative Writing. It's depressing, in a way, knowing Cruise won't be in any of my classes. That he won't be *teaching* them by proxy. All of those erotic, quasi-scholastic memories come flooding back and my lips curve with approval.

The Language Arts building is archaic to say the least; *decrepit* is a more accurate term, but it's the Gothic architecture that makes me love Garrison so much. I scan the lecture hall filled with mostly girls, a smattering of guys sitting lumped off to the side. A mousy-haired girl catches my eye, and I instantly recognize her skeletal frame, her thin, tight lips, that annoying little smirk on her face. It's Cheryl—the moron I had to deal with all last semester in my Gender Relations class. She's the one who kept bothering both Cruise and me with her deliberately annoying answers—even if they were correct.

"Kendall!" Someone hisses my name from down front. It's Molly, sporting an all-too-eager grin as she waves me over.

"Molly?" I make my way down and take up the cushioned seat next to her. It's stadium seating, the comfy kind they have in theaters, and I'm more than glad about the modern amenities. The last thing I need at the end of a long day is for my ass to go numb for a solid hour. "I can't believe you're in here." Never in a million years would I have guessed I'd have a class with Cruise's little sister. But then, she is a freshman, so I guess it's in the realm of possibilities—though an unfortunate one. Molly has a way of landing me, or more to the point, herself, in hot water without putting too much effort into it.

A dark-haired gentleman—hardly older than me—makes his way to the front and pans the room with a content look on his face. He pinches at his gold-rimmed glasses while squinting into the dimly lit room. He looks pleasant enough as he takes a seat on the edge of the desk. He's clad in khakis and a Garrison sweatshirt, so I'm betting good money he's the teacher's assistant. God knows I'm all too familiar with those.

"Hello, class." He belts it out with a clear projection and his voice reverberates off the walls in the back. "My name is Professor Kurt Ertose, but you can call me Kurt for short." He lets out a dimpled grin and half the girls swoon in response.

I lean into Molly. "You'd think they'd never seen a man before."

"Are you kidding?" Molly can't take her eyes off him. "Professor Curl-Your-Toes is going to be the highlight of this entire semester."

I gape over at her and she's all hopped up, curling her toes no less, like an estrogen grenade just went off in her pants. Clearly, Molly here has fallen under the spell of his ridiculously oversized glasses, which I doubt are even prescription, and that plaid scarf wrapped around his neck like a noose. He's a total hipster. I guess for Molly's sake it's a good thing I'm here. God knows I'm aware of the things a hot Garrison professor is capable of doing to a girl— not that this one qualifies as hot, not by a long shot. But, obviously, hot is in the eye of the beholder, as evidenced by the collective panting taking place in the sexed-up vicinity.

My stomach pinches with heat just thinking about all that steamy classroom sex Cruise and I had a few months back. And we'd still be having it if it wasn't for his wicked witch of an ex-girlfriend, Blair, who single-handedly took down his internship and scholarship, and simultaneously pulled the plug on any of his future scholastic endeavors at this fine educational establishment. The long and short of it: they kicked Cruise out on his ass. Damn bitch. To be fair, Cruise did break some scholastic code of ethics by having his way with me whenever and wherever he pleased on campus, but, nonetheless, Blair played her part in the final take-down of his teaching career. She tried pulling the same crap with Morgan, but my brother, much to his credit, has already hauled her before the school administration and now they're "looking into the matter." If they look into the matter any longer, she'll have a diploma to wave in their faces before they can properly kick her out the door.

Professor Kurt cozies up on the desk and casually glances out at the bevy of students. It's dark in here. The lecture hall is pretty much a cave, with the exception of drop lighting just above each desk. But the front of the room is lit up as bright as a spring morning, which might explain the severe squinting he's currently engaged in.

Molly waves at him like a lunatic until he finally gives a little wave back.

Great. He's going to think there's something wrong with her. And trust me, there might be. The jury is still out on that one.

"You might think this is just another stuffy writing class." He pumps a dry laugh as if it's too far-fetched to fathom.

I lean into Molly and whisper, "If it involves writing long, boring papers, it *is*."

Professor Curl-Your-Toes twitches in my direction.

"I'm sorry, would you mind repeating that a little louder?" He needles us both with a glare from those fake lenses, and I can practically hear Molly panting herself into oblivion. "I'm afraid the students in the back didn't quite hear you."

A series of *ooh*s circles the room. What is this, high school?

Not one to back down from a challenge, I clear my throat. "I *said*, if we have to write long, boring papers, then it will be."

Molly kicks me in the leg. Hard.

A series of sharp gasps emit from around the lecture hall.

Oh please. They all know it's true.

"Excuse me, what's your name?" He juts his chin in my direction.

Molly raises her hand. "Molly Elton, and I have a really light load this semester, so if you're ever in need of an assistant, I'd be more than happy to volunteer."

He pushes out a gentle laugh and nods at her like she's twelve. "I appreciate the offer. And your name?" He looks right at me.

Crap.

"Kendall Jordan."

"Well, Ms. Jordan, I look forward to proving you wrong. I assure you my passion for writing goes far beyond long, boring reports. In fact, there is no syllabus, no midterm, and no final exam in this class. Your one assignment is to simply write something. It must have a beginning, middle, and end, and must be at least fifty pages in length, but I'm sure most of you will far exceed the limit by semester's end.

"Fifty pages?" I gulp. "That's like an entire book." I have a tough time writing fifty words, let alone top-to-bottom *pages*. I suppose that whole plagiarism thing is still highly frowned upon. Face it. I'm screwed.

His back vibrates with a laugh. "No, I'm afraid fifty pages hardly qualifies as a novel. Don't box yourselves in. I want you to write freely, really pull the story from your gut. This is a show of creativity at its best. My eyes will be the only pair to admire your work unless you wish to share it with others."

Molly's hand spikes in the air, and I can't help but groan. I have a feeling this entire semester is going to be one long, drawn-out episode of Molly trying to land in his much-too-tight chinos.

"So what will we be doing in class?" She pumps her leg a million miles an hour. Molly is quickly morphing into a horse begging to be let out of the gate, and I know just whose stall she's hoping to kick her way into.

"Free-form exercises." Professor Hippie McHippie gives a cheesy grin in her direction. I bet he's the type to eschew public transportation in favor of some green retro bike he bought from a thrift store and renovated. "My desire is simply to assist in navigating your story in the right direction." Maybe I'm being a little hard on him, but I'll bet he's not above giving my soon-to-be little sister a private education that neither she nor her girl parts will soon forget.

Another student raises her hand, and he diverts his attention.

"Did you see that?" Molly jumps in her seat with excitement as if he blew her a kiss.

"See what?" I hiss it low enough for Molly's ears only, lest he call me out again on my vocal exercise.

"He looked at his crotch when he said 'right direction.'" Her eyes get all swirly and love-struck the way they do in cartoons. "He wants me."

"Would you stop?" I'd belt out a full-blown reprimand, but he's already passing around papers with a suggested book list. "The only thing he *wants* is for you to do some learning." Although I'm not sure "free-form writing" qualifies as anything particularly educational—sounds like more hippie-dippie nonsense and thus a waste of our tuition fees.

I wait until he and his roaming ears are safely situated at the opposite end of the lecture hall before leaning toward her again.

"He's not the one for you. Trust me, the last thing you need is getting mixed up with some professor. Look at those beady little eyes, that *beer* belly." Not really, but with the lighting just right, it might pass. "Besides, he's probably married. So keep your dating radar relegated to the Greek pool for a little while. Would you?" At least long enough for me to report her hormonal wanderings to her brother. There's no doubt Cruise will stomp out the scholastic flames before they have a chance to burn down another educational career. Although if Professor Kurt here tries anything with Molly, his career will be the least of his worries.

Professor Kurt sits on top of his desk and kicks off his shoes, exposing a pair of argyle socks worn threadbare at the toes.

So gross.

He proceeds to read out loud the list of reference material he's amassed. But all I hear is blah, blah, blah because he's just sitting there in front of God and every student in here with his stinky socks. I lean in to inspect him further. He's got a bona fide hole on his left big toe, probably from his disgusting long toenails clawing their way through the fabric. He finishes off the list and gives the class the all-exciting "tell me about your summer" assignment to busy us in our journals for the next solid hour while he dips into a bag of granola.

There's no way Cruise would ever let Molly get mixed up with that hole in the sock, wannabe edgy, shirking mass consumerism, sitting on his desk, granola eating professor.

But something about that dreamy look in Molly's eyes tells me it's already too late.

———

After class, I dart over to the university chapel, which sits tucked in a sleepy corner of campus. It's so beautiful, I sigh at the sight of it. There it is, surrounded by a sea of romantic willow trees and an aisle of bush roses that create white, ethereal clouds leading all the way to the entry. The architecture is Gothic in appeal and the doors arch skyward, with beveled glass windows cut into the center of them. Inside it's dark, and the air is heavily scented with frankincense and myrrh and . . . Well, I don't know what that overbearing smell is—for all I know there's a janitor here who really likes Old Spice—but underneath it all is a subtle layer of dust that tickles my nostrils, and I let out an obtrusive sneeze.

"Bless your heart." An older woman appears from nowhere, no bigger than a toddler. Her skin glows like a dulled-out flashlight against the dismal backdrop. "Can I assist you?"

"Yes, actually. I'm looking to book a wedding." My insides do a soft roll when I say it. Just having those simple words strum from my vocal cords has set an entire firework factory off in my stomach.

"Oh sure, right this way." She leads me into a nearby office and pulls out a large leather-bound register. "What date were you looking at?" She pushes back the yellow parchmentlike pages as if they've somehow offended her.

"Christmas Eve."

"Christmas Eve." She gives a warm smile as she brings her thumb over the date. "There."

"It's available?"

"Oh yes, it's available." She runs her finger down the tab and her brows flex with startled amusement. "In approximately six years."

"Six *years*? And here Lauren thought it would be booked a measly *three* years in advance," I say that last part to myself, but I'm so close to losing my mind I really don't care what I sound like anymore. I wanted my wedding here at Garrison, *this* Christmas Eve, and now it all sounds like a joke, even to this quasi nun sitting across from me.

"Your friend is right, generally speaking that is, but holidays in and of themselves tend to be a little more in demand."

"Do you have *any* date available whatsoever this year?"

"This year?" She ogles me as though I've just sprouted another head. "I'm sorry. I have nothing available. All weekends and most Fridays have been eaten up in advance."

Fridays? My heart humps with a ray of hope. We can totally have a Friday wedding. It says we're nonconformists, we do our own thing, we're free spirits.

Great, now I sound like Professor Kurt von Nut. Although, Cruise and I *are* sort of nonconformists, and we are rather free-spirited—both in and out of the bedroom. Come to think of it, that's my favorite part of us.

"Fridays?" I perk up at the thought. "That doesn't sound too bad. What's the next Friday you have available?" I'll pull something together quick if I have to. The important part is that Cruise and I will be at this lovely castlelike setting right here at Garrison where we met and—

"Next August."

"August?" I touch my hand to my chest. "We just finished August. Next August is an entire year away."

"You're bright. I can see why they admitted you," she says drily, annoyed by my matrimonial mathematics.

"What about Thursdays?" God, what am I saying? Trust me, no little girl in her right bouquet-loving mind ever dreams of getting hitched on a Thursday. Thursday weddings are the equivalent of the double-discount rack where they keep the moth-eaten clothes that have been cursed by the fashion gods.

"Sorry. We don't do weekdays."

Crap on a crap cracker. I was totally going to rock the Thursday wedding. I could see the invites now: *Thursday is the new Saturday!*

Lauren and her bribing father come to mind. "Can you tell me who has this Christmas Eve reserved?"

Her eyes widen. She hugs the overgrown leather book as if she's a protective mother keeping it safe from a roving matrimonial predator.

"We never divulge such delicate information. I'm sorry, but here at the Chapel of Truth and Light we never betray the trust of—"

I don't wait for her to finish her spiel. Instead I gasp and point out the window. "Good God, is that man *naked*?"

"Where?" She bolts over to the leaded glass while I dive on top of the holy of holies—the Garrison Chapel wedding calendar. "No!" She clamps on to my back like a cat in heat, but I continue to thumb my way through those pages until I hit December and trace my finger down to the twenty-fourth. *Blair Lancaster.*

"Blair?" I gasp, returning to an upright position and effectively knocking the tiny cage fighter off my back in the process. "Who in the hell would ever marry Blair Lancaster?"

—

I do the only thing I can think of and summon Ally and Lauren to an emergency meeting at Starbucks. Ally is already there since she works at the place, and as soon as I walk in she takes her break.

"Lauren's in the back." She steers us in that direction with a latte at the ready. Ally and Lauren have been better than friends to me since I arrived at Garrison last December. In fact, they feel more like sisters. And if Morgan ever proposes to Ally, at least one of them officially will be.

"Dish." Lauren gives me the crazy eyes while patting both Ally and me into our seats. "What the hell happened?"

"I went to the chapel to book Christmas Eve, and you won't believe who's already booked it."

"Cruise?" Lauren swoons like it's the most romantic notion. And, had he done so, it would have been.

A breath gets locked in my throat.

"Holy shit." My entire body seizes with panic as perspiration explodes under my arms. "It *was* Cruise."

"Really?" Ally leans in. "That's incredible. It's like he knew you were coming and so he booked years in advance."

"I bet he got his dad to pony up his millions and bought his way to the altar, like I did," Lauren quips.

"No, not my Cruise." I slump in my seat. He's far from the borrowing-millions phase of his relationship with his father.

"What other Cruise is there?" Ally brushes the hair back from my shoulders.

"Blair Lancaster's Cruise." I tell them all about the ninja nun who jumped me from behind while I dove into the calendar like some bridezilla on steroids.

The two of them lose themselves in a laughgasm.

"Oh, hon"—Lauren engages in some serious nose-honking into her tissue—"that doesn't surprise me about Blair. She's forever the planner."

"So I guess she and Cruise picked out Christmas Eve, too. Isn't that strange?"

"I doubt Cruise had anything to do with it." Lauren takes a few careful sips of her coffee. "It sounds like Blair just being her normal demanding self."

"Besides, she *is* getting married on Christmas Eve." Ally scoots her seat in. "I know this as a fact."

"To who?" I clench my coffee with a death grip. A remote part of me is afraid she's going to say Cruise.

"Rutger Crones."

"Rutger?" I pretend to sound incensed since Rutger is Ally's ex-boyfriend, but I'd be lying if I didn't say every cell in my body wasn't relieved it's not Cruise.

"Gross." Lauren turns her head as if she might be sick. "They totally deserve to be chained together for life."

"I wish she'd find another day to commence the shackling." I twirl my finger over the rim of my cup. "Anyway, something tells me even if I had a million dollars I wouldn't be able to buy Blair Lancaster off. She'd hold on to that date out of sheer spite."

"So true." Ally shakes her head, and Lauren knocks her elbow into her.

"No, it's okay." I sag in my seat. "I know all about Blair's ability to do things out of spite."

"Look," Lauren starts, "there are tons of other venues. You could have a seaside wedding. Or have it in a park."

"I thought about it, but it's going to be freezing out. And honestly, deep down I've always wanted a church wedding."

"I get it." Lauren reaches over and touches her hand to mine. "There are plenty of other churches right here in Carrington."

"You're right." I sink a little lower in my seat because I don't want any other church. I want the chapel at Garrison because it has meaning. "I'll get on the horn tomorrow and see if anything good comes of it. How are *you* doing? Everything coming together okay?"

"Are you kidding?" Lauren presses a well-manicured hand to her Ann Taylor blouse. "Trying to book a hall is a real bitch, not to mention attempting to reserve a caterer on New Year's Eve— and then there's the florist, the photographer, the videographer, the stylist, the wedding planner, and my yoga instructor."

"Yoga instructor?" Ally asks because, well, one of us has to.

"That's right." Lauren straightens defensively. "She helps keep me centered. Besides, she's charging me double because it's a holiday. They all are." She huffs as if the financial burden is too much to bear, but the truth is, the only one around here who can't handle the financial burden is me.

"Maybe Cruise and I should just elope." I crumple up my napkin as if I were crumpling up my dream of a big church wedding with a big, fluffy white dress. "I can't afford any of that."

"I think eloping is romantic." Ally swoons while gazing off at some invisible horizon. "If you want, guests can watch your wedding on Skype."

Lauren knocks her elbow into her again and smirks. "Nobody around here is Skyping their nuptials. It's not what Kendall wants." She flexes a weak smile in my direction because sometimes what you want and what you can afford are two very different things. And if you're me, it just so happens to be all the time. "Kendall wants all the things that come with the traditional bridal package, and we need to brainstorm and help her figure out how the hell to get them."

Well, now that she's put it so delicately, I can see it for the impossibility it's panning out to be.

Ally leans in. "A girl I know got married last spring and since she couldn't afford a traditional dress, she had one fashioned out of water balloons—white, of course."

Lauren and I just stare at her.

"What?" Ally shrugs. "It was cute. The guy who made it for her was a certified balloon artist. I could totally hook you up with him. And another way you can save money is by handing out a bunch of throwaway cameras at the reception and the guests can take their own damn pictures." She cinches a satisfied smile, but I'm still stuck on the words *water balloons* and *throwaway*, and the fact they're being used in conjunction with my wedding.

Lauren glares at her. "The water balloon artist isn't the only one who's certifiable."

"Okay, never mind. We'll figure out a way to raise the money." Ally takes a breath. "How about *bake sales*? We can bake a ton of cookies and cupcakes and sell them on campus. I bet with the Greek boys alone you'll score ten grand."

"It sounds like an awful lot of work." I bite my lip, trying to think of something—*anything*—that doesn't involve me inhaling mass amounts of carbohydrates moments before my big day. God knows I can plow through an entire sheet cake when I'm stressed, and not having a wedding dress, or venue, has me very much stressed.

"There's always posing as a nude model for the art department." Ally arches a brow.

"Been there done that." Like I would ever fall for that again. But then again, posing with Cruise as my partner would be rather symbolic, not to mention we'd score twice the haul. What am I saying? Only strippers and porn stars fund their nuptials by way of their naked bodies. "Besides, I happen to know Morgan is stuck taking that class this semester, and there aren't enough dollar bills in the world to make me drop trou in front of my brother." That horrible incident of me hanging from his closet in my G-string comes back to haunt me.

"You and Cruise should make a sex tape." Lauren hisses it out so fast you'd think it were a delicious piece of gossip. "You'd make a bazillion dollars with that thing."

"Oh, would you stop." Ally shakes her head, then freezes midflight. "Bazillions? On second thought, porn is all the rage."

"Both of you stop." I push the idea away. "Porn is *not* all the rage. It's dirty and sick and . . ." My mind starts to wander to those midnight moves Cruise employs and, dear God almighty, they are anything but dirty. Cruise Elton is a master both beneath and above the sheets. He can love me into oblivion with his tongue alone. Just the thought of his long, hard—

"Kendall, wake up." Lauren shakes me until I snap out of my sexual stupor. "The tape is *out*. We were only joking."

Ally takes a breath. "Maybe the sex tape is out, but that doesn't mean you can't tinker with the alphabet a little." She gets a wicked gleam in her eye that I'm starting to fear.

"The alphabet, huh? I do have a novel due for my creative writing class at the end of the semester."

"Who has time to write an entire novel?" Lauren is quick to balk at the idea. "At best you might squeeze in a few steamy chapters here and there, but how in the hell is that going to translate into a wedding dress and roses?"

"The book boards at school are rife with perversion." Ally perks up.

"Book boards?" I'm almost afraid to ask.

"Yeah, you know, where the bookworms go for guidance. I should know—I'm one of them." Ally's lips curve at the thought. "You can upload whatever fan fiction you want, and, trust me, my dorm sisters used to gobble that stuff up by the loving spoonful." She shrugs. "Okay, I did, too."

"Nobody pays for fan fiction, Ally." Lauren is right there with the sledgehammer of reality, ready to knock us over the head. "We could try marketing it like a subscription." She holds up a finger as if to signal her own genius. "A serial!"

Ally is quick to nod. "I see people uploading serials all the time. Mostly they're sci-fi or horror mash-ups, but I'm betting erotica sells like hotcakes, too."

"Erotica?" I jump back, taking my seat with me. "My mom would *die* if she knew I was peddling alphabet porn to fund my wedding."

"Oh relax." Lauren waves me off. "Consider it romance with open-door scenes. You know, invite the readers to sneak a peek beneath the sheets. God knows there's nothing wrong with two people enjoying each other's company. The Bible started off with an open-door scene."

"It did?" I'm practically clawing at my shirt. "How come nobody told me this?"

"*I'm* telling you, right now." Lauren snips. "Two people, in one garden, both very much naked. You can't tell me 'be fruitful and multiply' happened without a whole lot of lovin'."

"That's right." Ally is totally on board with the idea. "And not a person on this planet would exist without an open-door scene." She bites down on her lip and stares off dreamily as if she's imagining her own open-door scene with my brother as the lead character.

"But what will I do? What will I *say*?" This is all terribly exciting, and, truth be told, I've never been so damn electrified over a single shred of homework. "I'll never think up anything creative enough to make anyone's mouth water, let alone enough to outfit an entire subscription—or the back of a cereal box for that matter."

"You won't have to think of anything." Lauren needles me with her gaze like I should understand the subliminal implications of it all. "You'll be living it."

"Hear, hear! I can attest to that." Ally raises a hand like a Girl Scout. "Just the power tools I heard revving up back at that love shack of yours last summer were enough to pique my interest. Simply have a good time with Cruise, and jot down all the deets afterwards."

Lauren gives a sly grin. "And at the end of the day, I'm betting you'll have enough to fund both a wedding and a honeymoon to any exotic locale of your choice."

I scoop up my backpack and thank Ally for the coffee as I head for the door.

"Where you going?" Lauren shouts after me.

"It's time to start chapter one!"

Cruise

I pluck a soda out of the fridge, migrate to the couch, and flop down with a groan. I damn near broke my back crawling around under the bed-and-breakfast while trying to figure out where the hell that stench of death is coming from. The entire left wing is unlivable. Dad and Karen are still off on their extended European honeymoon; Mom is off helping my grandmother with her broken hip; and Molly, thankfully, is shacking up with a friend on campus. As much as I don't like Molly having free rein over Garrison while her hormones are on fire, I'd hate the thought of her sleeping alone in that overgrown house. And I do mean alone. Not a soul has booked it since before Dad and Karen's wedding three weeks ago. I pinch a wry smile. I still can't wrap my head around the fact that my father married Kenny's mother. Nevertheless, it was the last time the bed-and-breakfast saw warm bodies. There has to be something I can offer to help bring people in, but I just can't figure out what.

The front door rattles. Kenny bursts in like a hurricane, landing on my lap in less than two point five seconds, panting through that hotter-than-hell honeyed mouth.

"Whoa." A huge grin spreads over my face. First honest to God one I've had in a while. "Looks like someone had a great first day. Tell me all about it." I land a careful kiss on her feather-soft lips.

"It was *interesting*. Your sister is in my creative writing class, and the only thing she's plotting is how to jump the professor."

"What?" I sit up and Kenny bumps into my chest, then stays there. The last thing I need is Molly trying to hook up with faculty.

"Can you blame her?" Kenny hikes up her cheek, and that tiny dimple of hers goes off. "The faculty at Garrison is stunningly attractive." She drips her fingers into my jeans.

Hot damn. I do believe Ms. Jordan is happy to see me.

"Yes, I *can* blame her. And I will, first chance I get. I'm pulling the plug on this budding illicit affair with her creative writing professor, of all people. Who is this turkey anyway?"

"Some guy, Kurt something—*Ertose*, that's it. Molly nicknamed him Professor Curl-Your-Toes."

"Crap." I shake my head at the felony assault charges looming in my future. "You know I'm going to kill this guy if he touches her."

"I know." She growls it out as if it's the hottest thing she's heard all year. Kenny leans in and nips at my lower lip. *"Killer,"* she purrs warmly into my ear, and a shiver runs up my spine.

"You know I love it when you do that."

"That's why I do it." She straddles me with her knees on either side of my body and takes off her top. "I know you like this, too." Kenny unhooks her bra and the girls spring loose right here in the living room.

"Boy, you must have really missed me today." Kenny and I spent the entire summer in that bedroom—mostly trying to give Ally and Morgan the proper environment for falling in love, per

Kenny's orders—but nevertheless had an insanely good time keeping one another occupied.

"I miss you every moment we're apart. So"—she peels off my shirt and rakes her nails lightly over my chest—"we should take advantage of each other as much as possible when we *are* together."

There's a strange look in her eyes, and I can't quite pinpoint what's going on, but whatever it is, I'm liking the carnal implications of it all.

"What gives?" I'm only asking once before I get with the program. My boner was already protesting the words as they flew from my lips.

"I'm hoping *you'll* give." She unbuttons my jeans. "Then *I'll* give, then we'll *both* get deliriously happy, and we'll fall asleep in one another's arms. The end."

"The end?" A soft laugh rumbles from me.

Her eyes widen for a moment.

"Yeah, you know. Then a new day dawns and we start all over again." She sinks a kiss to my sticky, sweaty chest. Kenny must not care that I'm more than grimy after rolling around looking at rusted pipes all afternoon.

"I like how you're thinking." I catch a whiff of my body, and I'm shocked she's still smiling, let alone entertaining the idea of "giving" anything to me. "You know what *I'm* thinking?" I pick her up and head down the hall, spinning her slowly until her hair trails like a dark scarf. I can get lost in Kenny's hair. I have to thread it through my fingers at night or I can't fall asleep.

"The bedroom?" She flicks off her shoes in tandem.

"Close." I push open the bathroom door with my back and wince. "The shower."

"Oh!" She jumps over my hips, and I try not to groan. "How about a bath? We could light candles, and I'll throw in rose petals and it'll be all kinds of romantic!"

"Candles?" Do we even *own* candles? "Sure." I land her on her feet. "I'll start the tub."

Kenny runs around and turns the radio to some moody love song while I strip off the rest of my clothes and settle in the tub. The hot water runs over my aching back, and I settle into it. I run some shampoo through my hair and then dunk my head under the spout, accidentally turning it into a bone fide bubble bath.

Nice touch.

Kenny runs in with nothing but her jeans on, her boobs bouncing in rhythm—and holy hell, I can so get used to this.

"I vote we have topless Mondays," I offer.

"Very funny." She turns my yellow work flashlight on and lays it on its side. "It's the closest thing we have to a candle." She seems genuinely disappointed. Note to self: stock up on wax pillars. "And there's not a rose petal around for miles." She peels off her jeans, and I don't take my eyes off her for a second. I know for a fact there's a rosebud tucked between her legs, but then again I'm the only one lucky enough to see it.

"That's okay, we've got the poor man's rose petals." I toss a handful of bubbles into the air and a small cluster lands on her left nipple. "Nice catch. Come here, and I'll help you wipe that off."

"So what did you do today?" She dips her foot in, and I catch a glimpse of pink between her thighs.

"Looked up at pipes all day. Trust me, this is a much better view."

Kenny glides in, and the water sloshes slightly over the tub.

"Come to think of it"—I run my hands down her back and over her perfectly shaped bare bottom—"we've never once taken a bath together before."

"And it's damn near criminal." Her chest vibrates over mine as a laugh gets caught in her throat. "You know what we should do?"

"What's that?" My hard-on grazes over her thigh, offering her a pretty big clue of what I think we should do.

"We should challenge ourselves to have sex in all kinds of different places right up until our wedding day."

"Different places?" I'm pretty sure we've already covered an entire spectrum of spaces and places, but I'm up for the challenge.

"Yeah, you know—we can make a game of it. It could be our own private wedding challenge. Sort of a buildup to the big day."

"A climactic buildup at that."

"A happy ending to our never-ending story"—she touches her nose to mine—"every single day."

"Every single day?" I tweak a brow at her. Sounds ambitious.

"You complaining?" She reaches down and strokes her hand over my dick, and I let out a groan of appreciation. "Of course, you'll have to be the one dreaming up new things for us to do. I'm not really creative in that respect." She lowers her lashes for a moment. "Are you *up* for the challenge?" Her hand strokes over the length of me, and I give another little groan.

"Oh, honey, it's on."

"Really?" She jumps over me with enthusiasm and a wave splashes onto the floor.

"Yes, really. Prepare to have your wildest fantasies fulfilled." I reach down and run my fingers over her heated slick.

"Boy, you really know how to make a point." Her lids flutter as she lands a kiss over my lips.

I carefully spin her until I'm lying on top, and Kenny helps guide me in. The water pulsates to the rhythm of our lovemaking until an entire ocean sloshes out and onto the floor.

Kenny moves her hips with mine and moans right into my mouth. I reach down and work my thumb over her in slow and steady circles, bringing her right there with me. Her legs wrap around my back. Her heels dig into my muscles and it feels like the best damn massage ever. I take it easy until Kenny is about to lose it, then push into her as greedily as I've wanted to all night. Kenny lets out an aching cry and presses me in deep just as I tremble into her.

Kenny's legs go into lockdown over my back and we stay that way, with her limbs wrapped around me like she's hanging on for dear life.

"That was one heck of a first chapter," she pants hard into my ear.

"It's going to be an exciting new adventure with you every day, and I can't wait to turn the page and see what tomorrow brings."

Kenny bites down over her cherry-stained lip. "Me either." She digs her fingers through my hair and kisses me gently on the temple.

I'll personally make sure the next few months are exciting as hell.

I have a feeling the rest of our lives will be nothing but a long string of happy endings because with Kenny in my arms I'm already pretty damn happy.

3

THE BOOK OF LOVE

Kendall

’m up before dawn with my laptop open and my coffee waiting
patiently by my side as I hem and haw over details including pen
names and characters' names and towns and cities and planets.
God, this is all so complicated. Honestly, I thought I would just
have to employ my sarcastic superpowers and my bathroom sense
of humor and the whole crazy idea would be made of win. But it's
not. It's hard as all hell.

I slump in my seat and take in my surroundings. I love Cruise's
homey cabin. I love the rustic, woodsy feel, the large stone fireplace. My gaze dips to those sheepskin rugs lining the floor, and
a million erotic memories flood back to me. Cruise and I already
have it all—well, with the tiny exception of boatloads of money
and a wedding, and both look impossible now.

My phone buzzes. It's a text from Ally. **No hot water. Mind if
we shower at your place?**

I text back. **Not at all! ~K**

By the time Morgan and Ally come over, I still haven't written
a single sentence of chapter one because, for the life of me, I can't
figure out what to call my small cast of two. My screen is cluttered
with all kinds of ridiculous names I've jotted down as potential
monikers.

I give Ally a brief hug while Morgy heads straight for the shower. It still makes me smile that they're together, plus this way, I get to have my big brother in town, so it's a win-win.

Ally pulls her feet up onto the chair and hugs her knees. "I hope you don't mind I told Lauren to stop by. She's dropping Cal off at the gym and said she'd pick up coffee on the way."

"Sounds perfect. I've just been sitting here stumped over this whole naughty book thing."

"*So*"—her lips curve into a secret smile—"did Cruise provide any good material last night?"

"Doesn't he always?" I cut a quick glance toward our bedroom and a heat wave pulses through my body.

"Let's see what you've got so far." Ally leans in close. "Lacey Lovesalot—Ben *Dover*?" She makes a face and shakes her head. "Eh. It's cute but it's missing something."

The bathroom door rattles, and the distinct sound of two grown men shouting ensues.

"Holy shit," Cruise says. He stomps down the hall with a towel draped around his waist and gives Ally a sheepish grin. "Morning."

"Morning," Ally and I sing back in unison. Obviously, Cruise thought *I* was in the shower. God only knows the level of duress he's put my poor brother in.

Ally speeds out the reason they're here.

"Say no more." Cruise runs his fingers through his rumpled hair and my insides quiver. He's perfectly tanned from a long, hot summer, and his abs are so well defined I might just do a load of laundry on them later. "You're welcome anytime." He struts back into the bedroom with the towel dipping below his waist, exposing just enough of his bare bottom for me to wish we were alone.

"*God*—that man is dangerously sexy." I let out a breath.

The front door opens, and it's Lauren, bearing lattes for one and all. A cool breeze follows her in as she shuts the door with the heel of her thigh-high riding boot.

"What did I miss?" Her hair is up in a ponytail, and she's wearing her black Bebe sweatshirt with all the cute sparkly rhinestones. Lauren has a way of making questionable hygiene seem chic. She takes a seat at the table with us.

"Cruise just propositioned Morgan," Ally says, grabbing a cup and carefully taking a sip. "And Kendall here hasn't quite hit first base." She spins my laptop toward Lauren.

"No." Lauren shakes her head. "Those names will *not* do. You need something real, something gritty people can hold on to. You need to believe in these characters yourself or, trust me, nobody else will."

"Right." I avert my gaze for a moment. "But it's not like I can just call them Kenny and Cruise."

"I suppose not." Lauren slumps in her seat, and the three of us spend the next few minutes contemplating porn names that are quasi-believable.

Ally taps the table. "How about *Penny* and C-R-U-Z?" She tweaks her brows at the absurdity.

"Please." I shake my head at the idea—although I do find it wildly exciting to venture so close to the truth.

Lauren nods into the idea. "Penny *Whoredon* and Cruz *Shelton*."

"Shelton?" Ally ixnays the surname with a wrinkle of her nose.

A vision of me dangling in the closet the night of her and Morgan's housewarming party comes back to me.

"*Belton.*" I slap my hand on the table. "Trust me, no one knows how to wield a belt like my Cruise."

Their mouths fall open for a full three seconds in sheer awe of Cruise's mad strap-wielding skills.

"Penny Whoredon"—I bite down on a smile—"and Cruz *Belton*."

"Sounds like a bestseller in the works." Ally gives a little wink.

"Now we just need a pen name for *you*." Lauren thumps the table.

"Penny Whoredon," Ally insists.

Lauren balks. "You can't use the same name or it becomes yawnable nonfiction, or worse, slotted with all the self-help books."

"Kenny Spanx." I say it so fast it sounds like a hiss.

"Kenny Spanx?" Lauren's eyes widen with approval.

Morgan comes out wearing his sweats and a Garrison practice T-shirt. His tattoos stream out in a rainbow of color up and down both arms.

"What's up, sis?" He plants a kiss on the top of my head, and I'm quick to slap my laptop shut. The last thing my brother needs to see are the dirty details of my creative writing assignment, or, I should say, my creative *wedding* assignment. "I'll make breakfast," he volunteers, and soon the entire place fills with the scent of bacon.

The shower is running again, and I can only assume it's Cruise in there this time.

"I don't know how I'm ever going to get this done around here." I glance toward our bedroom.

"You're not going to tell him?" Ally's eyes widen like two emerald pools.

"No," I mouth. "And don't tell . . ." I nod over at my brother. God, the last thing I need is Morgan being apprised of my foray into erotica. "It's just a temporary stepping-stone—a monetary means to an end."

"Speaking of which"—Lauren drums her fingers on the table—"we need a title so I can start selling subscriptions. I've already contacted the book forum at Sorority Net and they're really excited to see what you've got."

Crap. I stare at the blank screen because what I've got is nothing. "Okay, um, how about, *The Sexual Adventures of a College Coed?*"

"Boring." Ally cuts the air with her finger.

"Overdone." Lauren closes her eyes for a moment. "And it's not like Penny is going to be sleeping with a million people. We need to keep it simple. How about *The Pleasure Me Diaries?* Or *My Romp with a College Professor?*"

Ally moans. "Too wordy."

"I got it." I straighten in my seat and note that Morgan is already creating a small mountain out of bacon. I lean into the girls. *"The Naughty Professor."*

They pull back as their mouths open wide—with awe, I hope.

"Now *that's* simple." Ally clearly approves.

"Lauren?" I hold my breath as she considers this.

"God, even I want to read this." She lets out a tiny giggle.

"Then it's settled." I click away at the keyboard until the words *The Naughty Professor* light up the screen. "Penny Whoredon and Cruz Belton are about to have the time of their lives."

Lauren salutes me with her coffee. "And so are we."

Ally and I do the same and respond in unison. "And so are we."

———

The clouds over Garrison swirl dark and ominous, like oily charcoal ready to drip onto campus. I was hoping to call Cruise in a bit and see if we can schedule a romp on top of the tower in the steel-caged globe the way we did a few months back. I glance up at the noble structure. It's Garrison's highest point. The entire building sort of watches over campus like a brick-and-mortar guard. I remember that day, the way he peeled my clothes off, the way our lips melted over one another as we made love with wild abandon. It was exhilarating and took away my fear of heights in grand style. But with my luck a downpour will ensue this afternoon and we'll both wash right out onto the lawn below with broken necks.

I just finished with my only class of the day—trigonometry. It's going to be hard as hell. I hate numbers for even existing, let alone tagging themselves with the alphabet to create a genuine mindfuck. None of it makes sense.

I duck into the bookstore to pick up the exorbitantly priced textbooks I'll need for the semester. I thought if I waited an extra day I'd miss the crowd, but no such luck. The entire place is teeming with bodies and the checkout line snakes around the entire facility.

Crap.

A tall, dark, and handsome man waves as he comes toward me—Morgan.

"Hey, sis." He holds out his bag for me to gawk at it, filled to the brim with a million books, most of them with a *USED* sticker stamped across the front.

"Did you break the bank?" I'm hoping he says no because in truth I could use whatever's left over to fund my own scholastic needs.

"It's covered with my scholarship. Why, you need help?" He nods for me to follow him deeper into the bookstore.

I hold on to his sweatshirt and his warm Polo cologne comforts me. It's the same scent he's worn since he was a teenager. For so long I'd flock to that cologne at the department stores just to hold my brother in my senses for a little while. Now he's here, and I still can't believe it.

"The books are on me." His dimples depress as if to accentuate his point.

"There's no way I'd risk you losing your scholarship over something like this."

"It's not a big deal. I picked up a book for Ally. They're never going to know. What do you need?" He takes the list from my hand, and I trail him around as he loads up on my textbooks. "This is maybe five books." He frowns at me. "How many classes are you taking?"

"Three." I shrug, snatching the list back from him. "I wanted a light load so I could focus on the wedding. Plus there aren't really any books for my creative writing class except for the one *I'm* writing."

"You're writing a book?" His eyes light up with a sense of pride.

Stupid, *stupid* me.

My mouth opens and just as I'm about to refute the idea, a shadow drapes over me, stealing the light from around us.

I glance back to find the demon of all wedding date stealing demons, Blair Lancaster.

"You still hanging around campus?" Morgan glares at her. She's the one who almost cost Morgan his scholarship by telling the coach she was his girlfriend, and then not relaying the coach's message that he'd made the team.

"Of course." Blair flicks at the pearls around her neck. God, she's so thin, she's downright wiry. Does the girl ever eat? Not that I feel the need to buy her a burger. She can live off birdseed for all I care. Her lips bleed out in a single red line and her blonde hair is gelled into a tight French knot. "Why wouldn't I be on campus? My father sits on the board. My grandfather has a hall dedicated in his honor." She pinches her lips in an arrogant manner. "My parents are 'platinum alumni,' which means they've given over five hundred *thousand* dollars to this school over the last ten years. We practically remodeled the very room you're standing in just last spring." She tightens her auburn-colored coat around her waist and narrows in on my poor brother. "Besides, what happened between you and me was simply a little misunderstanding." She flashes her ring finger at us, and I'm momentarily blinded by the obnoxiously huge rock on her hand. "Anyway, it's water under the bridge. Rutger and I are well into the final phases of planning our big day. We've decided to gift one of the most important things to one another this holiday season."

"The access codes to your bank accounts?" Morgan deadpans.

Blair cackles like the wicked witch she is. "Each other."

"I'd rather have herpes." Morgan pulls me along.

"With Ally by your side, you're almost guaranteed!" Blair shouts after us, and I can practically see the steam pushing through my brother's ears.

"Ignore her," I huff, trying to keep up with him.

"She's stealing my sanity."

"She stole *my* wedding day."

Blair crops up behind us in line with her own small pile of books in her arms. "Excuse me, *Kenny*—what did you say?"

"You heard me." I turn, trying to control my breathing. I'm about to add a major plot twist to my upcoming novel, the one in which Penny murders Cruz's ex and they have insane sex over her shallow grave.

"Sounds like a grapple for the chapel is about to erupt." Her eyes enlarge as though this is a real possibility.

"As if you'd ever move your date," I say as Morgan guides me toward an open register.

"You never know. Everything has its price."

"I seriously doubt there's enough money on the planet to buy you off."

"Maybe it's not money that I'm after." She bears into me with that animalistic gleam in her eye, and it makes her look downright rabid.

Morgan pulls me in close. "Don't entertain her. She's batshit. Sorry about your date, but I wouldn't hold my breath. You and Cruise will make it work." He hands me the bag full of my books, and we head outside to the crisp, cool autumn air. Blair seems to have disappeared in a puff of fog—probably back to the coven from whence she came.

"Look"—he offers me a brief hug—"if you want your wedding to go off without a hitch, do not, I repeat *do not*, expect an ounce of mercy from Blair Lancaster. She's only going to set you up for heartache. Promise me you'll stay away from her."

"Promise." I give him a good firm squeeze. "You're a good big brother, you know that?"

"I know." He tugs on his ball cap as he starts to take off.

"Thanks for the books!" I call after him.

But if there's any way in hell I can get Blair Lancaster to relinquish my wedding venue, then I'm going to do it.

The "grapple for the chapel." A huff of a laugh trembles from my chest.

It's *so* on.

Cruise

I stare out at the bed-and-breakfast with a can of varnish in one hand and a hell of a lot of misery in my heart. The entire damn place is falling apart, and if the vacancies keep up the way they are, it'll be a bona fide haunted house by Halloween.

A limo pulls up to the B and B just as I'm about to put a fresh coat of varnish on the front doors.

Great. Up until last week I was sporting my version of a monkey suit, and as soon as I throw on my paint clothes, royalty shows up. Just fuck.

The driver gets out and opens the door to the back and I wait for it. Obviously, they've landed at the wrong place, but if the driver was lost, wouldn't he have asked for directions?

A young woman comes out with odd-shaped high heels that look as if they invert in the back and a long stick hanging out of her mouth that has a cigarette secured to the tip.

What the hell?

She's got on dark sunglasses, and her short blonde hair is colored purple at the tips.

"You Cruise?" She nods like I should be expecting her.

"That would be me." Shit. I know I bedded my way through the Greek alphabet before Kenny was on the scene, and the only random thought flying through my head is that I'm about to get news that I'm a father. Maybe the kid's in the limo and they're dropping it off for good.

"My cousin Cal said my friends and I could crash here for a while." She gravels it out with a threadbare voice, and a swell of relief fills me.

That's right. He mentioned they wanted to rent the place out.

I let out a breath I didn't know I was holding—thankfully, the only DNA this visit holds is directly related to my favorite bald-headed bag of muscles. Not that I don't want kids. I do, but exclusively with Kenny. And, once I can figure out how to keep a roof over our heads well into the future, I'm sure we'll do just that. Just thinking about having a baby with Kenny—hell, about *making* a baby with Kenny—triggers a smile on my lips. "Sure." I put down the paint can digging into my fingers and slap my hands against my jeans. "When can I expect you?"

"I'm here, aren't I?" She starts in on a texting spree. "The rest of the band should arrive in a few hours."

Did she say *band*? I scan my memory, trying to remember if Cal mentioned a band.

"You want to step inside and I can give you a tour?" Take the deposit. My bank account has been on its knees for weeks and maybe this limo-kissing cousin of Cal's is the exact godsend I need.

She flips up her sunglasses, exposing her red-laced eyes while inspecting the place. She sets in on a frown and shakes her head. "I've seen all I need to."

"All right, well, I'll leave the place open. The fridge is stocked with drinks, and I'll run by and pick up some groceries to start you off. It's more of a do-it-yourself bed-and-breakfast."

"We have a chef." She waves me off as if I'm a fly.

"We have a chef" equals "We have more than a few dollars to rub together," and my blood starts racing with the financial possibilities.

"Be back in a little while." She retreats into the dark cave of the limo.

"Hey, what's your name?" I call after her but the driver has already entombed her inside, and they speed off as quickly as they came.

I'm thinking I should pay a quick visit to my good friend Cal.

———

The gym is overcrowded and surprisingly muggy. Ever since Cal initiated the hot yoga classes, every male, jock and Greek alike, has stormed the facility.

Molly bounds over and gives me a hug. She's not the little sister I'm used to. She's morphed into a model overnight and I don't like it one bit. It's nice Cal lets her pick up a few hours around here. At least that way he can keep an eye on her for me, and it gives Molly a chance to line her pocket with some change. I'd like to know what that feels like sometime.

"Hey, kiddo." I wipe my brow. "Geez, it's as hot as a freaking sauna in here. How's school treating you?" I know for a fact she's already crushing on one of her professors, because Kenny witnessed the event firsthand. Just the thought makes my stomach turn.

"School is *beyond* cool." She bounces on her Day-Glo–pink tennis shoes and the soft scent of baby powder emanates from her. Case in point, she's still a baby, or at least she smells like one. The last thing she needs to be doing is getting her hormones worked up over some guy. "By the *way*, I got busted at Mandy's. I guess I'm going to have to move back into the bed-and-breakfast." She wrinkles her nose, and I can see the ten-year-old still hiding out in her eyes. "Turns out people who aren't affiliated with the dorm are considered 'contraband,' and Mandy was put on probation."

"Crap. Yes, come back to the B and B." Then I remember why I'm here to begin with—the purple-haired cigarette eater and the band that's coming in later with their own sous-chef. "Wait, you can't." I suck in a quick breath. "I may have just rented out the entire facility."

"What about my room? *Mom's* room? And now your dad and Karen's?"

"Dad and Karen won't be back until after Halloween and Mom is helping grandma out for another few weeks. I've already locked those rooms and yours. Besides, there's no way I'd let you hang out with the entourage that's about to take over the place."

"Great." She puffs a breath through her cheeks and looks all of twelve in the process. "Now where the heck am I supposed to stay? Rush doesn't start for another two weeks and that only counts if I make it into Tri Delta. It looks like I'm freaking homeless now."

Shit.

"Okay look, you're not 'freaking homeless.'" I wrap an arm around her shoulder and pull her in. "You've always got me to depend on. You know that."

"Of course I know that." She folds into me, soft as a kitten. "You're always there for me, Cruise." Tears moisten her eyes, and this catches me off guard. "You're like a dad and a big brother all rolled into one."

My heart melts hearing that. I press a kiss over the top of her head just as Pennington barrels in this direction.

"Dude." He offers up a knuckle bump to both me and Molly. "Likin' the lovefest. Dad called, said he's having a blast in Spain."

I twist my lips. Dad called him. Figures. Not that I expect a phone call, but the truth is, I thought we straightened out our relationship a bit this past year. He's gone from an absentee father to taking up residency at the B and B. Anyway, I'm not going to be a pussy about it. He's closer to Pen, and that's the way it's going to be.

"Glad they're doing good."

Cal swoops by, immersed in whatever he's staring at on his clipboard, and I pluck him over by the back of his muscle T.

"Not so fast. Your cousin is in town. What's her name? Hell, what's the band's name? I couldn't get two words out of her."

"Lisa?" He perks up at the thought.

"Lisa seems too normal for her."

"That's because it is. She goes by 'the Skin.'"

"The *Skin*?" Molly jerks her head back. "Sounds disgusting."

"What's the band's name?" Pen, my younger, less-concerned-about-finances half brother, is suddenly interested.

"The Plague." Cal nods just as his phone goes off. "I gotta go. I've got another insurance adjuster looking at the basement." He pats me on the back and takes off. "Tell the Skin I said hello!" he shouts, zipping toward the exit.

I suppose the insurance adjuster has to do with the basement fire a few weeks back. Morgan's little nightclub endeavor pissed off the wrong people and nearly burned the place down. Bonehead.

Cal is lucky they didn't close down his entire business in the interim.

"The fucking *Plague*." Pen socks me in the stomach and knocks the wind out of me while he bounces around like a six-year-old. "This is going to be fucking badass."

"Watch the language," I reprimand. "There's a young lady around."

"I'm not a baby, Cruise." Molly cuts me a death stare before taking off toward the girl's locker room.

"I didn't say you were a baby." I *thought* it. "I'll see you tonight at the cabin," I shout after her.

"We'll see."

"Perfect. She's a ball of hormones on the loose. If you ever see her around campus, keep an eye on her for me, would you?"

Pen shakes his head. "I'm not hanging with the little girls if you know what I mean. I doubt I'll see her. I'm all about the Greek ladies this year."

"Yeah, well, if Molly gets her way, she'll be one of them."

"Got it. I'll make sure to steer the boys in the opposite direction."

"I appreciate it." For a second my brain ventures into the pity party once again and I wonder if it were Pen's B and B that was going down Titanic-style whether good old Dad would offer to come to the rescue. I thought about asking for a loan, with more interest than he'd get at the bank, only because I can't get an actual bank to lend me a pen, let alone some actual currency, but in the end I didn't bother. "Hey, how's your mom?" Rumor has it Jackie's been off celebrating the divorce from my father in grand style and with men thirty years her junior.

"Living it up. She just got back into town."

"Tell her I said hi."

"Will do."

He takes off just as my phone buzzes. It's a text from Kenny.

Expecting big things to come tonight. Namely you.

I give a little laugh. I don't remember her ever being so brazen. Now that's one ball of hormones I won't be protesting.

Kenny makes the world go round—that's for damn sure.

I pick up Chinese for dinner and hop in the shower before Kenny gets home. I've already initiated a plan of action for this, our first night of the fornicating challenge, and I hope to meet and exceed Ms. Jordan's expectations. I was hoping to work on my thesis a little tonight but I'll shelve that for another day. I'm hoping I didn't throw away the countless hours I spent on the thing, but I felt pretty passionate about it at the time. I hate not finishing something I start, so I'm pretty sure I'm going to see it through regardless of whether it proves to be a fruitless effort. I guess somewhere in the back of my mind I'm still holding out for a miracle. Getting back into Garrison would somehow add to the magic of everything that's already happened this year—namely Kenny. Besides, she's the real reason my thesis changed on a dime. My approach was to explain why love at first sight is a misnomer in modern society—how lust has threatened the infrastructure of true love. But now I happen to think lust and true love can go hand in hand, thus the revisions I'm planning. Not to mention that Kenny helped me debunk the theory of "the heresy of love at first sight." Kenny cured me of that on night one. I'm still feeling pretty damn lucky I went to that Alpha Sigma Phi party, or the entire last year would have played out differently. Most likely with me suffering the ill effects of some incurable STD and Kenny fighting off douche bags named Rutger or, God forbid, Pennington. Not that Pen's a douche. He's just not the one for Kenny. I am.

The door rattles and I can feel the cool breeze coming in. I snatch up a towel to dry off as best as I can and wrap it around my waist.

"Honey, I'm home!" She practically sings the words. I'd be lying if I didn't admit how fucking happy I am that she fell for someone like me.

I head into the bedroom and grab my tie off the nightstand.

"Close your eyes," I say before I hit the living room, and she's already got them squeezed tight with a giggle brewing in her chest. I shut the door and help her put down her backpack and a Garrison bookstore bag that might as well be laden with stones, it's so heavy. My stomach cinches when I see the total. Three hundred big ones. The fine print catches my attention. *Jordan scholarship fund.*

Shit. Morgan threw this on his tab. Now I really feel like crap. I had a few hundred dollars I meant to give her yesterday to cover books. Maybe I'll give it to Morgan instead.

"I went shopping and got the cutest baseball caps for us today," she chirps. "Mine says *bride* and yours says *groom.*" She squeals as I wrap an arm around her waist and land a gentle kiss on the back of her neck. "They're all sparkly and cute. Well, mine's sparkly and cute. Yours is sort of a baby blue and, well, not too emasculating—as long as you're not threatened by a stray rhinestone or two."

"As long as I get to be there on the wedding night I'm okay with sparkly." I slip my necktie over her eyes and secure it to the back of her head by way of a knot.

"*Ooh,* I like where this is going, Professor Elton." She purrs it out like my favorite song.

A demonic laugh gets buried in my chest. "Ms. Jordan"—I slip her coat off and unbutton the front of her shirt—"prepare to have your most thorough lesson of the day. Erogenous Zones 101."

"That's my favorite class." She unbuttons her jeans, showing me exactly how eager she is.

"I'm glad, because there's a hell of a lot of homework involved." I help her over to the fireplace while she gropes around like a blind man.

"Where are we?" She lets it out with a breathy laugh, and I just stand there admiring her for a moment. Kenny has a perfect body, with curves in all the right places.

"Never mind. You just take off the rest of your clothes for me, nice and slow." I drop my towel and my dick springs to life in anticipation of the big show.

Kenny fumbles with her jeans and flicks off her heels, nearly taking out the front window. She pulls off her top and leaves her G-string and barely there lace bra.

Hot damn. I shake my head while examining her.

She should be illegal.

My hands ride over her hips and she arches her head back and gives a little groan. I pull her panties down nice and slow until she steps out of them.

"Turn around," I instruct, and Kenny spins apprehensively. I know she's not crazy about me checking out her body with even a limited amount of light, let alone before sunset in the living room, but her skin calls to me, smooth like velvet. "You have a perfect ass."

"Please," she groans. "My entire body should be hidden from the free world now and forever. I'll have to write your eyeballs an apology later for subjecting you to the disaster at hand."

"No disaster here." I wrap my arms around her waist and pull her in until her skin sizzles over mine. "All I see is sheer perfection."

"I'm serious." She scratches at my chest. "I should go into hiding. I'm hideous."

I hold back a laugh. Kenny is fragile and vulnerable but she's pretty rock solid. She knows she's fine, and so do I.

"I'm okay with you hiding from the free world as long as I'm invited to view the show." I land a string of soft kisses on the back of her neck before securing her wrists together with her G-string "That should do you."

"Am I being arrested?"

"That's tomorrow night. I've got an entire hostage drama mapped out. Of course I'll be the one to rescue you." I land a kiss in her ear.

"I bet I'll be very, very thankful."

"That's the idea."

"So what's tonight's lesson? Set up the scene for me."

"The scene?" Boy, she's into this.

"I mean, Professor Elton, what exactly is it that you're going to *teach* me?" She drops her voice into a lower register and my hard-on extends farther than I could have ever imagined.

"Tonight's lesson is all about lingual affection." I run my tongue up her spine and she quivers into me. "Bend over."

A choking sound emits from her throat and Kenny complies without wasting a second. I lash my tongue over her neck, across her shoulder blades, wet my way down to the perfect bottom and pause.

I could swear I heard the faint sound of a girl laughing. It's probably just "the Skin" disease that's moving into the bed-and-breakfast. Maybe I should go out and see if everything's okay.

Kenny nestles her body into me, and I shake all thoughts of the B and B out of my head.

I run my tongue lower, all the way to her left thigh, and Kenny moans as if I'm killing her. I give a few careful licks leading up to her inner thigh and the laughter outside intensifies, followed by a very loud "Cool! I'll call you later," and this time I distinctly recognize the voice as Molly's. A rustle erupts at the door, and I scoop Kenny up and carry her into the bedroom without giving it a second thought.

Shit.

"Who's that?" Kenny squirms in my arms as I lay her gently on the bed.

"My sister." I hop into my sweats and toss on a T-shirt.

"Cruise?" Molly shouts from the living room. "Geez, you guys live like pigs." The sound of a backpack being flung to the floor thumps through the tiny cabin, then footsteps heading in this direction.

"Molly?" Kenny bites down over her ruby-red lip.

I lift the tie off her head, leaving her hands still bound.

"Let me say hello, and I'll be right back." I run my finger down her chest and circle over her left breast. Kenny is soft as a dream. "Don't go anywhere."

I zip into the living room running my hands through my hair, only to find Molly already raiding the fridge.

"You've got the diet of a six-year-old." She smirks as she pulls out some brownies from the freezer and a soda. Nothing beats a frozen brownie at midnight. She pulls out some bread, too, and starts making a sandwich. "So I'm crashing. Do you care?"

"Nope." I glance down the hall to make sure I shut the door. "Kenny and I are glad to have you. You can take the spare room if you want." Crap. It sounded like a much more reasonable offer when I didn't have Kenny hog-tied in the next room.

"Thanks." She gives an unenthusiastic eye roll. "I really can't wait to get my own place. Maybe I'll start looking for an apartment next week."

"An apartment?" I'm stunned she could even entertain the idea with a straight face. "With what—your good looks? Last I checked, landlords want a mint to lease a room out."

"Well, it's not fair you get to live here for *free*. What about me? What do *I* get?"

She's got a point. Almost. "I live here in exchange for running the B and B. Plus I can keep an eye on you."

"Maybe I don't want you keeping an eye on me. What if I have a date and I want to bring him over to the house?" She's red-faced and yelling and what the hell just happened? "I *can't* because everyone knows you'll go ballistic and yank his balls out of his ass."

"I'm your big brother. It's my job." I pull back my shoulders, damn proud of her astute assessment.

"It's all your fault I lost Morgan," she seethes, and suddenly I fear for *my* balls. "And now he's chained at the hip with that ditz Ally and I'm stuck all by my lonesome here in Siberia." She throws her hands in the air as if the cabin is the equivalent of middle-earth. "I'll never have anyone, and I'll die an old lady. But that's okay because deep down inside you know that's how you want it!" She slaps her sandwich together and hightails it to the back bedroom, then slams the door.

Shit. I shake my head, putting the mayo back in the fridge.

I return to the bedroom and find Kenny has worked off her cotton cuffs and is flipping channels on the television with the covers pulled up to her nose.

"What was that about?" She gives a wry grin like she knows.

"Moll needs a place to stay so I offered her a room."

"Molly is going to be living here?" Her mouth opens wide, and it's clear she's shocked by the revelation. "Now we're never going to have exciting sex." She lets the remote slip through her fingers.

"What are you talking about?" I lock the door and bounce down next to her on the mattress. Kenny looks perturbed, and I can't help but smile. She's cute as hell when she's angry.

"Face it. Being confined to these four walls—our sex life is going to take a nosedive and fast."

"Not true." I pull back the cover and wrap my arms around her waist.

"It *is* true. We'll be locked in this bedroom and nothing exciting will ever happen again and we'll be forced to elope."

"Elope?" What does that have to do with being confined to the bedroom? "Hmm . . . Well, if it makes you feel better, the entire time Morgan was here we had an outstanding, and might I add *thorough*, exploration of our erogenous zones." I reach in the top drawer of the nightstand and turn on the electric-blue vibrator Kenny brought home one day last summer. At first I was offended, but she innocently thought it was a couples' game, so we turned it into one. Nightly.

"And now you're getting back at me by having your sister here?" She pushes my arms off her hips. "I *knew* you hated Morgan."

"Whoa. *Hate* is a strong word." First Moll, now Kenny? Maybe there's a severe case of PMS going around. "I like your brother— hell, I think he's a great guy." True story. Most of the time.

The sound of a fist pounding emits from the other side of the wall. "It's true! You *hate* Morgan!" Molly shouts it out like a battle cry.

"Holy crap, she's listening," I whisper.

"These walls are paper-thin," Molly belts out. "I can hear every darn word. Keep it down, will you?"

"Will do." I don't bother shouting. Apparently there's no reason.

"So what now?" Kenny shakes me as if we've got a serious problem on our hands.

"It's all right. Don't worry about it. It won't be for long." My fingers demand to drift lower over her soft skin, but I resist the urge.

"Don't stop." Kenny wrinkles her nose as she wiggles into me. "I kind of like where you're going with that." She says it a notch below a whisper.

I place my lips next to her ear. "Once I move Molly we can resume our challenge. She's ruining my mojo." I hate to admit it, but my little sister hardly fits into the hostage standoff I've got planned for tomorrow.

"Oh no you don't." She shakes her head emphatically. "I've got papers to write and a wedding to plan. You are going to fuck me tonight, Professor Elton, and quite proficiently." She says it like she means it, and the last thing Kenny does is whisper.

A hard groan comes from the next room.

I give Kenny a weak salute and switch off the lamp. Suddenly I'm half-afraid Molly has garnered X-ray vision and soon we'll be a visual disturbance as well. I swipe the remote off the bed because the TV affords just enough light for me to enjoy Kenny's body, and I turn up the volume a good few notches.

"There." I glide in next to her and Kenny ravenously tears off my clothes. "Looks like someone's hungry."

More pounding ensues. "Then make her a sandwich!"

Shit.

I shake my head at Kenny, wild-eyed. I'll never get it up with Molly joining in on the festivities every few seconds.

Kenny pulls me into a violent kiss and yanks at my cock like she's about to pull it right off my body.

"I want you to do something totally insane," she pants. Kenny looks hotter than hell with her lids hooded, her hair melting around her in a shadowed puddle. Lucky for me my hard-on has decided to wake up and take a look for himself.

Kenny pants into me. "Take my body and make it your own." She shakes me by the shoulders when she says it and the thumping resumes.

Crap.

I compress a smile and start in on kissing every square inch of Kenny's beautiful body while Molly complains to a friend on the phone.

I hope at least one of us has a good time tonight.

4

IMAGINE THAT

Kendall

Storm clouds hover over Carrington, dark and thick as molasses. I pull my cardigan tight around me as I stare helplessly down at my laptop in the early morning hours at Starbucks. I keep looking out the window for inspiration—hell, for a skywriter I could quasi-plagiarize—but nothing.

Crap.

I highlight the entire last page and hit delete.

"This isn't working." I shut my laptop with a bang, and I wouldn't be surprised if it never blinked to life again. Not even Starbucks and all its fresh roast–scented magic can draw another sentence from my sexually weary soul.

Ally comes over and hands me a hazelnut macchiato, extra caramel, easy ice. I love how well she knows me.

"So? How's it going?" She doesn't bother taking a seat. She's working her shift, and the last thing I want is for her to get into trouble because of me. No point in both of us being incapable of pulling an income.

"I've got half a scene. Molly came over last night, and the chapter went right out the window along with my dream wedding."

"Don't get so down over it. It's no biggie. You mentioned Cruise and you had a good time last night."

"True." I happened to say those very words as soon as I set foot in this heavenly scented establishment.

"Well, there you go. Just embellish a little. This isn't a documentary. No one is going to rewind and check for accuracy. This is a work of fiction, remember?"

"*Embellish,*" I say as if the word isn't even in my lexicon, and at this point it may as well not be. "Embellishing requires an imagination, and obviously I wasn't present the day they handed those out."

"Oh, come on. You can make last night whatever you wanted it to be." She gives a little wink. "You can even throw in a little annoying dog named *Polly* if you like."

"Right." I make a face as she scuttles back behind the counter.

I open my laptop and take a deep breath. I can totally embellish. It's a perfect idea. I mean, God knows I had all kinds of crazy thoughts about what might happen last night, and *Molly interruptus* was nowhere near the short list. I scratch my head and take a sip of my drink. Mmm, so much damn caramel—Ally knows I love me some caramel.

Ooh, here we go. I start back in with Penny and Cruz. She's just entered his apartment, looking forward to that "extra credit" he offered, and of course he's wearing nothing but a towel.

A private smile warms my lips. I love it when I come home to find Cruise in nothing but a towel.

Penny gets on her knees and begs for one last assignment. She needs a passing grade or she'll be kicked out of school forever.

No, wait, that's a bit dramatic.

She'll lose her scholarship and have to hoof tuition like the rest of the peons at Garrison.

Wait—I'm not actually going to reference Garrison, am I? I could get sued and find myself in all kinds of legal misery over this. They'll take me to the cleaners. I'll be liable. Not that there's much to clean. Oh hell.

Harrison University. There. That's better.

I continue the scene with Penny begging Professor Belton to have his way with her. And Professor Belton, perv that he is, demands she take her clothes off before dousing the two of them with vats of caramel.

I take another careful sip for inspiration.

Penny drops to her knees and engages in the most calorie-laden blow job known to man while professor Belton thrusts himself freely—

A pair of warm hands cover my eyes.

"Boo," Cruise whispers in my ear, and I bounce in my seat, spastically slamming my laptop shut and christening a three-table circumference with my extra caramel, easy ice macchiato. And judging by the brown goo dripping off the coat of the girl in front of me, Ally may have added extra, extra caramel.

"Oh no! I'm so sorry!" I jump out of my seat and try to clean the mess with nary a napkin in sight, but the girl makes a dash for the restroom before I can destroy her coat any further.

"I've got this!" Ally makes big eyes at me before darting over with a dozen dish towels.

"Let me help." Cruise insists, but she bats him away.

"That's why they pay me the big bucks. Why don't you take your girlfriend on a mystery date?" Ally winks at me. "I'll handle the rest. Now go on, get out of here."

I bite down on my lip while quickly putting away my things.

Cruise hands me one of Ally's dish towels, and I wipe down my hands.

"I was just thinking we've got some catching up to do." He's got that come-hither look in his eyes, and I'm hopeful that a whole new storyline is brewing for Penny and Professor Belton. "Are you free?"

I've got class in less than ten minutes.

"Of course I'm free. My next class isn't until two o'clock." If I'm missing sociology, I may as well miss trig, too. "Creative Writing." My lifeline to a beautiful wedding and, apparently, an exciting sex life.

"You're really enjoying that class, aren't you?" He leads us out into the brisk fall air.

"More than you'll ever know."

Cruise and I stroll around campus hand in hand, and for a minute it feels like last semester, as if we had somehow passed through a time portal and were right back at the beginning.

I tug at his arm as I snuggle into him. "How many things would you change about us if you could go back to the day we met?"

Cruise blows out a breath and ponders this for a moment.

"Exactly zero."

"What?" I jump a little at his answer. "Really?"

"More than anything I would want us to end up right here, doing this." He plants a quick kiss on my lips. "I'm a big believer in things ending up the way they're supposed to."

I gaze up at him, this handsome man that destiny somehow thought to plant by my side.

"Me too," I whisper.

Cruise meets me with a kiss that says thank you to fate and destiny, and maybe even Cupid, for bringing us together, right here at Garrison—safe in one another's arms.

Creative Writing drones on for the entire livelong hour while Molly busies herself contorting her body into every sexually suggestive position possible. I'm not sure what makes me more nervous, the fact Molly is so ready and willing to lie down for the professor or the fact I'm going to ask him to help me in my own creative writing endeavor—which entails having him review the naughty thoughts I've committed to paper.

I wait until most of the class clears before pulling myself off my seat.

I turn to Molly. "Look, I need to speak to the professor for a second. You mind hanging out a minute? Maybe wait by the door?" God, I'd die if she tried to listen in. The last thing I need is for her to blurt out to Cruise that I'm documenting our sexual shenanigans. He'll think I'm perverted or, worse, clinical, and that sex is nothing more than some scientific experiment I'm partaking in while jotting down my findings.

I head over just as Kurt is about to buckle up his briefcase.

"Excuse me," I say, leaning in, and noting Molly less than ten feet away.

Crap.

I press in close until my lips are practically in his ear. "If you don't mind, I have a tiny favor to ask."

He blinks up in surprise. "Ask away."

"I'm writing this book—for class, of course—and I want to know if you could help review for me as I go."

"No rush for perfection." He pushes his glasses up with his finger. "Take your time with it. The assignment's not due for months."

"No, you don't understand. I'm very into this book, and I can't wait to share it with my girlfriends. In fact, I'm putting it up on Sorority Net to share with *all* my friends, chapter by chapter as I write."

"What's the hurry?" He looks stymied by my rush to publish.

"It's sort of a specialty book, an explicit specialty book detailing what goes on behind closed doors—you know, of some fictional couple that isn't real."

He straightens, and it's clear I had him at "explicit."

"Anyway," I continue, "I have a very active imagination and dozens of sexually frustrated friends who are begging to read this book right this minute. They're all itching to get their hands on it so they can finally get some damn relief, if you know what I mean. They're desperate and lonely."

His brows rise, a nervous grin flitting across his lips. "Well, if it's for a good cause, I'll edit the chapters as quickly as you can get them to me." He darts a glance at Molly. "I'm more than willing to help the desperate and lonely any way I can."

A dull laugh thumps in my chest.

I bet.

Cruise

After I drop Kenny back at Garrison, I head home and find a barrage of moving vans clogging up the driveway.

Moving vans? I frown at the eccentric display. Kenny had my head tucked firmly in the clouds for the past few hours, and now the sight of a dozen U-Hauls has efficiently shot me back down to earth.

"What the?" I park on the shoulder of the road above the B and B and head on over to the chaos.

Lisa, aka the Skin, is down below, barking out orders at the movers while they haul couches out of the bed-and-breakfast.

Wait one fucking minute. Those movers are working in reverse. That's my stuff going *into* the vans.

I jog on over. "Hey, Lisa," I say, trying not to let on that I'm as pissed as I am. And for damn certain, addressing her as "the Skin" is out of the question. I'm not fostering anyone's junior high fantasies, with the exception of Kenny's, of course. Instead, I get right to the point. "What the hell?"

"Keep it moving!" she howls at the arsenal of buffed-out boys she's got crawling along the property like an army of sugared-up ants. It's then I notice she's got one pale milky eye, and the other is nothing but a big black pupil. Something tells me that's a manufactured look, and judging by the new rainbow added to her hair, I'm willing to bet there aren't too many genuine things about the Skin in general.

"You gotta relax, man." She huffs as she snaps on her sunglasses. "The Plague likes things a certain way. We're sending this junk to storage and putting it all back in place just before we split. What the Plague destroys, the Plague rebuilds, man." She shakes her head at the B and B as if she feels sorry for it, and, right about now, I do, too. "Someday you're going to get on your pretty boy knees and thank me for this."

"It's doubtful," I deadpan. "Look, you need to knock this off. That's my grandfather's furniture. Everything you're tossing in the back of those trucks needs to be put back where it belongs right now. They're like"—I shake my head as my grandmother's desk is carried into the hungry mouth of a moving truck—"antiques!"

"It's just the living room and three upstairs bedrooms," Lisa counters. "The chef thinks the kitchen's pretty cool. We'll throw in an extra ten K once we shore up the bill, so don't sweat your pretty little balls over it."

"Ten K?" Holy shit. It takes everything in me not to help clear the old crap out of there faster.

"The Plague has a strict rider for their dressing room, and every detail needs to be just so."

Did she just refer to the B and B as the band's dressing room?

"The Plague runs a lot smoother when things are exactly the same in every location across the country."

"Like a traveling home." I nod into her lunacy.

"That's right—they can't be home so they bring home with them."

One of the guys carries in a strange-looking chair with leather and chains dangling from it.

Normal people who use hotel rooms are satisfied with basic creature comforts like a bed and bathroom.

Two movers haul a mirrored coffee table out of one of the trucks and muscle it inside while another pair drags in a bed frame with mirrored paneling.

"You've got a theme, huh?" I ask.

"The Plague believes mirrors are the pathways to new realities," the Skin replies. "The soul cannot breathe if it cannot transcend into new dimensions night after night." She strums her long black fingernails over her chest.

"Yeah, well, tell 'em to keep their interdimensional jaunts quiet, and I'd like every soul asleep by ten. We've got neighbors around here, and we've never given anyone any trouble."

She glances up and snarls at me like a rabid dog. "You're a negative spirit, and I won't have you influencing the Plague with the cheap lyrics bleeding from your lips. Nothing pulls them into a bad frame of mind before a show more than someone trying to sell your brand of bullshit." She claps her hands over her head and lets out a cry of agony.

"You okay?" I'm not sure I'm buying her brand of bullshit, either.

"Get away!" The words bleed from her lips with a moan—like cheap lyrics to be exact. "You're repugnant! You're *cynical*. You're uninterested in everything we're doing." She bites the air between us, and I take a full step back. "For God's sake, you sound like my father." She belts it out so loud, I'm half-afraid the cops are going to haul my ass off to jail for assault.

"All right." I continue to back up with my hands in the air. "Do your thing. I'll be in that little tiny cabin behind the property. See me before sunset about leaving a deposit."

I make tracks down to the house, shaking my head as I pass the moving trucks.

She's a nut, but she had me at 10K.

———

A couple of hours drag by, and the moving trucks keep coming and going. I'm worried that soon I'll look out the window and the entire bed-and-breakfast will be gone—even though it would be a relief on some level.

One of the reasons I went to Garrison this morning was to track down Dr. Barney, one of the grant directors for my now nonexistent fellowship. He said Professor Bradshaw was still in remission and returning to his old ornery self and spending his days on the golf course, which made me glad. Memories of filling in for him and teaching his class last semester make me shake my head. I loved teaching that class—being with Kenny in that class. Anyway, I asked—just this side of begging—if there was any way he could get me back into the graduate program and was met with an emphatic N-fucking-O. Strangely, I'm okay with it. There was something freeing about Garrison cutting me loose last spring. And, truth be told, I don't mind running the B and B. People kill to have their own businesses, and I've had one handed to me on a silver platter. The real trick is getting it to produce a profit. I'm grateful for the B and B, but I can't let go of Garrison, either. I guess a part of me, my ego to be exact, was sort of hoping to be published once I'd finished up with grad school. It was going to be the icing on the scholastic cake.

Kenny and her insatiable appetite drift to mind. I much prefer my hands full with trying to please Kenny rather than the board of education at Garrison. An entire slew of ideas on how to do the former runs through my brain, and soon the lower half of my body is getting in on the action. And now I want nothing more than for Kenny to walk through that door.

The door rattles, and I jump up to get it.

It's like she read my mind.

I swing it wide open and Molly stares up at me, her arms weighed down with boxes full of her stuff.

"Good timing," she says, handing them off to me. I spot Kenny behind her with a matching load in her arms.

"Do you believe this?" Molly points hard at the B and B while I set the boxes down. "It's the freaking Plague! This is going to be so cool! They're finally going to put this sleepy town on the map. I hear they're *huge* in Japan."

"I bet." I kiss Kenny on the lips as I take the boxes from her, too. "There's something I need to show you out back a little later." I give a quick wink. The last thing I want is Molly listening in while I drive Kenny out of her mind, and I do plan on inducing a heavy bout of insanity in her. "So how was class, girls?"

"*Kenny* here"—Molly smirks over at her before continuing—"is vying for teacher's pet."

"What?" I seriously doubt this. The only teacher's pet Kenny is allowed to be is mine. I give her a quick wink.

"Oh, be quiet." She brushes Molly off. "I had a few questions about the assignment, and he wanted to take a look at my work after class. I think your sister here is just jealous that I actually had a conversation with him."

"You were whispering in his ear. Your body was pressed against his. I saw the whole thing." Molly sticks a finger down her throat and mock gags.

My body temperature spikes. No reason to panic. That's his job. Kenny is his student, and it's her job to ask questions. Nothing more than a scholastic exchange took place. The last thing I'm going to do is make her feel bad about it.

"I bet he wanted to see everybody's work." I frown over at Molly for trying to make something out of nothing.

"Nope." Molly pops open a bag of chips and shoves one into her mouth. "Just *Kenny's.*" Molly only calls her "Kenny" when she's trying to get under my skin.

I glance up at Kenny, and she shakes her head dismissively. "We'd better get the rest of the boxes out of my car before it gets dark."

Molly and I help unload the rest of her things, and soon the living room looks like a storage facility.

"I'll move these into my room tonight." Molly starts sliding a stack of boxes to her bedroom, so I take over. By the time I finish, my back feels like it's about to snap in two, so I crash on the sofa.

"Hey, cowboy," Kenny purrs into my ear from above. "I believe you promised me a trip to the barn a little earlier. Got a wild mustang in the corral you want to show off?"

A dull laugh pumps from me. "You sure know how to get me fired up." I hop off the couch and shout to Molly that we're going for a walk. The truth is, the only thing I'd like to do with Kenny right now is a little mattress rodeo, but because the walls are made of onionskin, that's going to be impossible for a good long while.

I take Kenny's hand and head out into the night, shocked as hell to see that the movers are still working away as vigorously as they were this afternoon.

"What the hell?" I take a step toward the melee, dazed by the sight.

A dozen oversized spotlights ignite the area like a football stadium, and a glow emits from the vicinity as if the bed-and-breakfast has become a nuclear reactor.

"*Shit.*" I let out a breath and a plume of vapor emits from my lips. It's freezing out, and I'm not sure the weather's conducive to helping Kenny reach that nirvana I planned on taking her to.

"Do you really think it's a good idea to let these guys just come in and take over like this?" Kenny presses into me as we walk briskly past the mayhem.

"No. I know for sure it's not a good idea, but I'm hoping the financial payout will far exceed the risk." Speaking of which, the Skin never did stop by to discuss the deposit. Then again, she is Cal's relative—I suppose this arrangement is a little more casual than for an ordinary tenant. Only something tells me the fact she's related to Cal is precisely why I *should* have taken it up front and double.

I wrap my arm around Kenny's waist, and we follow the stream up the property a way. The noise from the traffic and the movers drifts farther and farther away until it feels like a memory.

"Peace at last." I press a careful kiss over her cheek and take in the scent of her hair, chamomile and honey. Kenny is sweet tea in the flesh. "I like it like this. Just you and me." And yet already I miss it being just Kenny and me back at the cabin. I'd never ask Molly to leave, but I'll be glad when this Plague that has taken over our lives finally clears out and things get back to normal around here.

"I like it like this, too." She clasps her hands around my waist and lays her head over my shoulder. "We're going to have this forever."

We take a seat under the overgrown pepper tree, and I pull Kenny onto my lap.

"You know what the best part of each day is?" I hum it low into her ear, and her spine shivers over my chest. "Falling asleep with you in my arms—knowing you'll be there in the morning."

"Mmm," Kenny purrs. "I feel the exact same way. What we have is a gift." She wiggles her hips into my lap, extending the invitation to yet another gift. "I wouldn't trade it for all the riches in the world."

"I'm glad you feel that way. At the rate I'm going we might be stuck in that cabin longer than you think."

"Cruise . . ." Kenny twists in my arms and looks up at me with those crystalline eyes. I could sink a thousand years just staring into Kenny's beautiful eyes. It's as if God stole a piece of the sky and let her have it, because she's just that beautiful. "I'd be happy to spend the rest of my life in the cabin with you. It's perfect. It's our home. As long as you're with me that's more than enough."

She traces out my features with her finger, and my boxers start to tick. I wasn't really planning on bringing the boys to the party tonight. I really want the focus to be one hundred percent on Kenny and her needs. That's what I plan on doing for the rest of my life, putting her needs first.

A tiny breath escapes her. "Of course, I still want a really nice wedding." She says that last part a little louder, and my mind replaces the word *nice* with *expensive.*

"Did I tell you?" Her face lights up. "I found an amazing bone-colored Vera Wang that's to die for! Only that particular shade washes me out because my hair is so damn dark. I was thinking of cutting it real short in one of those asymmetrical styles to offset the sweetheart neckline and really bring out my—"

"Whoa, princess." I rock her in my arms and give a gentle laugh. "Please don't think you need to cut your hair to match your dress. Cut it only if you want to. I'd love you without hair, but I'd hate to see you get caught up in the wicked web of live bands and DJ combos just yet."

"Just *yet?*" She snaps her head up at me and her eyes blaze with an unfamiliar fire.

Something tells me we've strayed onto dangerous terrain.

"What's that supposed to mean?" She snaps it out so fast that instinctually I want to reach down and cover my balls. "We're getting married in . . . Less. Than. Three. Months. *Three months!*" She shouts that last part out and her voice comes back to us as an echo.

Holy shit. Something tells me I've lit the very short fuse to a bridal bomb.

Why doesn't life have a "Rewind" button? There's nothing more I'd like than to rewind and take back the words "just yet."

"It's like you don't even care," she goes on without missing a beat. "I bet you want one of those 'backyard weddings,' and you want me to sew my own wedding dress and bake my own cake. I bet you'd love it if Cal barbecued and we all sat around afterward watching ESPN."

ESPN? Is that big at weddings?

Her lips quiver like she's about to cry, but I can tell she hasn't discounted the idea of ripping my balls off—so I do the only thing I know. I land my lips over hers and slip my hand up her skirt. It's high time I put my body to work to untangle her nerves—defuse her before her world blows to bits over dinner arrangements and music. Kenny is perfectly wet, waiting—*wanting.*

I run my fingers along her heated slick and Kenny moans into my neck. I work in deliberate, slow circles, working my way up to a pressured pace until she's clawing at my chest.

"Enjoy it, baby," I whisper into her ear. "This is all about you." I want to make this happen for her just like I'd love to see her dream wedding happen. I don't know how, but I plan on ensuring each one of her wedding dreams comes true.

I ride over her harder and faster until she snaps her neck back, trying hard to keep from losing it.

"Take it." I whisper. "Let it out. I want to hear you."

Kendall bucks into my chest and gives a heated cry that rips from her lungs like a drill. She digs her nails into my arms as her legs clamp down over me, and I gently bring my hand up and rub a warm, wet circle over her belly.

"I love you, Kenny Jordan." I kiss her over the ear and leave my lips there.

"I love *you*, Cruise Belton."

I give a little chuckle at her surname slipup.

She's so damn cute.

5

IN THE SWING OF THINGS

Kendall

A week zips by and I've spent countless hours writing, editing, and effectively freaking out over my first short story in the Naughty Professor series . . . serial . . . whatever. Honestly, the word *serial* evokes all kinds of crazy thoughts in my head, like Cruise chasing me around with a hatchet. It's definitely not a word I'd voluntarily attach to our lovemaking, but then that was Lauren's doing. Anyway, I digress, I've sent countless drafts to Kurt—or as Molly insists on calling him, Professor Curl-Your-Toes—and he's graciously been editing them to perfection for me. Lauren had me send her a final copy last night. She's insistent on handling all the "details" that will magically make my read-by-the-chapter book appear on the Sorority Net website.

God, people are actually going to read this! It's like I've opened our bedroom door and sold tickets to some invisible peanut gallery, and Cruise has no idea how deceptively delicious it all is. But, to be truthful, I'm not so sure he'd find my deception so delicious. I have a feeling he'd be outright pissed and rightfully so. In fact, maybe that's when the hatchet chasing ensues and the reason Lauren insisted on calling this a serial comes to light. My enterprising erotic ramblings will have unwittingly turned my sweet fiancé into a homicidal felon.

I breeze into Starbucks after my last class of the day, or more accurately, my latest meet-and-greet with my editor. I giggle to myself at the thought. It all sounds so official it's almost scary. I give a brief wave over at Lauren and Ally. The sharp scent of fresh brewed coffee infiltrates my sense, and I can feel the weight of this entirely too long school week dripping off my shoulders like a lead coat. I just want to get home and relax with Cruise—and, well, get started on chapter two.

"Hello, ladies." I plop into a seat and mouth "thank you" over to Ally for having my drink at the ready. I admire the caramel dripping down the inside of the translucent cup and curl my lips. Penny and Cruz sort of have a caramel fetish going on at the moment. It's pretty exciting. It's like I get to have two sex lives and they're both with Cruise. If that isn't win-win, I don't know what is. "So what's new with you guys?"

Ally perks up. She's so sweet and beautiful—I'm really happy for her and Morgan.

"Well"—she chews on her lip—"I may have told Penelope Sandoval that I'd take one of her puppies off her hands."

"Dogs aren't allowed in our building." Lauren shakes her head like an irritated parent.

"But they're Siberian *huskies*. They're going to have those piercing blue eyes and black-and-white coats. It's basically the canine version of Morgan. They're the sexiest dog on the planet and believe you me, I'm getting me one."

"Sexiest dog on the planet?" Lauren lets out a groan like she's physically in pain. "No dogs, Ally. Before you dabble in bestiality, I need you to realize that the rental agreement I signed on your behalf was watertight. You're going to get yourself kicked out, and you'll be homeless again. You'd better tell Penelope and her puppy they're both out of luck."

Lauren helped Ally get the place and now they're neighbors. They used to be roommates at one of the dorms, just last semester. So much has changed so quickly. My engagement ring catches the light and I admire it—white platinum and a simple diamond. I know it probably seems like things are moving at the speed of light for Cruise and me, but when you find "the one" you're just happy to go along for the supersonic ride.

"I love dogs," I offer, still staring dreamily at my ring. "I realize this doesn't help"—I touch my hand to Lauren's for a moment—"but, back in California, we had one growing up. He really did add stability to our lives. He was always there to greet us when we came home. He sat right next to me while I did my homework. We ate all our meals with him there by our feet. He was like a member of the family. My mother used to tease that he took my father's place." Rat bastard. "Anyway, I'm sure the dog added much better stability than my father ever could have." True story. Hey? Did I just admit to being raised by a dog? Nevertheless, I'm positive it was better than his human counterpart.

"Relax," Ally quips in Lauren's direction. "The dog isn't for me, it's for *Ruby.*"

Ruby is Ally's four-year-old daughter, whom she gave up for adoption. It's an open adoption, so she gets to see her at least once a month. Morgan had the chance to meet her a few weeks back, on Ruby's birthday. He said that she was a living doll, that he helped teach her how to ride a bike. Just the image alone melted me. Morgan is going to be a great father one day.

"Ruby? Oh, that's a great idea." Lauren nods. "And that way you'll still have a roof over your head, and I'll still have my favorite neighbor." Lauren slings her arm over Ally's shoulder, pulling her into a headlock of a hug. Come to think of it, that's sort of Lauren's signature embrace.

"Speaking of a roof over your head . . ." I segue into the trials and sexual tribulations of having Molly stay with us. "The quick and dirty of it? She's killing Cruise's mojo. And get this! She actually applauded when I climaxed last night and shouted, *"Now I can finally get some fucking sleep!"*

Lauren and Ally both lose themselves in a bout of choo-choo train laughter.

"It's not funny. If this keeps up, she'll totally put a damper on chapter two. By the way, Kurt says I've really got a knack for this. He's amazed at the level of detail I've managed and he says—"

"Kurt?" Ally is stuck on first, and I've already run home with the conversation.

"That's my creative writing teacher," I tell her. "He's kind of out there, but he's the one I had edit the story. Once I managed to overlook his spontaneous desk-sitting, the taking off of the shoes, the holey socks, which he may or may not change, his granola-eating ways—Kurt is actually a really nice guy."

Lauren dips the tip of her finger in her mouth. "Kendall gave me chapter one last night, and I've already uploaded it to Sorority Net."

"It's up?!" I slam both my palms on the table and our drinks jump a few inches to the left. You'd think I was excited about Cruise's fifth appendage the way I belted that out. Belted . . . see what I did there? "People are actually going to see it? *Read* it?" God, now I feel completely foolish for hardly making an effort to veil our identities. "Word *is* going to get back to Cruise and he's going to kill me." Hatchet Cruise rears his gorgeous felony-in-the-making head at me.

"Oh, he is *not.*" Lauren is quick to brush off the idea. "Besides, I've been tracking sales and if you continue to climb like you have been, you're going to have the most sought-after serial on the book forums. Popularity equals subscriptions, so keep up the good work.

And, I took the—" She clamps her mouth shut and manufactures a smile.

"And you took the what?" I lean in, suddenly very interested in what would cause Lauren Tell-'em-What-You're-Really-Thinking Ashby to clamp shut on a dime. Lauren's not one to shy away from anything. She's got lady balls of steel.

"I took the liberty to add it to a few other sites." She lets the words dribble out the side of her mouth. "It's no big deal. It just gives you more visibility. I'll keep you updated on sales. Trust me, if things go well, you'll have plenty to fund your wedding. Speaking of which, did you find a church?"

I crumple my napkin and pitch it across the table. "I spent all week calling every church in Carrington, and they all gave the same answer: Christmas Eve service trumps Christmas Eve weddings. Not to mention, they all preferred if I were a member of their congregation for at least six months. It looks like it's a trip to the courthouse for me."

"That's not so bad." Ally rubs her warm hand over my shoulder.

"In blue jeans no less," I add. "I've gone online and nearly died at the price of some of those wedding dresses. And the Vera I'm after will cost me a liver on the black market."

Lauren nearly spits out her coffee. She never wiggles with excitement, so immediately both Ally and I are amused. "Speaking of wedding dresses," Lauren says, "come with me next week. I've narrowed it down to three, and I'd really like your opinions."

"Of course." I can barely manage the words. It's going to kill me to be around all those creamy, dreamy wedding dresses, knowing that I can't have a single one. It's like taking a diabetic to a bakery and shoving her face in a vat of buttercream frosting.

"How about eBay?" Ally offers. Ally and I are both up Poor Man's Creek without a sound financial paddle, so I appreciate all her suggestions.

"Well"—I'm half-afraid to admit this—"I did go on eBay and I found the exact sweetheart neckline Vera that I've got my eye on. And I *can* afford it." I try to summon all the faux enthusiasm I can muster, sort of the way I do with Molly in the morning. "There's just this one tiny detail . . ."

"Spill it, Jordan." Lauren axes the words out.

"The bride may or may not have been jilted at the altar—"

"Mmm, mmm." Lauren wags a finger with her latte still pressed to her lips. "Hell to the *no*. You just back away carefully from that haunted auction. Trust me, the last thing you need is bad dress juju following you around."

Bad dress juju—that's exactly what I was afraid of.

"It's too late," I snap. "I've already put a bid on it. It's my size and it's my *Vera*!"

"God, a *Vera*? How'd you get the money for a Vera?" Ally's face is alive with color at the thought of the matrimonial miracle.

"I didn't," I say flatly. "It'll take an act of God for me to win. There were at least thirteen other brides throwing their desperate Italian veils into the ring. Anyway, if I did manage to pull it off, I'd simply put it on my credit card." Never mind the fact I've been hitting all the sales around town, purchasing little knickknacks here and there in hopes of making my big day a little brighter. Of course, once I nail down a theme, all the prebudget spending will be much more streamlined. Not that I have the money for a budget.

Lauren needles me with her beady-eyed judgment.

"Don't look at me like that. I couldn't resist—it's like *ninety* percent off! And God knows it's my only shot at walking down the aisle in style. Not that there will be an actual aisle where I'm headed." Way to make it sound like I'm getting hitched in a penitentiary.

A brief yet vivid scene of me and Cruise having hot prison sex wafts through my mind like an erotic summer's breeze, and I fan myself with a napkin.

"You're not getting married in hell, Kendall." Ally closes her eyes for a moment. "I'll create an aisle for you if you want."

"You'd do that for me?" I get all teary-eyed and weepy, and just as I'm about to blanket her with a big old hug, Blair walks in with the douche bag she's leashing herself to for the rest of her life, Rutger Crones. "Asshole alert, twelve o'clock." Surprisingly, I managed to get the time orientation right.

Ally turns momentarily. "Bleh."

I wrap my fingers around the edge of the table and continue with our conversation. "How's your wedding, Lauren?" Truthfully, the way Lauren's been prepping and spending, you'd think she were in heavy training for the Bridal Olympics. But really I'm only half interested at this point because the disease that's hell-bent on destroying my happily-ever-after with Cruise is staring me down. I don't take my eyes off Blair. There's got to be some way to get her to relinquish my wedding date at the chapel. Maybe I can convince her to have a cliffside wedding? And maybe afterward, both she and the groom could take a nice swan dive into the Atlantic as a gift to the rest of the world.

"Oh, I forgot to tell you!" Lauren jumps in her seat. "I've booked the grand ballroom at the Carrington Country Club. I'm going for a masquerade theme, so you'll both be in full period costume. It's sort of Regency masquerade fusion with an Oriental flair because Cal is addicted to Chinese food. But I'm more into Japanese, so I'm compromising and having a sushi chef flown in from Hong Kong." Lauren looks to me. "How are you handling the reception?"

I swallow hard.

"Actually, it'll be small. Like less than ten or so. I was thinking we could go to the Della Argento after and have a nice dinner and a champagne toast."

Lauren lifts her chin at me and nods as if I've just spoken some mysterious new language and she hasn't a clue what just flew from my mouth.

"What about your cake, Lauren?" Ally leans toward her like this is the dirty detail she's waited all day to hear.

"Marzipan." She wrinkles her nose. "Traditional Swiss on the inside, but we're going to the Cake Chief and having him do something designer just for me. We've already talked to the producers, and our episode will air a few weeks after the wedding, just in time for Valentine's Day."

She says it so nonchalantly that both Ally and I are left openmouthed.

"You're going to have your wedding featured on *The Cake Chief*?" My stomach pinches with jealousy. "Lauren, that's amazing!"

"God, yes." Lauren lowers her cup to the table like a gavel. "I wouldn't trust anyone else with my wedding confection. This is the cake to end all cakes in a person's life."

A cake to end all cakes. And here I hadn't even thought of that pile of flour and eggs up until this moment. Maybe I don't deserve a wedding. If I care at all about my wedding, I should make a beeline for the nearest bakery right this fucking minute. Of course, I won't have to feed the masses—maybe just a *small* cake from the Cake Chief would be enough. After all, it's the cake to end all cakes.

I lean in. "So how much does your average cake run at the Cake Chief?" I bet whatever it is I can cut that number in half by the simple fact I'll have less than a dozen mouths to feed.

"At least five or six for a primo wedding design. But I want the recipe and blueprint destroyed afterward so there'll never be another like it, and there's a nominal fee for that as well."

"Five or six hundred?" God, that's a ton of money, but mine would be far less than that. I smell a cake adventure for Penny and Cruz.

"I wish." Lauren looks to the ceiling and lets out a hearty guffaw.

Five or six *thousand*? I bite down over my lip to keep from letting the expletives fly like I want.

"Oops." Lauren glances at her phone for a moment. "I gotta run. I'm auditioning stylists this afternoon."

"What's the stylist for?" Ally asks.

"Oh, hon"—she tousles Ally's hair—"you can't just expect me to show up at all these appointments in a T-shirt and jeans. I've got to look presentable, especially on television. I'll see you later! Ta-ta for now!" she sings as she heads out into the street.

"Ta-ta for now," I say weakly.

"Hey"—Ally shakes me by the arm—"cheer up, girl. You've already got what you need to pull off the perfect wedding and his name is Cruise Elton."

"You're right." I twist my lips into something just shy of a smile. "Cruise is by far enough." I drum my fingers against the table so hard my bones rattle. "It's just . . . I've always dreamed of having a *perfect* wedding. You know, it's sort of a one-shot deal. Too bad it's coming up at a time we're both pretty broke. And sadly, I really don't see that changing anytime soon."

"I hear you. Morgan and I are pretty tight ourselves."

"How about you, Ally? Do you have your heart set on a fancy wedding?"

"Nope. Never have, never will. Morgan and I will probably elope one day." She scoops up her things. "I've got to run to class.

Catch you later." She bullets out the door before I can contest the idea.

Elope? They'd better not. I have every intention of witnessing my brother and Ally tie the knot. I'd feel cheated if I didn't.

Ally seems perfectly content without having her heart set on some stupid fancy wedding.

Why can't I be more like Ally?

Blair swoops in and takes Ally's seat. She's buried in a thick furry coat that looks like it cost thousands of chinchillas their lives, and that crimson lipstick smeared over her face looks as if it cost one or two of them some blood as well.

"I have something you want." Blair's eyes ignite like a pair of wildfires.

"Yes, you do."

"It must hurt to know I took something you wanted so badly. Just like you took Cruise from me."

She gets up and leaves, and all my hope of having a Christmas Eve wedding at Garrison leaves with her.

Cruise

It's been one week, dude," I say to Cal as he helps me lower my weights back onto the press. I've been busting his balls for a little over an hour about his nonconformist trespasser of a relative.

"Pound on the door." He wipes the beads of sweat off his face with the back of his hand. "I don't know what to tell you."

I've been more than patient with Lisa "the Skin," but she hasn't come through with the deposit, and a part of me is sure I've let a bunch of squatters settle into the bed-and-breakfast.

"I thought maybe you could talk to her." I sit up and wipe my face down with a towel.

"No can do. Our families have a lot of bad blood between them. I haven't talked to Lisa since we were kids."

"What?" I'm not sure why this surprises me. "You talked to her a few weeks ago when you set this whole thing up, didn't you?" Why do I get the feeling I'm not going to like the answer.

"Not exactly."

Shit. My stomach acids churn with his admission. If I vomit, I'll be sure to aim right for his shiny new gym shoes.

"She texted me the night before, and I gave her your address. It was less than a text, really, so I wouldn't count that as communication. Besides, if my mother finds out, she'll revoke my invite to Thanksgiving dinner. There's no way in hell I'm missing that."

"Great." I run my fingers through my hair. It looks like the only real turkey around here is me. "So you're telling me I've gotten myself and my business caught up in some familial revenge scheme. Why do I get the feeling a gun battle that rivals that of the Hatfields and the McCoys is about to erupt on my property?"

"No way. We're past the gunslinging phase of our relationship."

My eyes bulge out of my skull because, for one, I was fucking kidding.

"After my grandfather did some time, we put away the shotguns. That arm of the family isn't worth even walking past the shadow of a penitentiary."

"What the hell did you let me rent the entire B and B out to her for?" I'm panicked. "She made it sound like they were setting up shop for months."

"She might be." He wipes the sweat from his brow. "I did a little research the other night, and the Plague has a gig near Carrington scheduled for the next three months. They're headed to LA just before New Year's, or I would have booked them for the wedding."

"*Three* months? The bed-and-breakfast will belong to the bank if they don't pay before then. I'd better hunt down the Skin infection and make sure she coughs up some green stuff. I'd hate to lose the business the first year it was entrusted into my hands."

"So how things going with you? You pretty happy running the place?" He knocks back half his water, and I wait for him to finish.

"You didn't hear a word I said, did you?" I swat him on the chest with my towel. "I'm in the shitter. I need to pull the bed-and-breakfast out by the balls and pray it makes some cash, or Kenny and I will be penniless and homeless. Some husband I'm going to make."

"Relax. Everything will kick into gear. You'll see. Why don't you go around and spy on all the other B and Bs, see what they're doing right, and steal their ideas? That's what I did with the gym."

"Did it work?"

"I don't have the top-selling membership in the tri-city area for nothing. You're damn right it worked. Check out the competition and believe you me, once you start implementing all their genius ideas, things are really going to turn around for you." Cal smacks me on the back. "I better run. Lauren wants me to meet her downtown to approve a monkey suit for the big day. You get the monkey suit yet?"

"Nope. But I think I've got a suit tucked away from my grand-father's funeral."

Cal barks out a laugh. "Grandfather's funeral! You got me good." He hoots all the way out of the weight room.

Too bad I wasn't kidding.

Kenny comes home right after her last class of the day with Molly in tow. They've been commuting to save on gas, and it's kind of nice to have both of my girls home at the same time.

"Just FYI"—Molly makes eyes at Kenny as if she wants her to keep quiet about something—"I might have a guest over tonight."

"Go ahead." I wrap my arms around Kenny and seal my lips to the back of her neck. She tastes as sweet as an apple. "You're welcome to have your friends over anytime. And if you want to overdose on chick flicks, you're welcome to do that, too. Kenny and I will steer clear."

"It's not that kind of friend," Kenny whispers into my ear.

"What?" I can feel my big bro overprotective superpowers kicking in. "No way." I shake my head at my sister. "Don't even think of bringing boys around here. I might be moved to commit a felony."

"Cruise!" Molly bites the air when she says it. "Stop treating me like I'm a baby."

"Yes, Cruise." Kenny spins in my arms until she's looking up at me with those sea-silver eyes. "Whether you like it or not, Molly is an adult. She has as much right to date as you or me."

I shake my head just barely at Kenny. In no way do I want her to join in on the Molly-gets-to-bring-dates-home parade.

"Look"—I sigh at my sister with her beautiful blonde hair, her little body wrapped in not enough clothes—"I understand the fact you want companionship. That's what friends are for. You can talk all night on the phone—heck, have a girlfriend or two spend the night. You can have as many slumber parties as you like. But as far as boys are concerned—I don't think you need to be wasting any time with them."

"Cruise"—Kenny pinches my ribs—"you've got to be kidding." She turns to Molly. "You're welcome to date. Just bring the boy around so your brother can approve. And for God's sake, be aware he's probably going to have a one-track mind. No one-night stands. You hear me? You need to look for a solid guy who has eyes and a heart just for you. You need to fall in *love*, Molly. When you're in love, sex can be this amazing—"

"Whoa." I cover my ears for a moment. "Kenny, why don't you take a walk with me down to the B and B for a minute. I need to see about getting that deposit. If they see your beautiful face, they might actually come out of hiding." She blushes as we make our way to the door. "As for you"—I narrow my gaze over at my sister—"don't go looking for love. When the time is right, it'll just happen. Focus on school, would you?"

"Oh, I will." She nods with that "you'll regret this" look in her eyes. And trust me, I already do. Crap. Anytime Molly agrees with me, it's cause for alarm.

Kenny and I make our way out the door, and the icy air cuts right through my clothes. I collapse my arms around her and rub my hands over her arms as we head toward the B and B.

"Boy, you're really tough on your little sister, you know that?" Kenny's dark hair blows back against the gray day, and she looks like a poem written over the landscape.

I press a simple kiss over her lips. "I just want someone to love her the way that I love you. I don't want to see her heart broken ten thousand times in a year, because she's trying so hard. And for damn sure I don't want to hear the sound of grunting coming from the next room."

"Speaking of grunting." She pulls a strand of her dark hair into her mouth and slips it out seductively. "I'm sort of in the mood for some grunting myself."

"Forest or beach?"

"Cold and colder." She makes a face.

We walk up the steps to the porch of the B and B and give a brisk knock on the door. I can't think of a single time that I've knocked before entering.

We hear the sound of footsteps scuttling upstairs, then nothing but silence.

"They're in there but they're ignoring us." I say, this time giving a series of powerful blows.

"You think the band is in there?"

"Doubt it. They take off every day at four, and I have no idea what time they get back." For the most part they've been dream tenants—except for the tiny detail of nonpayment.

"Let's just go inside." Kenny turns the knob but it's locked.

I pat my jeans down. "I left my key back at the cabin."

She points to the living room window that's open a few inches and makes her way over. Kenny slips it open farther and unhitches the screen. In less than a minute she has the B and B's front door open.

"You're the sexiest cat burglar I've ever laid eyes on. Remind me to arrest you later for trespassing." I run my tongue over her lips and she gives a little laugh.

"You've got to see this place." She pulls me in, and I shut the door behind me. It's quiet as a tomb. Gone is the dark cherry-stained furniture of my grandparents, replaced with clean, art deco lines. Most everything is stark white, with enough mirrors set out to make you feel like you're lost in some sci-fi fantasy. This stuff qualifies more as pieces in a modern art museum than furniture in a B and B.

"Thank God my mother is away," I whisper, taking it all in. "She'd have a coronary if she saw what I let happen to the place."

"You're going to get it all back, right?"

"I'd better." I glance down the hall and note that the grandfather clock that's been watching over the B and B like a soldier all these years is missing, and my heart sinks like a brick. "Anybody here?" I project my voice enough to carry throughout the facility because I damn well know Lisa and her delinquent Skin are hiding out upstairs.

"I guess she's not in the mood to deal with you." Kenny wraps her arm around me and sighs.

"Are you in the mood to deal with me?" I brush a kiss over her ear.

"Why, whatever did you have in mind, Professor Elton?" She bites over that pink lip of hers, and I take a nibble right alongside her.

"Let's make sure the upstairs is still intact." Something tells me it's not.

I lead Kenny up the steps and give a hearty knock at the door of one of the rooms they're "leasing." Again we hear the sound of footsteps from inside, then nothing.

"Crap." I shake my head. I venture on down the hall to the next room I've foolishly given away and the door is cracked open, so I push it in a few inches with my finger. "Holy shit," I whisper. Gone is the four-poster Victorian furniture my mother took pride in, and in its place is a steel rack with a giant leather swing, with stirrups attached on either side. The irony that this was once my grandparents' bedroom is not lost on me. I'm sure my grandfather is looking down and shaking his head right about now. To say I've fucked up good this time would be letting me off easy.

"Oh, this is going to be fun." Kenny pulls me in and locks the door behind us.

"We can't use this."

"We can." She strips down to nothing in less than twenty seconds, and it's damn hard to argue, with her tits staring me in the face. "And we will."

"Hello, girls," I whisper, giving them each a gentle squeeze. "But no, we can't."

"Oh, Cruise." She averts her eyes for a moment, pulling me in by the tie. "Imagine all the great stories that will come from this." She picks up a riding crop off the table and swats me on the ass with it.

"I hardly think these are stories we'll want to pass down to the grandchildren one day." My dick just voted that I shut the hell up and get with the ass-whipping program. Then again, my dick has never been one to think clearly under sexual duress.

"Oh?" Her fingers run over my lips like a feather. "Our grandchildren. Who else?" She takes me by the hand and walks us over to the cagey-contraption. Kenny sits herself down and lifts a leg into one of the straps. That dark triangle at the base of her pelvis flirts with me as a sliver of pink exposes itself in this dim light.

"Holy hell." I tear off my clothes and help her other foot into the stirrup. There's a bar up top, so I place her hands on it. "Hold on, sweetie, this is going to be one hell of a ride."

Kenny leans her head back and the ridges of her neck call my lips over with a private invitation. I lean in to kiss her, only to send her swaying in the opposite direction.

"Oh, wow, this is fun." Kenny giggles and brings a finger to her lips.

My erection bolts out because the thing that amps me up ten times more than needed is Kenny playing hard to get—but in this instance she's just plain hard to get a hold of. I brace her by the hips and carefully push into her, but she slips away and my dick ticks in the air as if asking, "What the fuck?"

I know, dude, I want to say. I pull the metal chains toward me and try again, achieving that deep level of penetration I've waited all day for. I groan, enjoying the hell out of the warm, wet squeeze she offers. Kenny has a way of always being ready for me. Just as I'm about to initiate my first full thrust, she slips backward as the swing pushes out.

"Tricky little fucker," I say, inspiring Kenny to break out in a fit of giggles. I grab on to the chains again, albeit lower and with a much firmer grasp, and plunge into Kenny with a victory thrust.

My foot slips, and I land over her and we both go flying back, only to rock gently forward again. "Are you okay?" This is actually kind of nice. I can't quite see her because my face is buried in the top of her head at the moment, but I'm hoping somehow she's enjoying it, too.

"God, yes!" she bleats. "This is *fantastic*! It's like we're flying. We're flying and having sex all at the same time."

"Hey, we're giving a flying fuck," I say, amused by my own little quip. I hike my knees on a pair of leather loops that dangle from the chains. "That must be what these are for," I say, straddling her and thus freeing my hips to thrust on command. I glide in and out freely as we continue to swing back and forth.

Kenny closes her eyes and moans. "This feels amazing! I think I want one of these for Christmas. It's like a ride at an amusement park."

I start in a little quicker and the swing starts to gyrate, losing its once-smooth rhythm, replacing it with a jerking motion that has all of our loose parts jiggling out of control. I watch as Kenny's tits bounce from her chin to her belly, and I can't say that I'm not enjoying the hell out of it. Kenny expels a few choking sounds from her throat, and I can only assume she's loving the shit out of it, too. Hell, maybe I *will* invest. Of course, I'll need a dungeon to store equipment like this. It's not the kind of thing you'd want your mother, sister, or, God forbid, future brother-in-law to stumble upon.

"Oh, Cruise," Kenny moans.

The flash of red and blue lights from the mirror in front of me catches my attention, and I wonder if we've alerted the sexual trespassing response squad—but I'm just about to have the most electric orgasm of my life, so I don't analyze the situation too deeply.

"Cruise!" Kenny shouts with abandon so I speed up my efforts. This might be one way to bring us both to a climax without any extra effort on my part. "Oh, Cruise, oh no . . ." She lets out a moan just as I hit my limit and tremble into her.

The door bursts open.

"Police!" A red-faced officer whips out his weapon and points it right at my bare ass.

Kenny lets out an ear-piercing belch and the distinct sound of vomit splatters to my left. I pull out and carefully ease Kenny from the contraption.

"Sorry." She sits up, covering her mouth. "Motion sickness. It gets me every time." She shrugs.

The officer hands me my Levis before replacing his weapon.

"You're both under arrest."

6

SWEET RELEASE

Kendall

4**00 downloads!**

I glance at Lauren's text while Cruise speaks to the officer at the midtown branch of the Carrington Police Department. It took two hours for Cruise to prove he's the owner of the bed-and-breakfast, and that we were simply making sure the new tenant hadn't broken anything.

As soon as the officer takes a full—highly detailed and, might I add, embarrassing—report, he informs us we're free to leave.

"You might want to lawyer up," he suggests to Cruise as we're about to head down the long hall to freedom. "Breaking and entering is a serious offense."

Cruise gets that swirly look in his eyes like he does sometimes with Cal or Molly. "Again"—his voice is tight—"it's my property."

"Doesn't matter." He shakes his head. "Tenants have just as much rights as landlords do these days. Probably more."

"So you're saying you can't help me get rid of them?"

"It's a civil matter," the officer says with a shrug. "Bring it to the courts."

"Crap." Cruise presses his hand into the small of my back and speeds us along. I'm sure the last thing he wants to think about is legal fees.

Cruise called Molly, of all people, to pick us up, and now I'm assuming we're bound to have yet another interesting conversation with his sister this evening. I tried to get him to call Morgan but he wouldn't hear of it. He said Morgan would have his balls if he knew what happened, and he's probably right. "They can't sue," he points out with a twinge of doubt in his voice. "We didn't break anything."

"*And*"—I wrap an arm around his waist—"I cleaned up the mess before we left." Cleaning up my own vomit after sex is an act I pray I will never relive. I doubt I'll be including that little tidbit in next week's installment of *The Naughty Professor*. Penny and Cruz's little twirl-till-you-hurl routine will be kept under wraps for now and, well, forever—at least the hurling portion.

I pull out my phone and hold it low while I text Lauren back. **400 downloads? Fantastic!**

Cruise's phone buzzes and I'm half-afraid I sent him the text instead. "Molly's here," he says.

"Oh, right." We step out into the cool of the evening. Cruise has his T-shirt on backward and I've lost an earring in the debacle, but who the hell cares. I've got great material for the next chapter in Penny and Cruz's steamy adventure. And trust me, there was enough heat in that room to steam any sorority girl's glasses.

Lauren texts back. **No, my friend, it's fan-tucking-tastic.**

I give a little laugh.

"What's so funny?" Cruise sighs as he pulls me in. It's hard to see him down like this. This whole thing with Cal's cousin has really been stressing him out. Clearly he could use some cheering up right now, and I have to bite my lip to keep from telling him how great the book is going. I mean, I will tell him—*eventually*. The last thing I want is for us to start our marriage off with secrets—and with a sexual exposé of our love life, of all things.

God, he's going to think I'm all kinds of twisted if he ever finds out on his own. He'll think I've been using him this whole time for entertainment purposes, or worse, to turn a profit on the side. A part of me thinks he might be amused and another, far more logical, part believes he'll put the kibosh on the entire thing, and I'll be back to my denim-disaster wedding at the courthouse. Not that I wouldn't be happy to marry Cruise in blue jeans—it's just that the tiny Vera sitting on my shoulder disapproves harshly, and I happen to agree with her.

"Oh . . ." I shake the tiny Vera out of my head. "Nothing's funny. Lauren's just texting me details about her wedding."

"That's nice. Hey, Molly just texted that she's here, but I don't see her car anywhere. Do you?"

Technically, Molly doesn't have a set of wheels to call her own. She's borrowing her mother's car while she's away.

A horn goes off, and one of those tiny hybrid vehicles pulls up beside us with Molly waving from the passenger's seat.

"Hop in!" She motions to the back.

"What the—?" Cruise opens the door for me, and I gasp when I see who's at the helm of this green nonluxury ride. Gah! It's Professor Curl-Your-Toes himself.

"Hi, Kendall." He gives a light wave. He's wearing his gold-rimmed glasses, and he's got his button-down sweater with a pink dress shirt peeking out from underneath, his signature khakis completing the look.

"Cruise Elton." Cruise extends his hand from the backseat and Kurt is quick to accommodate him with a handshake.

"Nice to meet you. I'm Kurt," he says, then turning his attention back to the road. "Molly says nothing but nice things about you." He glides back into traffic and good thing he has to focus on the road. I'm pretty sure one wrong word and Cruise will introduce an entirely not-so-nice side of himself.

"So"—Molly spins to face us—"what the hell'd you two get arrested for?"

Cruise swallows hard. "We didn't get 'arrested,' Molly. It was simply a misunderstanding. We were just looking for the people I rented the property to. Nothing more."

"And they hauled you all the way to the station just for that?" Kurt glances back at us through the rearview mirror. "There's a perfect example of how the Carrington PD is wasting taxpayers' hard-earned money. We should take this to the media. I've never heard of someone being arrested in their own home."

"So how'd you and Molly meet?" Cruise is quick to take the focus off media attention. I'm a little impressed. He did it with such finesse and dexterity, he should really consider politics.

"I teach creative writing over at Garrison. Molly and Kendall are actually both my students."

Crap. The next thing you know he'll be commending me on my exceptional erotica skills. Then, of course, I'll have to shove my fist down his throat, and he'll lose control of the wheel and we'll all die in a fiery crash. It's safe to say I have no problem taking this secret to the grave—and not just my grave.

Cruise tips his head, suddenly a bit more interested in the date his sister has scored for the evening.

"So what's going on?" He looks more than mildly alarmed. "Did Molly leave something important in class and you were driving by to drop it off?" Cruise is hopeful that a missing purse is at the end of this scholastic rainbow.

"Nope." His attention never leaves the road. Kurt doesn't seem the least bit concerned that the granola bits in his tighty-whities are in peril. "Just thought we'd catch a quick bite."

A deafening silence fills the car as Kurt drives us closer to the spot where Cruise is about to bury his body.

"First date?" Cruise glares over at him.

"Oh, no, Molly and I've been out a couple times around campus—nothing that qualifies as dating. I simply like to go above and beyond with my students." He chuckles softly to himself as if reliving a private memory. Crap. I can practically see an entire movie reel of all the private times Cruise and I shared back at Garrison spinning through my poor fiancé's eyes. God knows Cruise Elton is well aware of what can be done and where at that not-so-sacred institution. "It's weird"—Kurt goes on to seal his fate—"every time I turn around, she seems to be standing there. It's just one of those kismet things, I guess."

Or stalker things, but I keep the commentary to myself. I wouldn't put it past Molly to have staked out his comings and goings with the finesse of an upper-echelon PI.

"Anyway"—he continues to walk farther down the plank—"I thought, why not? She was after me to take her off campus, and it *is* Friday night." He tweaks her knee, and I can feel Cruise's entire body tense up at the sight of this bona fide faculty member molesting his not-so-sweet baby sister. "Hey, you guys hungry? Want to join us?"

"No!" It roars out of me without meaning to. "I mean . . ." I glance to Cruise for help. Surely he doesn't want to endure more of Professor Curl-Your-*Sister's*-Toes.

"Yes," Cruise says with much more force than my "no." He nods at me so I shrug in agreement.

"Good." Kurt's eyes widen for a moment as he looks back at Cruise in the rearview mirror. I think he's finally catching on that Cruise isn't all that impressed with how willing he is to go above and beyond for his students. "We're headed to Della Argento, but if you'd rather go somewhere else, I can turn this ship around." He laughs like he's trying to add levity to the situation. God knows, this Tinkertoy qualifies as more of a rowboat—a *paper* boat to be exact.

"Della Argento sounds perfect." Cruise gives him a hard look. "Perfect," indeed. Cruise knows exactly what goes on at the Della Argento. We may or may not have partaken in some bodily desserts the past few times we were there. Poor Kurt might as well have said "Motel Six," the way Cruise is digging his fingers into his pockets to keep from breaking his neck.

Thank God Kurt hasn't said a single word about—

"I've been meaning to talk to you about your book, Kendall!" A toothy grin takes over his face as he gives a quick glance back. "That's one wild kitten you're writing about!"

Shit.

"Book?" Cruise is suddenly interested.

"Just some silly class assignment." It speeds out of me as we turn into the restaurant parking lot. "It's about kittens and how crazy in love they can fall with one another—sort of an animal-bonding piece."

Animal-*fucking*-bonding piece? Way to stretch the truth to the man you're about to marry.

Kurt glances at me for a moment, and I take the opportunity to shoot him a look that says, *Breathe another word and I'll knife your balls off.*

"Oh look, valet parking! I'd hate for you to miss it." I practically jump to the front seat as I help steer him to the right. The sooner we're out of this tin can, the sooner I can inform him to zip his granola-loving lips when it comes to me and my kitten porn.

"I, uh, wasn't going to park in valet," he stammers, but I nearly mow down an entire herd of people waiting for their cars and he's forced to brake abruptly. "It's six whole bucks and they expect a tip on top of that."

"It's on me!" I sing as I evacuate the vehicle.

Cruise comes around and helps me to the curb. "Are you feeling okay?"

I'll go with that. "No, come to think of it I feel terrible." I touch my hand to my forehead.

"We'll be quick."

"What?" I thought for sure he'd whisk me back to the cabin without a second thought.

"There's no way in hell I'm letting this guy paw all over her at dinner. We'll use you as an excuse and end the night early." Cruise seems satisfied with his plan to shoot down his sister's evening.

"No, it's fine. I suppose one quick meal won't kill me." I glance over at the marble statue of a naked woman covered in Christmas lights just outside the entry. "Besides, we've made a lot of nice memories here. Hey, maybe we should sit at a separate table. You know—give the lovebirds some privacy."

"Oh no." He shakes his head, adamant. "We're definitely sitting with them."

"Perfect." It comes out weakly as we make our way inside. It's only then I notice that Molly has on a pair of my leather FMs, my lace miniskirt, *and* my leather vest. "Hey"—I catch up to her and whisper—"what's with the wardrobe heist?"

"All my stuff is in boxes. It was sort of a last-minute thing, so I just helped myself. I figured since we're practically sisters you wouldn't mind." She inverts her lips and looks up at me with those puppy dog eyes.

Even though she's a total buzzkill on my mojo, my heart melts at the idea of being "practically sisters" with Molly. That means I'm one step away from being Cruise Elton's wife, and I cannot wait for that magical moment. It'll be the best damn moment of my life.

"You can borrow anything you want." I give her a little hug as we enter the establishment. It's breathtaking inside, dimly lit with candles quivering against the crimson wallpaper, the carpet rolling from the entry into the dining area like a red velvet tongue.

The hostess seats us, and Kurt quietly excuses himself to use the restroom. Perfect. Here's my chance.

"I'll be right back as well." I press a quick kiss into Cruise. "I need to freshen up."

I chase Professor Curl-Your-Toes down before he can hit the men's room—just the act of chasing a man who isn't Cruise down these halls makes me a little sad. He and I have been known to fornicate freely here—well, everywhere, come to think of it.

"Sorry to stalk you like this," I pant, glancing briefly over my shoulder in case Cruise thought my abrupt exit was an invitation.

"Not a problem. Can I help you?" He leans in, inspecting my disheveled state. I probably should have run a brush through my hair on the way over.

I grab him by the sweater and yank him in. "I beg of you to keep the assignment I'm working on in class private."

His eyes enlarge as he takes in my fists balled up on his chest, so I relent and smooth him back to normal.

"You see, my fiancé isn't quite aware of it just yet."

His forehead wrinkles with confusion.

"We're getting married in a couple months and the whole thing is sort of a wedding gift." Ha! I guess it could be, although I'm pretty sure shoving a tell-all book in his face isn't the first thing I want to do as his new bride.

"Interesting." He frowns at me as if he smells a rat.

"I'll have the next chapter done next Tuesday. Do you think you can get the edits back to me by Thursday?"

"If it's just as short, I don't see why not. In fact, if you like—"

Cruise comes barreling down the hall, so I spin around and duck into the ladies' room before poor Kurt can finish his sentence. I take up residency in a stall for a small eternity, just killing time before we can leave this damn place. I hope to God that Kurt got the message loud and clear. Kitten sex is off the list of topics for sparkling dinner conversation. I splash some water on my face and head back, only to smack into one of my favorite hard bodies, Cruise Elton himself.

"Fancy meeting you here." I give a wry smile.

"Are you okay?" He looks genuinely concerned, and now I feel bad for texting Lauren and Ally for the past ten minutes while he was busy out in the hall worrying about my intestinal health.

"I'm fine." I swipe my finger over his cheek. "I promise."

"Come here." He pulls me back behind a dark velvet curtain where we've been known to instigate some quick coital activity and wraps his arms around me lovingly instead. "I just want to hold you a second."

There's a sadness in him, like he's got the weight of the entire universe on his shoulders and all he wants is a nice firm hug. Come to think of it, so do I.

"Everything okay?" I whisper, almost afraid to ask.

"Let's see. I just got arrested for trespassing on my own property, which, embarrassingly, I did. I inadvertently mooned an officer while he threatened to pump lead in my ass, and I made my bride-to-be sick to her stomach while trying to make love to her on bastardized jungle gym equipment. I'll leave out the part about my sister getting felt up by her creative writing teacher in front of me. It's about all I can take for now."

I pull back and drink in his gloriously blessed features. Cruise Elton is a god among men.

"I'm sorry." I give his shoulders a tiny massage before dropping my arms around his waist again. "It's all going to work out—I just know it is. Sort of like we did."

He dots my nose with a kiss.

"I want to hear all about your book when we get a chance."

My stomach clenches and reenacting my earlier vomit incident feels like a real possibility.

"You do?"

"Yes." He tucks his head back a notch. "You're the most important thing in the world to me, and I want to encourage and support you in whatever you want to do. And if writing about kittens makes you happy, then that's what I want you to do."

"*Aww!* You just melted me, you know that?" I push him in by way of his bottom. "And what if it's hard-core kitty porn?" I give his buns of steel a squeeze, but to no avail—Cruise is hard as granite.

He pushes out a dry laugh. "I'd love you even more." He touches his lips to my forehead. "As long as you're not starring in any kitten porn, I'm fine with it."

I swallow hard.

He doesn't really mean that. In fact, I will give him my book as a wedding present—as soon as we come back from our honeymoon.

No reason to rock the boat during a perfectly good epilogue.

———

As soon as we get home, Cruise hits the shower and I hit eBay. I've got about another ten minutes and, last I checked on the drive home, I was still the highest bidder. Sadly, this, too, is another tidbit I'm keeping from Cruise but I don't feel too bad. Everybody knows it's rotten luck for the groom to see the bride-to-be in her wedding gown, and I can only assume that means him gawking at her eBay purchase of said dress as well.

I log in, only to be met with *Sorry, you've been outbid!*

Crap.

I click on the picture again. The dress is a perfect size six. Technically I'm an eight, but everyone knows you can get those things adjusted. Plus I plan on cutting out the lattes and mixing in a few salads the closer it gets to the wedding. Although I sort of need to feed my Starbucks addiction at the moment because it just so happens to be the only thing keeping me sane.

I zoom in on the image. The dress sits neatly tucked into a box, with a clear view from the neckline to the waist. Next to it is a picture of a runway model wearing it. It has a sweetheart neckline and a clean hourglass waist that sweeps out in layers of delectable sheer fabric, luscious as buttercream. It looks like one big delicious fairy tale ready to unfold. The retail price of $7,000 has a giant red X through it, and just below, the bid reads $200. Of course it's at $221 at the moment because some skinny bitch thinks she's about to outbid me. Little does she know I've got my Visa out and I'm not afraid to use it. I frown a little at the idea. I don't exactly have the means to pay it off all at once. But it's not like I sit around nightly, outbidding people on designer dresses. This whole financial fiasco is sort of a one-off. I type in $250 and hit "Place Bid." There.

Cruise comes into the kitchen and I'm quick to close the laptop.

"What's up?" He nods at the computer while grabbing a water bottle from the fridge.

"Just checking my emails. I'll be back in a bit."

He comes over and kisses me on the top of my head.

"I love you." He tucks a tiny grin in his cheek. He's showered and smells like mountain spring soap, mouthwash, and the slightest hint of his seductive cologne, which calls forth all kinds of erotic memories. "Don't ever feel like you need to hide anything from me. I promise I'd never read your emails."

"And I'd never read yours," I purr as he heads off to the bedroom.

I open my laptop in haste, and it takes a minute for the damn thing to blink to life.

Outbid! And only three minutes left.

Shit!

Molly saunters over, oblivious to my real-world worries because she's been floating on cloud nine ever since Professor Curl-Your-Toes gave her a rather warm and intimate embrace good night when he dropped the three of us off. Cruise nearly had a vomiting session of his own at the sight.

Crap. It's up to $251. Who in the hell is this whore who thinks she's about to swipe my Vera?

"Back off, bitch," I whisper, typing as fast my fingers will fly—$280.

"That's not enough." Molly pipes up from behind, and I jump in my seat. "If you really want it, put in some outlandish number to ensure the win. Are you really going to let 'crazyeights' steal your wedding dress?"

She's got a point.

"Hell-*fucking*-no." My fingers glide across the keyboard—$5,001—and I place the bid.

There.

"Holy shit." Molly belts out a laugh. "You'd better hope crazyeights is as insane as you are or—"

Congratulations, you're the highest bidder!

"Ha!" I hold out my hand, just waiting for Molly to slap me some skin but she doesn't. Instead, we both stare dumbfounded at the idiotic number I've managed to conjure up on the screen. "Five thousand dollars?" I croak weakly. "Actually, five thousand and one."

"God, Kendall"—Molly staggers backward—"you've just spent more money than Cruise has made in his entire life."

"Crap. Just crap. What am I going to do now?" I bite down so hard on my lower lip, I'm about to draw blood, and I wish to God I would. I should start stabbing myself with a pen and pulling my hair out in clumps, running around eating artificial houseplants because, unless I plead insanity, I'll never in a million years be able to pay off this wedding dress.

"Wow." Molly leans in. "Do you see the shipping on that thing?"

"What's this?" I scroll down. "Five hundred dollars to ship?"

"Congratulations, Kendall, you've just been fiscally screwed. There's no way it costs that much to ship something. I mean, where are they sending it from, Siberia?"

I swallow hard and scroll a little farther down.

"Patagonia." That's like Siberia's cousin.

Fuck.

"Estimated arrival January third? What the hell . . . Is she *walking* it over?" I shake my head at the insanity of it all. "Screw it. I won't pay. I'll just say my child did it. You hear about toddlers running up their parents' phone bill into the thousands all the time on the news, and everyone laughs it off."

Molly raises a brow in amusement. "Only you don't *have* a child unless, of course, you're counting yourself." That hint of sarcasm in her voice lets me know she's enjoying this on some level.

"I'm counting *you*, Miss 'If you really want it, put in some outlandish number to ensure the win.' This is all *your* fault." Not really, but it feels good to spread the blame.

She averts her eyes toward the ceiling. "Well, you have to pay them or they can take you to court." She squints into some invisible horizon and a devious smile tugs at her lips. "But you can always turn around and tell your credit card company that your card was stolen, and—*ta-da!*" Her eyes narrow in on mine and she looks eerily like Cruise's evil twin. "You're suddenly free of a five thousand—dollar mistake that's better off in Patagonia where it belongs. And, sadly for them, they'll still send you the dress. It's made of win—a devious win."

I gasp. Is this what it's come down to? Internet fraud? *God.* I clasp my chest. I'm going to land myself in prison for some stupid bridal crime that Molly dragged me into.

"Lauren was right," I whisper. "This dress is rife with all kinds of bad juju. I guess I'll just contact the seller and explain the entire thing was a mistake. I'm sure she'll be reasonable."

I waste no time before diving into a psychotic manifesto that depicts my ill state of mind after vomiting on a sex swing, when what I wanted to say was: *I wasn't thinking straight, because who pays five thousand fucking dollars for a used dress when I can buy a perfectly new Vera for as low as twenty-five hundred?* But instead I round it out with: *Please excuse my three-year-old daughter, Molly, who accidentally bid on your beautiful wedding dress. She has a bad habit of landing herself in places she doesn't belong. I wish you much luck with finding a buyer!*

Less than five minutes later: *Congratulations on your purchase of an original Verra Wang designer wedding dress! Please complete payment promptly to ensure this case does not continue to the resolution center. If a prompt payment is not made, due diligence will be made to legally pursue the collection of funds. You have entered into a legal and binding contract and will be pursued to the fullest extent of the law to fulfill your financial agreement. The item you have purchased will be sent to you upon payment.*

The message may as well have read: *Congratulations on your new dress, sucker!* I read it over again and balk at her misspelling of *Vera.* It doesn't matter. She's got me right where she wants me. She could spell it with just dollar signs, and it wouldn't change the fact I'm a fool.

It's like she's going to come after me and my future children as well. Cruise will probably lose the bed-and-breakfast because we'll be sued into oblivion, and it'll be all my fault.

"Screw it."

I whip out my Visa and pay for the damn thing.

I think my credit card is about to get stolen.

And, much to my mortification, I just may have my wedding dress—albeit two weeks too late.

Cruise

A few days go by and bodies start filtering in and out of the bed-and-breakfast at all hours—girls in ultrashort skirts and bare-chested guys with their shirts wrapped around their necks, their boxers hanging out the back of their pants. I've effectively turned my grandfather's sweet little lodge into a full-fledged brothel. Not to mention that a cash transaction has yet to take place.

The Plague has arrived in full force and is ready to have one hell of a good time on the sexual playground they've turned my nest egg into. Mom called yesterday and I assured her I have every-thing under control, because I didn't have the guts to say otherwise. She mentioned Grandma was still in need of her help, so that took some pressure off. She asked about the beauty parlor, which is on autopilot thanks to a competent staff. I did promise to drive by sometime to make sure it's still standing.

Late in the afternoon, Kenny and I decide to head to the gym.

She pulls me in just shy of the weight room. "I think I'll hit hot yoga," Kenny purrs while pointing across the way.

"Save some of your hot moves for me, will you?" I wrap my arm around her and drop it low until I'm cupping her ass. She heads off in the other direction, and I stride into the weight room, where

I find Morgan with a disapproving smirk on his face. Great—just what I need: a little grief from my soon-to-be brother-in-law. I head over and take a seat on the bench next to him.

"Ho hey," he says unenthusiastically as he slaps his weights on the bar. "Rumor has it you nearly landed my sister in the big house the other night. Care to explain?" He wipes the sweat off his brow with his heavily tatted up arm.

I'm not sure what Kenny told him, or if he got wind of what happened by way of Ally. Either way, he might know more than I want him to.

"Misunderstanding." For a second I consider bolting and running laps on the track outside. I like my balls right where they are, and Morgan seems to be in the mood to do some anatomical rearranging.

"Ally mentioned there was a breaking and entering charge."

"It was at the bed-and-breakfast. It's not like we broke in." That was easy enough. I lean in to adjust the weights.

"And a *fuck* swing," he deadpans.

Shit.

I shoot him a look just as Molly comes up and lands a nice fresh towel across his shoulders.

"And how are you this fine day?" She bats those baby blues at him and my stomach turns. On second thought, I'd rather be discussing a "fuck swing" and contemplating the ways he might disembowel me rather than watching Molly try to lure him into bed.

"Why fine, thank you." He buries his face in the towel for a second. "And since I'm not the one who was taken downtown for performing an indecent act on private property, I guess I'm *really* fine, thanks for asking." He has the nerve to smile up at her.

"It was *my* property," I hear myself say, and I can't believe I fell for that.

"So you admit it." He glares at me.

"Anyway"—Molly runs her hand across his shoulders like she's dusting him off—"I just want you to know I'm in a committed relationship now, and things are moving pretty quickly. If you want to have any chance with me at all, I suggest you act fast before I'm out of your arms forever."

Again, I'd rather be discussing perverse playground equipment than listening to my sister sell herself as a blue-light special.

"You're very sweet, you know that?" Morgan looks up at her. "I'm happy for you, Molly. I'm really glad you found someone special. Make sure he treats you right, or I'm going to have to come after him." He brings his fist to his palm playfully, and Molly's lips twist into a reluctant smile.

"And you're really a nice guy, Morgan. I can't wait for you to meet Kurt. But don't go scaring him with your muscles. Okay?"

"Deal."

She skips off, content with his gentle kiss-off.

"Thanks," I say. "I agree with Molly. You really are a nice guy."

"I'm not *that* nice." That look of annoyance returns to his face as his features harden. "You get my sister thrown in jail again, and yours will be the only ass I'm interested in kicking." He leans in. "I roomed with you for the last three months—I know you're a sick fuck," he says, serious as shit. "Kendall is a good girl. And for whatever reason, she's drawn to you." His fingers flick through the air as if he can't find the right words to actually describe the dung that sits before him. "Treat her right. If you have to indulge in that shit, keep it in your own damn house. But breaking into other people's bedrooms to entertain yourselves is flat-out wrong, Cruise. You got that? It's fucking *wrong*. So if it's some new fetish you're into, I suggest you cross it off your wish list. My sister's not some prop you can drag around from place to place to get your rocks off."

"Look, I don't make it a habit of breaking into other people's bedrooms," I say. "It was a onetime thing, and it'll never happen again." And why the hell do I suddenly feel the need to justify my actions to Morgan?

"'Onetime thing'?" His chin dips as if I'm shitting him, and that night at his housewarming party comes back to me.

"That night at your place was something totally different. We've never done that before." Had we? An entire montage of places and spaces that Kenny and I have defiled runs through my head.

"What about that night you took Ally and me to that uptight Italian restaurant? If I remember correctly, you and *Kenny* took a little potty break together. Was that a fluke, too? Or what about the time you screwed your way around campus and got thrown out of the graduate program? You going to tell me *that* was some unfortunate quirk?"

Crap.

I just stare at him a very long time.

"Look"—he digs his palm into his eye as if talking to an idiot like me is an exhausting effort, and it probably is—"I get it. You're crazy about her. And trust me, I'd rather have it that way than you being some indifferent asshole. But when you put her in that position, you're still sort of being . . . an indifferent asshole." He sighs with exasperation. "I want you to love my sister—just not in public, or in other people's bedrooms, or closets, or any other nooks and crannies I don't even want to think about. I'm not asking you to keep it in your pants. I'm asking you to keep my sister safe—be responsible. Keep it in the bedroom. Got it? Stop being such an ass and love her sweetly—like a real man, not some perv." He gets up and stalks out of the room.

Keep his sister safe. Something about his please-keep-my-sister-out-of-prison speech hits home with me. What if it were "Professor Kurt" who had done all those things with Molly? I'd knock some teeth out and save the speech for later. Looks like Morgan let me off easy, seeing as my balls are still intact. Maybe I'm not treating Kenny as well as I should be. Maybe the last thing I need to be doing with Kenny is having outlandish sex with her every chance I get. I think I'll take things down a notch. I think I'll stick to making love to Kenny right there in the confines of our bedroom like Morgan suggested. And, ironically, that turns me on even more than thoughts of swinging with her on perverse toys in my grandfather's old bedroom. I shudder at the imagery.

Morgan was right.

I need to love her sweetly.

That night I make an all-you-can-eat spaghetti dinner with meatballs the size of oranges and garlic bread guaranteed to linger on your breath for days. I break out a bottle of two-buck Chuck, and Kenny and I enjoy the hell out of ourselves on a meal that cost less in total than a single appetizer at the Della Arm-and-a-Leg Argento.

"Too bad Molly missed out," Kenny says, leaning in. Her cleavage bows into me, practically begging for a kiss. But she doesn't look sorry at all about Molly's absence, and right about now neither am I. "You, my love, are a five-star chef. How *ever* will I repay you for this meal?" She bats her lashes at me, and my dick comes up with an entire roster of suggestions she could systematically check off.

The old me would have raked off the table and had her on her back in less than three seconds, risking the possibility that Molly might come home early after being molested by her English professor. But the new me, the one my dick is not so fond of at the moment, has paused and is regrouping to figure out how best to lure her to the bedroom.

"Wanna fuck?"

"*Oh . . .*" She laughs darkly. Kenny pushes the dishes to the far end of the table and hops on as if she's read my mind. "I thought you'd never ask."

I shake my head just barely. Poor thing. I've practically trained her like a circus poodle to go to the most perverse plausible option. I'll have to sexually reprogram her to be loved and cared for like the sweet woman she is.

"Come here." I pull her up and wrap my arms around her waist. "You're the love of my life, you know that?" I walk her backward toward the bedroom and plant a kiss on her lips.

"And you're the love of *my* life." She nods, edging me back toward the table.

"*And*, I think we should share our appreciation for each other right this minute." My hard-on is about to bypass any altruistic motives my heart might have, and I want to bend her over before we get to either the bedroom *or* the table. "Let's get to bed."

"'Bed'? What's the matter?" She looks genuinely concerned, like maybe a medical issue might be at the heart of my mattress motives.

"No." I hold back the urge to laugh. "I want to make love to you. In our *room*, on our *bed*." I give a gentle tug down the hall, but she's rooted her feet to the floor.

"Well, I don't want you to 'make love' to me." She gives me a hard tug in the opposite direction. "I want you to *fuck* me on the table like a man!"

Good God, I've ruined her. I close my eyes for a moment, just this side of despondent.

I bring her hand to my lips and lay a gentle kiss over the back of it. It's becoming pretty clear just how much perverted damage I've caused. Poor Kenny doesn't think she's worthy of being made love to behind closed doors and in a bed, of all places. I've warped her image of sex so that it's become some near-violent act that ends with weaponry pointed at our naked bodies while she vomits her brains out.

She folds into my chest. "You want to make love to me?" She says it almost disbelieving.

"Just as much as you want to fuck me," I tease.

She glances down as if truly disappointed. "Okay, but just this once."

My heart drops like a stone because every part of me wants to make love to Kenny over and over again, and never "just this once."

"I'm all yours." I reel her into me and brush my lips over hers. Kenny comes at me hungry, like she's never tasted my kisses before. Her tongue lashes over mine like a punishment as she devours me from the inside out. I pull her back gently until we're safely tucked away in the confines of our bedroom, then turn out the light.

Kenny rips off her clothes like they're on fire, and I can't help feeling bad, like I've sent her the message that every time she's with me it's a near assault. I am, after all, her first, her *only*. I have a responsibility to shower her with affection, but I've spent the better part of the past year taking her like a frat boy every chance I got.

I peel off my clothes and bring her heated body over mine. Kenny is smooth as velvet against my skin, like something precious to be cherished, not an object to be tied down with leather and chains and spun into stomach-churning oblivion.

My mouth finds hers once again, and we indulge in a lingual exchange that spans a small eternity as we stand there in the dark, in the confines of our own bedroom, and it feels far more erotic than the broom closet of some restaurant—or her own *brother's* closet.

Kenny runs her warm hands down my back and drips down to my thighs before rounding to the front and taking me in her hands. I walk her back and lay her gently on the mattress, trailing kisses from her neck to her chest, down to her smooth, soft belly. I rub my face over her stomach and indulge in the simple act of loving her in this innocent way. There are so many new ways to love Kenny that feel satisfying, though just a week ago I would have brushed them all off as juvenile.

The nightstand drawer opens and closes, and Kenny tosses down what sounds like jewelry, but it's the chains we've used from time to time. I pick them up and gently lay them on the floor, far away from our tender moment.

"Excuse me." She balks at how quickly I've dismissed them. "That was a hint, by the way." She rubs her foot over my back, and I'm half-tempted to hog-tie her in less than three seconds, just the way she likes it.

"Maybe not tonight." I press my lips into her belly button and Kenny quivers beneath me.

"Um"—she clears her throat—"there's a can of whipped cream in the refrigerator, the new chocolate kind. Would you like me to get it?"

Chains? Whipped cream? Poor Kenny doesn't even know that sex without some added prop is possible.

"No, I think we've got this handled." I dip my tongue into her belly button and start in on a slow rotating circle until a groan wrenches from her.

"Oh yes, right there." A string of giggles reverberates through her body, and a smile sails to my lips at the innocent and yet soulful seduction of Kenny. I trail lower, creating an *S* over her skin with my tongue before pressing her knees back and settling her legs over my shoulders. My mouth finds its way to her wet slick, and I indulge in a kiss that rivals any I've ever given her before.

"You taste damn sweet, Kenny. You're all I need." I run my fingers over her stomach until she catches my hand and kisses it.

I love Kenny in that same sweet way, all night long.

7

DRESS TO IMPRESS

Kendall

Weeks slide by. For starters, Aunt Flow made her monthly debut and did her best to kick the storyline back a notch, but, thankfully, the Penny Whoredon in me rose to the occasion and turned her appearance into a fellatio funfest for all. Needless to say, Cruz Belton was more than pleased, or should I say *pleasured*? Anyhoo, Lauren and Ally are picking me up so we can all go to Lauren's fitting together. Everything is falling into place for her dream wedding, though mine is sort of falling apart at the seams and frothing at the mouth, just seizing and begging to be put out of its misery. The courthouse should have a sign over it that reads: "Abandon all hope ye who want a dream wedding." Not that I was dreaming of much to begin with—just a beautiful dress and the chapel at Garrison.

Lauren pulls up in a brand-new silver Range Rover, and I'm quick to hop into the back. The butter-soft leather gives off that magical scent that only new cars know how to expel, and I relax into it.

"God, this smells like heaven!" I take in a lungful of that fresh-from-the-factory deliciousness as Ally turns back to look at me and rolls her eyes.

"You've just inhaled every chemical known to man, plus the dead flesh of some unsuspecting bovine. If I were you I'd stick my head out the window before I ended up with mad chemical cow disease."

I roll down the window and buckle up as Lauren pulls onto the highway.

"We need to discuss business." Lauren glances at me briefly in the rearview mirror. She's got her hair back in a chignon, with a silk scarf tied around her neck. She's wearing big Jackie O sunglasses. Hanging out with Lauren is like living in the glossy pages of an expensive magazine, and in this case, it's one of those oversized, heavy as a brick bridal varieties that, ironically, I'm always trying to figure out how to crawl into.

"Business?"

"The Naughty Professor had another record-breaking week. I'm close to getting every sorority in the country to sign on for the subscription. I'm telling you—you've got one hell of a pornographic hit on your hands."

Ally nudges her. "Tell her about the—" We pass a construction crew jackhammering on the side of the road, and I miss the last crucial part of her plea.

"Tell me about the *what?*"

"Oh, it's nothing." Lauren shakes her head in that aggressive way that lets me know it very well *is* something.

"Spill, Ashby, or I'll be the last to tell you the truth at the fitting." I know for a fact it's down to three dresses, and Lauren and her mother are deadlocked. She's totally relying on Ally and me to secretly side with her, only she won't tell us which dress is her fave.

Lauren's eyes enlarge for a second. "I—" She closes her mouth and shakes her head just enough to let me know she's having a silent argument with herself. "Oh yes, there was one thing. The chapter you sent me last night? What the hell is up with that?"

I sink in my seat a little because I know exactly what she means. "You didn't like it?"

"*Like* it? It put both me and my vibrator to sleep. Where's the passion? Where's the sex swing? Bring back the belt, for God's sake, and spank that man's ass. We're going to lose the attention of all these sex-starved girls. We simply can't use it."

Crap. She's right.

"I don't know what's happened." I throw up my hands, at a loss as to what went wrong. "I mean, I'd like to blame it all on Molly moving in, but the first few chapters took place while she was there. It's like Cruise just turned off one night and it hasn't been the same since."

Ally gasps as she spins toward me. "Has he stopped sleeping with you? I mean *sleeping*, sleeping."

"No, no, nothing like that. We still, you know, and quite nicely. In fact, I guess in that respect it's been better than ever. It's just everything is taking place behind closed doors, our bedroom door to be precise, and it's not like him. Not to mention the fact I've offered an array of battery-operated, latex-loving, intended-to-inflict-some-serious-punishment apparatus to him, and each time he's gently refused."

"Oh no." Lauren slams her hand on the steering wheel. "No, no, *no*!" She moans as if she knows exactly what's gone wrong.

"What?" I grip her shoulder. *"What is it?"*

"The boring bomb went off way too early in your relationship. I mean, you haven't even gotten to your wedding night and he's already trimmed the party favors. He's traded in the great outdoors and settled for a quick romp on the mattress before bedtime. The next thing you know he'll be asleep before you ever hit the sheets, and you'll have to slap his dick silly if you even want to think of getting any action." She sighs hard, as if she's speaking from experience—and knowing Cal, she is. "This isn't going to work. I'll need all of chapter four rewritten before Tuesday."

"What'll I say?" Crap. My entire body tenses up at the thought of letting down countless sex-starved sorority girls, and it's all boring Cruz Belton's fault.

"Draw on the past. Certainly you had insane sex with Cruise all over campus. Rumor has it security has replayed some of that footage on a loop."

"Oh." I perk up at the thought. That's right. Cruise and I inventoried all the hot spots around campus with our bodies. One particular day in his classroom comes back to me, and I flood with heat. God, I wish he were here to relieve a little of the tension.

"Not to mention"—Ally twists her head back like an owl, her *Exorcist*-like skills freaking me out a little—"have you tried to lure him out of the cabin? I bet it really *is* Molly that's toning down your thigh-slapping shenanigans. I'm telling you, Morgan couldn't get past listening to you pant your way into sexual oblivion."

Just the thought of my brother listening, even if was accidental, makes my skin crawl.

"That's a great idea." Lauren bobs with approval as we pull into the strip mall that contains both Cruise's mother's hair salon and the bridal shop. "Plan out about six great adventures. Ally and I will help you think up some really steamy scenes. That ought to help give Cruise his groove back."

"Yeah," Ally agrees. "It's not like he's suddenly uninterested. He's totally still into you, I can tell."

A sinking feeling settles in my chest as we park and head out.

God, I hope Cruise Elton is still "into" me. The alternative is too tragic to even think about.

We head into the expansive bridal salon, which takes up most of the strip mall. The interior is done up with sparkling white granite, and pearlescent stone flooring expands at our feet. Mirrors are set everywhere you look and oversized marble statues dot the area, wearing the creamiest, most scrumptious-looking wedding gowns you could ever lay your eyes on.

Then I see it. An entire Hallelujah Chorus breaks out in the heavens, and the whole store seems to dim as the white-hot spotlight of God shines over my perfect Vera.

"My dream dress," I whisper as I feel its magnetic pull and walk over. Its miles of satin and lace have cast their spell on me, and the only thing that can break it is love's true kiss—but Cruise isn't here to give it to me, so I suppose it's safe to say they'll need security to remove me from the premises. Then Lauren locks her arm through mine and spins me in the opposite direction.

A tall, pencil-thin girl with thigh-high boots, a bustier, and skinny jeans escorts us to an oversized room with a series of pincushion sofas.

"My name is Ella. I'll be your fitting consultant for the afternoon." She punctuates her statement with a giggle. "The champagne will be here shortly—make yourselves at home." A string of titters unleashes from her, and I'm only one chortle away from questioning her sanity.

I glance around at the cavernous room filled with opulent furniture and people clustered on small sofas, but not a mannequin in sight.

"God, where are all the dresses?" I want to run up and down the aisles and try each one on, just like when I was a little girl and played dress-up in my mother's closet. And sadly, yes, my mother's closet was bustling with wedding gowns.

"Oh, they're in the back." Lauren flicks her wrist. "They would never let you see them all—it would be too overwhelming. You simply describe your dream design and they bring you a limited selection to choose from."

"Really?" Ally doesn't look convinced as she takes a seat. "I'd probably want to try them all on just to be sure. I mean, most wedding dresses cost more than some new cars. It sounds ridiculous to let someone else decide."

"It's not ridiculous." Lauren refutes Ally's logical theory. "They're thinking with a clear head. You, on the other hand, would be thinking with emotion."

"I can't think of a more emotional event than a wedding." I whisper it so softly I hardly hear the words myself.

"Hey, hey, the gang's all here." Blair pops up like a demonic apparition, effectively sucking the joy right out of the room.

"What do you want?" Ally crops up beside me. Blair has pissed the two of us off enough to last a lifetime. It's hard to believe she was once friends with Lauren and Ally. Well, mostly with Lauren.

Blair flips back her brassy blonde hair, exposing the fact she's in desperate need of a touch-up, and too bad she can't touch up her personality.

"I'm picking up my dress." She darts a look at Lauren. "I saw your name on the roster, and I thought I'd come by to say hello. Really, Lauren, you're cutting it down to the wire. To not have a dress this close to the wedding, you might as well give up."

A knot builds in my throat. I don't have a dress, so should I give up?

"And how is your wedding coming along?" Blair steps over to me. You could cut glass with that sharpened look of hatred in her eyes.

"What did I ever do to you, Blair?" Honestly, I'd like to know.

"You did something I could never do." She glances down for a moment. "You stole my boyfriend's heart." Her voice grows small, and for the love of all the fictitious drama in the world, I swear she's harnessed the ability to manufacture tears.

"Oh, *please*." Ally steps between us. "Cruise and you were ancient history by the time Kendall stepped into the scene. She was quite the plot twist."

I give a private smile to Ally for her quasi-literary reference.

"That's not what I'm talking about." Blair gives a few rapid blinks and dabs her pinkies onto her tear ducts. "Things were already cooling off between us while we were still together."

"That's because you cheated on the poor guy." Lauren plucks a tissue off the table and hands it to her—a move I classify as something just this side of treason.

"Before that." Blair flails her arms as if she's genuinely coming unglued by her relationship with Cruise, of all people. Although I'll be the first to admit Cruise is totally worth coming unglued for. "It's like his kisses changed."

My stomach cycles at the thought of her ever laying those yarn-thin lips over my precious Cruise.

"He used to be so daring, so fun, and things sort of took a nosedive." She honks into the tissue, and Lauren proceeds to hand her the box.

Crap. She's pretty much describing what's happening between Cruise and me right now. Only, the last thing in the world I'd do is cheat on him. I'd die before I even gave one wayward look to another guy. Face it, there's not another man out there for me. Never was, never will be.

"Anyway, I started thinking I wasn't enough and that's when Rutger noticed me, and one thing led to a case of wine coolers and we sort of ended up having a good time in the back of his sports car."

Blair lost her virginity to Rutger in the back of one of his father's roadsters? Serves her right.

"Ms. Lancaster?" A tall woman who closely resembles an uptight librarian calls her to the front, and suddenly it feels like we're all in trouble with the principal. "Your gown is ready."

"I'll be right there." Blair looks over at me with those red-laced eyes. The hurt of losing Cruise is still fresh in her heart. "I guess I never really had Cruise Elton to begin with. I mean, he hasn't gotten sick of *you*."

I swallow hard. God, I hope he hasn't.

"Cruise and Kendall are a forever kind of deal." Ally is quick to link elbows with me. "Now surrender her wedding day and no one gets hurt."

Just great. My wedding has entered into hostage negotiations. I've officially eclipsed the worst-case scenario—a bridal standoff at high noon with Blair.

Blair smirks as the color comes back to her, the fire of revenge alive and well in her cheeks. "That's highly doubtful. That happens to be my birthday." She scuttles over to me. "I put that date on hold two years before Cruise broke it off with me. There's no way in hell I'm bending over and letting you screw me with my own wedding date. Find somewhere else to tie the knot. The last place it's going to happen is that chapel. You may have Cruise, but Garrison is *mine*."

"Is that why Rutger is marrying you?" I shake my head at the idea. "Because you've had a space reserved in advance and you need to fill it?" A tiny part of me is feeling sorry for Blair, but I'm quick to bitch-slap that tiny part of me and I'm right back to doling out the appropriate measure of disdain. It's obvious she's so desperate to keep her spot at the chapel she doesn't care whom she's walking down the aisle with.

Blair's open palm sails across my cheek for what quickly becomes the slap heard around the bridal salon. She turns on her heels, grabs her dress, and storms the exit.

"Holy shit!" Lauren dips a tissue in a glass of champagne and offers up a bubbly facial to take the edge off.

"She just bitch-slapped you for no reason." Ally can hardly control her breathing.

Maybe she did, but I can't get past what she said about Cruise cooling things off with her. Is that what's happening between us?

Nevertheless, I insist Lauren try on her dresses while Ally and I knock back the rest of the champagne and try to ignore the handprint welt forming on my face.

The first dress is a halter and it gives a summery feel, so we thumbs-down that one pretty quick. The second is a heavily ruched number that swoops down into a fabric-laden fishtail.

"Mermaid falls into vat of whipped cream—film at eleven." Ally shakes her head, ixnaying the gown.

Lauren comes out in the third dress, and both Ally and I stand and gasp.

"Oh God, Lauren." I can hardly get the words out. It's an off-the-shoulder gown with delicate lace cap sleeves and a plunging neckline that gives away just enough, while the dress puddles into a smooth pool of perfection. "You look amazing."

Ally snatches a tissue from off the table. "You look better than amazing. You look like one of those wedding cake toppers. All you need now is Cal and a cake."

"Speaking of cakes"—Lauren gets that devious gleam in her eye like she does just before she demands I vomit out the naughty details of my not-so-private love life—"I want you both to come with me on my visit to the Cake Chief. That way, we'll all get on TV together."

"Sweet!" Ally squeals with delight while my enthusiasm wanes around my vocal cords. Not that I'm not happy for Lauren, it's just that I seem to have lost my ability to squeal. I blame Blair for losing both my wedding venue and my squeal.

"So *this* is my favorite." Lauren holds her hands out, looking an awful lot like a princess.

"It's perfect." I blink back tears. I'm genuinely happy for Lauren.

"Then it's settled." She looks back at herself in the mirror. "This is my dress."

Ally and I press into her like a pair of bridal bookends, and the three of us blink back tears at how stunning Lauren is. All her dreams are effortlessly coming true, and a tiny part of me selfishly wishes we could trade places just for a moment.

After about an hour, Lauren changes and antes up with Ella at the front counter, but my heart is kicking and screaming because not one ounce of me wants to leave.

"Why don't you two go ahead?" I bite down on my lip as I take in the nirvana that is bridal heaven. "I'll have Molly swing by and pick me up. I've got a hair appointment next door." I can't believe I just lied to Lauren and Ally. And I feel like a fool for doing it.

"You sure?" Lauren gives me that look like she can see right through this wedding-inspired white lie.

"I'm sure." I wave as they take off out the door.

Ella in the thigh-high boots comes over and offers a placid smile. "Can I help you?"

"Yes. I'd like to try on some dresses."

Cruise

I'm just about to head home from the gym when Cal catches up to me in the lot. He's sweating, and panting, and now I'm half-worried I'm about to witness a cardiac episode.

"What's up, sweet cheeks?" I unlock my truck and it burps to life.

"Just talked to Lauren." His bald head reflects what little sun there is today. His muscles bulge from his tank top with prime definition. Cal is the best damn advertising around for this place, especially since he's looking cut, lean, and mean these days.

"Yeah? She leaving you for the leader of the geek squad?"

"You wish." He mock socks me, and swear to God, I might get a bruise. "She was just at the fitting for her dress and mentioned Kendall seemed pretty down. Thought I'd relay the news before you wondered why your balls were being nailed to the wall."

"Got it. Thanks for the heads-up. I'll head home. Maybe I'll bring her some flowers."

"I don't think you'll find her there. Lauren mentioned she left her at the bridal shop—said something about getting her hair done after."

"Thanks." I hop in the truck and head down toward the only bridal shop in town, the one that happens to be next to my mother's beauty salon. I know for a fact there's no way in hell Kenny would get her hair done there. The last time she tried, she came out with "skunk streaks," as she put it, and gray isn't her color.

By the time I arrive, the sun has already dipped behind the hillside, melting over the landscape like an orange Popsicle, and the light in the bridal boutique illuminates the strip mall with a peach glow. I hop out of the truck and pause to see a brunette with long hair through the window—Kenny is still in there at the far end of the boutique. I don't waste any time and head inside, where I find her holding out her arms while looking in a mirror. She's wearing a long white gown that accentuates her perfect hourglass figure and a pair of satin gloves that travel up past her elbow.

Wow.

I take a minute to catch my breath.

God, she's so beautiful. Kendall Jordan is a dream come true in every possible way.

I head over just as she spins around and the smile plastered to her face slides right off the instant she sees me.

"Cruise?" She lets out a shriek and dashes behind the oval framed mirror standing in the middle of the shop.

"Whoa." I head over and peer to the side. Kenny frowns and suddenly I feel like a jerk, so I do the only thing I can think of and give a little wave.

A tall woman with boots that ride past her knees comes barreling toward us, and for a minute I think she's the bridal bouncer getting ready to kick me out on my testosterone-laden ass.

"I have a few other Veras you might be interested in," she says to Kenny without paying me or my male parts any attention.

"Oh"—Kenny emerges from hiding and literately takes my breath away—"that won't be necessary. But thank you." She glances down with a heavy gaze like she's getting ready to cry.

"Please," I say, reaching for her hand, "don't let me stop you. It would be my pleasure to see you in each and every one of them."

"*No.*" Kenny swats me over the wrist until I let go. "This is all kinds of crazy bad luck with you here." She reverts her attention to Boots. "I'm done, thank you. I'll be in the dressing room in just a few minutes."

Boots cuts me a look that lets me know my balls are on the line. I've committed some major gender-bending infraction, and if I don't comply with the rules, my man parts are going to pay.

I hold up my hands. "Looks like I should have called."

"Come here." Kenny pulls me in and lands a warm, inviting kiss on my lips.

"You are so fucking beautiful." I keep my eyes closed for a moment before blinking back the tears. "God, Kenny how did I ever get so lucky?"

"You haven't yet." She curtsies in her snow-white gown.

I take her by the hands and take a step back to fully inspect her. "Is this the dress?" My heart thumps just soaking her in. Kenny has transformed into a genuine storybook princess.

"Not anymore. It'd kill the entire future of our marriage if you saw me in my wedding dress."

"Doubtful." I flex a dry smile. "I'd better step up my game and get a tux or I'm going to feel like a frog come Christmas Eve."

"You could never be a frog." She presses in another quick kiss before pulling away with a devious look in her eyes. "Hey . . ." She glances around. "I've got a dressing room back there the size of the entire cabin." She wets her lips nice and slow. "You want to help me take off my dress, cowboy?"

Kenny shoots me that lusty look and a flash flood of hormones unleash in me.

"Now what kind of gentleman would I be if I didn't help a lady out of her dress—I mean, *in distress?*" I give a quick wink as she begins to whisk us off in that direction.

Morgan's face crops up in my mind, about as wanted as a swarm of angry bees.

"On second thought"—I pull her to a halt and let out a heated breath in lieu of cursing her brother out loud—"I think maybe we should have a celebratory dinner." I draw her into a kiss while trying to decompress my dick from its upright position.

"Great idea. We can do *dinner* after we do each *other.*" She pulls me toward the dressing room as if pulling me out of a fire.

"No, no." I glance around. "We'd better not. I'd hate to get you in trouble with the boot lady. She might actually *give* us the boot if she knew what I was really helping you with." My breathing grows erratic because every part of me wants to have her ten million different ways in that wedding dress. Morgan's face blinks through my mind again, and this time I imagine punching him in the neck just for the hell of it.

Her lips quiver like she might cry. Kenny looks over her shoulder for a moment.

"Last chance for love," she whispers, barely audible.

I shake my head once because I don't have the balls to say no. As much as I hate to admit it, Morgan is right. I would have happily followed her back there and broken ten different matrimonial commandments without thinking twice. I've got "fucking" on the brain twenty-four seven, and I've unwittingly dragged Kenny into my carnal world of perversion.

"Let me take you somewhere special." I clasp her hands and kiss each of them in turn.

"You want to *take* me somewhere?" Her eyes pick up that spark again. "Oh, Professor Elton, I thought you'd never ask!" She rises on her toes and dots my cheek with a kiss before running off to change. I watch as she makes her way down the long hall. The next time I see her in a big white dress, she'll be coming toward me, and I cannot wait. It's amazing to think that the best days of my life are still ahead of me. It's going to be Kenny and me forever.

And, for us, forever began the first night I laid eyes on her.

―――⌒◯⌒―――

Kenny and I settle on a sushi restaurant just south of Garrison, and from where we're seated we have a clear view of the steel-caged globe sitting on the university's highest point. A dull smile plays on my lips. That's yet another place where I had mindless sex with Kenny. Wait, what am I saying? That was one of the most exhilarating experiences of my entire life, and I'm damn glad it was Kenny I shared it with. Morgan's smirking face haunts my brain again, and this time I don't hesitate to give him a black eye.

"It's a clear night," I say, wrapping my arm around her. Kenny loves to sit on the same side of the booth with me. I think it's adorable and sweet, just like Kenny.

"The stars spray out like magic here in Carrington." She rests her head on my shoulder. "Back home there were only streetlights and smog, but here we have the universe sparkling like jewels right over our heads."

"You have a way with words." I land a kiss in her hair. Kenny holds the scent of vanilla and roses.

"And you"—she rides her foot into my pants leg and the feel of her skin over mine sends a heat searing in my chest—"have a way with your body." She tweaks her brows. "I happen to know for a fact the ladies' room here is a single lock-off." She runs her tongue over her lips and they glisten in its pretty pink wake.

Shit. I bounce in my seat because I'm half-tempted to do it. Morgan spikes up and no matter how many times I knock him down, he bounces back like a judgmental punching bag.

"So I was thinking"—I clear my throat, trying to ignore her foot edging its way to my knee—"I think"—her hand fumbles its way to my crotch and I scoot in the opposite direction a few inches—"I'm going to see a lawyer about getting the Plague the hell out of the B and B. It's like a freaking beehive now with bodies coming and going at all hours of the night."

"Beehive." She blinks a smile because we both know she didn't catch two words. Kenny's got a one-track mind, and according to the hard-on blooming in my jeans, it seems to be a catching condition.

"Not to mention they haven't even paid us yet." I like using the term *us*. It feels natural—official.

"*So*"—she gives a husky laugh—"you want to walk me to the bathroom?"

Before I can answer, the waitress comes and takes our order while I shake my legs in an effort to defuse the boys. As soon as she walks away Kenny is back to massaging my crotch to the point of no return.

"Where were we?" She slips her hand down my Levis and latches onto the one-eyed snake faster than I can throttle her effort.

Fuck. Here we are in public and she's about to willingly toss me off. How the hell would I feel if some idiot made Molly believe that this was how rational adults act in the real world? I can't believe it took Morgan Jordan to help me see the imprudent light.

"Cruise Elton." She dives in and lands a barely there kiss on my neck. "If I didn't know better I'd swear you were rejecting me." That thinly veiled look of hurt in her eyes lets me know she believes this. She runs her hand down to my balls and cradles them.

ADDISON MOORE

My head knocks back and I let out a groan that garners stares from the diners at the next three tables.

"Rejection?" I whip out my wallet and toss forty bucks on the table. "Hell no." I speed her out the door and to the truck, navigating the road back to the cabin like it's a speedway.

"The cabin?" She tilts her head into me as I narrowly miss the entry to the bed-and-breakfast. The entire roadway is clogged with cars taking up both sides of the street. A loud thump vibrates the dashboard, so I roll down the window and listen as the B and B pulsates into the night with its own damn heartbeat.

"Shit." The easement is backlogged three cars deep, so I jump the curb and drive over the landscaping, and to my chagrin two other cars follow my moronic behavior. "What the?" I glance over the B and B lit up like a football stadium as the music ricochets off the forest and amplifies itself so loud that I'm sure the entire state of Massachusetts will be treated to a little of the Plague tonight.

We jump out of the truck, and for a second I contemplate going over there and raising hell—but judging by the spontaneous mosh pit in the front yard, I think the Plague beat me to it.

"It's so loud!" Kenny screams as we make our way into the cabin.

I shut the door and the walls vibrate in rhythm to the music.

"I think this is exactly what we needed," I say, still shouting over the damn racket churning in our once-sleepy neighborhood. I put in a quick call to the Carrington Police Department and give a sly grin over at Kenny once I hear they're sending a unit out to investigate.

"What'd they say?" She shouts over the noise. Her cleavage ripples as she brings her hands to her ears to muffle the noise.

"They said I'd better do this." I carry her all the way to our bedroom and shut the door. If Molly is next door, she won't hear a damn thing. Thanks to the Plague, Kenny and I can turn up the mattress music as loud as we want. "I've been waiting to do this since I saw you in that dress." I strip off her sweater and she wriggles out of her jeans. "Kenny, I swear I've never seen anyone look so damn beautiful."

"Shut up and kiss me!" She pulls me in by the face and I laugh as our mouths find one another. It's not going to be easy learning to hold off on our lovemaking until we land safe in our bedroom, but Kenny is worth the wait every single time.

She rakes off my clothes as if there are only minutes to live, and judging by the sirens barreling down the street, she might be right. Kenny jumps up onto my hips with her bare skin against mine, our bellies meeting with an unromantic slap—that was mostly *felt*, thanks to the Plague's best effort to be heard on the moon.

I gently push her into the wall and she guides me in. Kenny ravenously peppers my face with kisses as I give that first forceful thrust.

"Yes!" She cries it out at the top of her lungs. Kenny wraps her legs tight around my back, hanging on to my shoulders for dear life.

I head into a barrage of full-throttle blows as I spear into her again and again.

"*Harder.*" Kenny arches her head so far back she accidentally slams into the wall. She pushes me in by the small of my back while I rail into her, and each time I do she gives my dick a little squeeze by way of the inside of her perfectly fit body.

"God, yes, that," I pant.

Kenny claws at my back like she's trying to scale a building, her cries of delight climbing toward the ceiling as if they're trying to escape.

"Fuck me, Professor Elton! Fuck me!" She screams it so loud the window rattles from her shrill effort.

A loud thump emits from the other side of the wall, and Kenny bites down on her lip. Her face flushes a severe shade of crimson. It's only then I note the music has ceased and the sound of silence clots up our ears, but I really don't care because Kenny just gave me a command that I plan on carrying out to completion. I continue my aggressive assault, knocking Kenny into the wall with every other thrust and Molly returning the favor each time with a thump of her own. Thank God I'm too far in to let Molly kill my good time. All the blood in my body and every emotion, feeling, and lust-filled sentiment I've ever had for Kenny is culminating in one fantastic explosion that rockets out of me and straight into her. I clutch on and squeeze so tight I think she's going to crumble while I throb over her body.

"Oh wow." She throws her arms against the wall and lets them slide lazily down to her sides. Her hair is gloriously messy and her mascara is smeared just enough to give her that sexy-as-hell look that I live to see each morning.

I'm still holding her up with my hips pinned against hers, my hands locked under her thighs.

"That was definitely worth coming home for." I press a heated kiss over her dewy skin.

"I'll say." Her lids flutter dreamily. "But I have a confession." She bites down on her finger as if she's ready for round two.

"What's that?" I pant, never taking my eyes from hers.

"I've been a very, very bad girl, Professor Elton. I've cheated on all your exams."

"Really?" I hike a brow, amused at her role-playing antics. I guess it's enough to break her of public lewdness for now. No point in taking away her not-so-innocent fantasies as well. "Too bad for you because I have a zero tolerance policy against tampering with letter grades."

"Well then, Professor Elton, I deserve to be punished to the fullest extent." Kenny gives my bottom a firm squeeze. "I expect nothing less than a firm paddling."

A brisk knock erupts at the door.

"Get your pants on! And put the damn paddles away," Molly shouts. "There's an officer out here, and he wants to speak with you."

I jump into my sweats and head out to talk to the cops. It turns out all they could do was quiet the Plague for the night and file a report. As luck would have it, I'm liable for all the noise pollution, so any complaints the neighbors have will fall squarely on my shoulders.

After an hour of legal bullshit that ran in the favor of the squatters who set up shop at the B and B, I make my way back inside. Apparently dollars changing hands by the landlord and tenant is merely a detail here in this late, great state I live in. The words "lawyer up" were used, and I swear I saw dollar signs sprout from the cop's mouth as he said them.

I head into the bedroom and find Kenny curled up in a ball, already fast asleep, and I don't have the heart to wake her up for that "firm paddling" she's looking forward to. A part of me wonders if the old Cruise would have done it, and deep down I know I would have. I'd have Kenny on her knees, pretending to beg for mercy until five in the morning, and we both would have enjoyed the shit out of it.

Instead, I glide in next to her and wrap my arm around her waist. Kenny's bottom nestles in my stomach and I soak it all in. Here we are—my future bride and me, our happily-ever-after just a few months away.

I fall asleep and dream of Kenny hog-tying me with garter belts while spanking the shit out of me with a white satin heel.

8

THIS ONE TAKES THE CAKE

Kendall

Creative Writing just let out and Molly said she wanted to stay a little later to speak with Professor Curl-Your-Toes—she told me not to bother waiting, that she'd find a ride.

I speed out into the brisk air. The kaleidoscope of fall has taken over Garrison, and you can't take two steps without hearing the satisfying crunch of brittle leaves underfoot. It already looks like evening, with the sun hidden behind a veil of midnight-colored clouds. It keeps threatening to rain, but defers the idea to another time—sort of the way I've been putting off my schoolwork, other than creative writing. That happens to be going swimmingly because I've devoted every spare moment to jotting down copious details of my sexcapades with Cruise—or more to the point, Professor Belton. God knows I've had to pull some oldies but goodies from the vault, but Penny and Cruz have been none the wiser.

I pass the bookstore and spot an entire row of giant paper ghosts lining the window. In a few nights it'll be Halloween, and Pen is throwing one of his epic parties at Alpha Sigma Phi and made Cruise promise we'd be there. It's a costume party, so already it sounds like it'll be fun by default. Still, I wish I could miss it. The truth is I haven't really cared to go to any parties since Cruise and I have been dating. Of course, I went to Rock Bottom when

Morgan was responsible for the hottest party in town. That was before Ally's ex-boss at the strip club went ballistic and gassed the entire facility, nearly killing both Ally and Morgan. Thank God they're both okay. I don't know what I'd do if anything happened to Ally or my big brother.

A pair of strong hands dig into my shoulders. "Boo."

I turn to find my gorgeous and very-much-alive big bro.

"Boo yourself. Where's your better half?" I glance around for signs of his gorgeous girlfriend. I hope he's pinching himself at least twice a day. He's that lucky to have her.

His brows rise in response. "I'd argue with you on that, but you happen to be right. She's pulling an evening shift."

"Oh! Come home with me. Cruise is making dinner. I know he won't mind."

"Mmm." His dimple digs in on one side of his mouth as he considers the idea. "I'll pass. I don't want to be anyone's third wheel."

"You won't! Molly will be there, too."

"Exactly why you won't be seeing me." He gives a wry smile. Molly was a little more than obsessed with him last summer— still is on occasion. "Hey, I talked to Dad today. He wanted me to extend his congratulations. I told him you're getting married."

"Who?" I'm genuinely confused. Does he mean Mom? I bet he means Mom. But she already knows that I'm getting married.

"*Dad*. You know, the rat bastard who ran out on us when we were kids." He tickles my ribs for a moment, and I'm quick to brush him and his crazy conversation away.

Morgan and my father—a term I use loosely—have spoken regularly for the past few years. Morgy attended school for a while in Oregon, where said rat bastard lives with his new, unimproved family.

"That's nice." I continue to make my way to the parking lot and Morgan follows.

"He says he'd like a chance to talk to you one day if you let him."

"Really?" I cut a quick glance to the forest. "I doubt he even knows who I am." He's long since replaced us. As soon as he left my mother he remarried and had a whole gaggle of brand-new children.

"He knows you, Kendall." Morgan pulls me to a stop just shy of his truck. "He's more than sorry for how he left things with us. Trust me, he wants in—at least a little. If I can talk to the guy and not explode in a fit of rage, I know you can, too. You're a much nicer person than I am."

"Not when it comes to idiots who abandon their families." I unlock my car from across the lot. "Look, I've got enough stress planning a wedding that at this point has no hope of panning out the way I want. The last thing I need is him trying to worm his way back into my life."

"You don't have to let him in all the way." Morgan leans toward me, a pleading look on his face. "He just wants a chance to say sorry and maybe get to know you. His kids really want to know you, too. The girls had all kinds of questions about you the last time I was there. You have four little sisters, two little brothers. We shouldn't hold it against them that our father is an ass."

My heart sinks just thinking about it.

I leap up and wrap my arms around his neck.

"There's no way I could love any other sibling as much as I love you."

"Sure you could." He presses a quiet kiss to the back of my head. "Your heart is huge, Kendall. You could love a lot of people if you let them in."

He walks me to my car, and I give a little wave before driving off.

I think it's heartbreakingly sweet that I have brothers and sisters on the opposite coast who would love to meet me. But, in all honesty, I wish my father would stay in the past and keep his heartbreakingly happy family with him.

I'm not ready to let him or anyone else he created in.

Not now, not ever.

———

I pull up to the bed-and-breakfast both physically and emotionally spent for the day. A trail of cars line the street, and the entire parking lot in front is clogged. God I hate this. I should barge in there myself and demand that those cretins leave. I can't believe poor Cruise has to get a lawyer to chase the lowlifes away. It's beyond ridiculous that anyone would think they could just move into someone else's property and refuse to pay them. Some people believe they're entitled to everything.

I squeeze the car down to the cabin and narrowly escape scraping it up against a fencepost on the right. I'd feel horrible damaging Aunt Jackie's luxury car in any way. I shouldn't have taken the risk.

I make a face as my nonwedding flashes before my eyes. I know I'm taking a lot of risks I shouldn't be lately, like picking up knick-knacks for an all-but-nonexistent wedding and further placing myself in debt that I'll never be able to dig my way out of. Maybe I'm the one who feels entitled. Maybe Cruise should get a lawyer to evict the credit card from my purse. God knows it's smoking from all the errant purchases I've made of late, i.e., the gently used Vera that I'm going to have to sell my liver to pay for. And if my own chaos wasn't enough to set me on edge, the malfeasance caused by the Plague has really got my blood boiling.

I scoop up my backpack and burst into the cabin. The scent of grilled vegetables and steak enlivens my senses, and I spot Cruise hovering near the stove while a cloud of steam rises from the pan in front of him. He's wearing his faded Levis and a plain white T-shirt, and his five-o'clock shadow gives him that late-night, scruffy look that's so damn hot on his perfectly tan face. A half smile rides on his lips and he's bedroom-eyeing me with a leer that suggests an array of unholy thoughts are running through his mind—and dear God, do Penny and I ever approve.

"You know what they say"—I go over and wrap my arms around him from behind—"there is not a damn thing sexier than a man in the kitchen."

"Well then . . ." He spins in my arms and lands a kiss on my lips. "They haven't met *you*. How was your day?"

"Weird. How was yours?" Quite frankly I'm not in the mood to discuss my father or his newfound desire to say he's sorry.

"Ditto on the 'weird.'" He brings the food to the table, and I follow him with plates and forks—all the while inspecting the way his rock-hard bottom looks in those blue jeans.

Cruise's long, commalike dimples dig into his cheeks. "You ready for the world's best fajitas?"

"Only if I can eat them off your body." I'm not teasing. Cruise has washboard abs that I plan to sit on later tonight. I swear I can orgasm just using his body as a luge. "We can start now if you like." I pat the table with the carnal invitation. Methinks the next chapter of Penny and Cruz's adventures should be plated for the readers in an exceptional fashion.

Cruise proceeds to dole out a serving of his gourmet fare and literally ignores my proposition. I can't for the life of me figure out why he has lost his erotic edge lately.

"So tell me . . ." I pick up my fork and stab at my food with no real desire to dive into Cruise's exquisite cuisine. The old Cruise would have had me twelve different ways by now. "What was so weird about your day?"

"Well, I saw six attorneys and they all said the same thing. It could take up to three months to get them out if things move quickly, and they all want thousands of dollars to make this slow-moving miracle happen."

My hand flies to my chest. "That's terrible. Why is the law always on the side of the criminal?" Well, not always, but it is for sure in this case.

"I'm not worried. We'll get through this." Cruise pours me a glass of red wine and taps my glass with his before taking a sip. He's always so positive and uplifting—it drives me wild in a get-in-my-bed sort of way.

"On another note"—he takes a bite of his meal—"I took Cal's advice and drove to a few B and Bs in the area. I had a chance to speak to a couple of the managers to see what their thoughts on the business were."

"*Ooh.* Covert ops. I kind of like you as a private dick." I rub my foot over his leg, and he leans in and gives a little sexy growl. There's my boy. "What did they say?"

"Oddly, they said they heard about a bed-and-breakfast in south Carrington that's hosting private parties each night with a live band and DJ, and that it's opening a whole new market to a younger generation."

"Really? That sounds fantastic! Where is this place?"

"It is fantastic. It's sheer genius." His affect sharpens, no smile. "It's us, Kenny. We're the hippest, coolest B and B in town."

"Oh my God!" I slam my hands on the table with glee. Then it hits me. We're not actually capitalizing on the whole affair.

"Oh . . . oh my God." It comes out more of a desperate moan. "This sucks."

"It does suck." Cruise looks past my shoulder, despondent. "I've already depleted my bank account, and by next month I'll have wrung out the final reserves in the line of credit I have as well. After that, we're just moments away from a bank seizure."

My mouth falls open. My appetite takes a nosedive. No matter how hard Cruise slaves away in the kitchen. I may never want to eat again. "That's terrible."

"It is terrible, considering they'll take the cabin right along with it."

I press my lips tightly together. I can't believe this is happening to Cruise—to *us*.

Tears start to come, and I blink them away.

"No, no, no." Cruise's eyes are wild with panic. "I swear to you, this will all work out. I was just venting. There's no way I'll let us be homeless on our wedding day. I've got a few surefire tricks up my sleeve. Once I evict these clowns, and I *will*, I'll have us back in the swing of things. I'm not at all complaining about my life." He reaches over and clasps both of my hands. "With you in it, Kenny, the best is yet to come."

"You're a prince among men, you know that?" I chew on my bottom lip until it feels like I'm going to bite right through. "I can't help feel like I'm some bad luck bomb that went off the moment you met me. I'm the reason you got kicked out of Garrison."

"*I'm* the reason I got kicked out of Garrison," he's quick to correct.

"*We.*" I smile sweetly at him.

"Nope." Cruise smolders into me and my heart melts. "Just me. What's new on the wedding front?"

"Absolutely zero. No venue, no dress, no reception, no photographer, no videographer, no cake, no reality TV show to document our efforts, and no stylist to make me look good weeks before the big day." God that sounded horrific coming from my own more-than-slightly-entitled lips. I hate sounding like a spoiled brat. I've never been handed anything, so I'm not sure why the reality of having a simple wedding isn't sinking in. Damn all those fantasies I bought over the years that sold me on the fairy tale of it all. Besides, who needs a fluffy white dress when I've got Cruise Elton waiting for me down the imaginary aisle at the courthouse?

His features soften. Now Cruise looks like he wants to cry and it's all for me.

Just great—way to further deplete his mojo.

"Let's solve some problems." He gives my hand a tug. "I thought we were getting married at the chapel?"

"Blair Lancaster has the date marked as her own." Just saying her name makes me feel as if I'm about to conjure her wickedness right into the room. "She reserved it *years* ago. I guess it was supposed to be your wedding date." Even thinking about Cruise and Blair planning for their happily-ever-after makes my heart sink, heavy as an anchor.

"Blair and I never set a wedding date." Cruise bears into me with his powder-blue eyes. "Not real or imagined. The topic never came up. We never got that far."

"She said it was her birthday." I shrug. The truth is, Blair killed me a little the other day when she talked about how things cooled off between her and Cruise. And judging by the steady decline in bedroom antics, I'm a little afraid things might head in that same direction with us if I'm not careful. It's becoming painfully clear that I'll have to go above and beyond to keep our relationship alive.

"Her birthday is in April," he deadpans.

"That lying bitch." A wave of fury sears through me. "Do you know she slapped me the other day in the bridal shop? And here she lied to my face? I'm going to kill her."

His eyes round with rage. "Let me. There's no way in hell I'm going to let her run around assaulting you." His gaze darts around the room like he's trying to process exactly how the pending homicide will take place.

"Don't bother. I'd hate to reduce our relationship to conjugal visits."

"I'll talk to her. I'll see if I can't get our wedding date back. Have you thought about other churches?"

"They all have wait lists. And Christmas Eve isn't available anywhere on the planet. Face it, we're doomed to the county courthouse."

"*Kenny.*" He tugs at my hand, trying to get me to perk up. "I would be happy to marry you at the courthouse. I'd marry you in a jailhouse, an outhouse if that's what it took. How about the beach? Or a park? We could do a cliffside ceremony if you want. It'll be beautiful."

"They all sound great." Too bad I can't muster an ounce of fake enthusiasm. "But with my luck it'll rain and we'll be swept to sea." You read about it every now and again on the news. I can practically see the sharks circling me now, and, oddly, each one has a striking resemblance to Blair.

His lips curl on the sides because a tiny part of him knows this to be true.

"Okay, how about the reception?" Cruise dips his chin. His eyes are practically pleading for me to glom on to any ray of hope because we both know he's having a hell of a time trying to see the silver lining himself. "Have you thought about what you might like for that?" Cruise creates tiny circles with his thumb over my palm, sending a warm tingle right up my spine.

"I was sort of hoping we could all go out to the Della Argento after." I bite down on a naughty grin. "You and I can make a quick trip to the back for *dessert* and kick-start our honeymoon a few hours early." I give a little wink. How's that for shooting down the negativity? All I have to do is remind myself of the ray of sunshine Cruise has in his pants, and suddenly every cloud has a sexy silver lining.

His face smooths out as if he's genuinely worried for me. "Della Argento sounds perfect."

"It will be," I whisper. His lack of enthusiasm for my dessert dalliance leaves me wondering if we'll ever get back to where we were. "But it'll also be expensive. I'd like us to pick up the tab for our family and friends." True story. I'm sure somewhere my Visa is cringing.

"Of course we will. We'll just cut back on the spending and we'll be fine."

A flood of relief washes over me. "Then we're going to the Della Argento?"

He gives a brief nod.

"Plus it's a once-in-a-lifetime thing," I'm quick to add. *Finally,* something is going my way. Cruise doesn't mind one bit. "Besides, I don't overspend," I gently correct. "I'm totally frugal. Really it borders on scary. I'm practically addicted to the dollar store. It's a wonder Lauren even speaks to me."

Cruise glances behind the barstools, eyeing the bags piling up that I keep meaning to put away.

Crap.

"Um . . ." I clear my throat, trying to garner his attention before he decides to delve into them. "Those are just the necessities." I take a sip of my wine, never taking my eyes off his judgmental stare. "*What?* They are. Plus they were on sale and double-discounted, so it would have been fiscally irresponsible for me to have passed those deals up." God, that was brilliant. I should go into law. "You don't want me to run around town, buying things at full price, do you?"

"Heavens no." He's mocking me. I can tell.

"Look." I spot a stack of mail and head over to find my AmEx, MasterCard, and Visa bills. "There's not one of these that I can't handle." The truth is I've dwindled my savings to nil, and the tiny detail of no actual job is about to land me in the red if I'm not careful. I rip open the AmEx and proudly display my zero balance for his fiscally judicious eyes to witness. The same with the MasterCard, which I forget on occasion that I even have—and it's a good thing, too. Then my Visa, which I know I've used for oddball purchases—the all-important wedding stuff, and a few back-to-school clothes, but I tend to favor that card because of the frequent-flier miles it lets me accrue. Right now I have enough to get me to Cincinnati with about twelve layovers. "See?" I hold out the final summary of my prudent spending, and his face bleeds dry of all color. It's obvious I've impressed the hell out of him.

"Kendall?"

For a second I want to ask who the hell Kendall is, because Cruise is pretty consistent in calling me Kenny, and truth be told, my formal name sounds foreign coming from his lips.

He snatches the page out of my hand and begins reading voraciously.

"What?" I yank it back with an explanation already bubbling from my throat. "You can't really blame a girl for getting excited about a few back-to-school supplies. All those colorful notebooks and pens just scream, *'Buy me!'"* My eyes drop down to the balance and the room starts to spin and fade.

"Crap," I whimper. Six thousand and eight hundred dollars. God almighty. I forgot all about that bitch in Patagonia. "Shit," I seethe.

"So you did a little shopping." Cruise forces a smile, and it's quick to glide right back off his lips. "There's nothing wrong with that." He swallows hard. "Let me help you pay that bill," he offers sweetly.

Crap. Not five seconds after I tell him how financially responsible I am, I prove myself to be a walking disaster in the shape of a dollar bill.

"No. I've got this handled." I can officially add lying to my roster of deception. "Anyway, I'll be looking into all those wedding venues you mentioned and we'll have all the details hammered out soon. I promise." I sniff, holding back tears while my entitled inner child happily strangles Blair Lancaster and evicts her from the Garrison chapel. This is all falling apart. It's like Blair figured out a way to go back in time just to piss me off. And now, Cruise and I are in this awkward place. Where's that damn silver lining when you really need it?

I give a forced grin. "Wanna have sex?"

———

"What kind of sex did he have with you?" Lauren leans over her steaming cup of pumpkin-spiced coffee while Ally finishes up her shift behind the counter.

"The good kind." It speeds out of me as only the truth can.

"You mean the boring kind."

I sink a little in my seat, guilty as charged. "What's happened to us?" I've spent the better half of the last fifteen minutes relaying my night of fiscal horrors to Lauren, who looked genuinely con-fused. I think I'd have a better chance of making her understand by drawing it out in hieroglyphics—lots of red dollar signs might get the message across.

"And not only do you have a love life that's not subscription-worthy, you're short one used wedding dress—which, by the way, isn't due until *after* the ceremony." Lauren sputters it out, harsh as a reprimand. "What are you going to do now?"

"I called the credit card company this morning and told them my card was stolen."

"You *what?*" Lauren's forehead breaks out in a series of worry lines, and this alarms me because I know for a fact she Botoxed her face into oblivion a few weeks back. Disabling an entire line of credit is one fucking boundary you do not cross in her world.

"What'd I miss?" Ally pants as she plops down between us.

Lauren strings it all out for her, swift as a hummingbird, and now I feel like a pervert for even looking at wedding dresses on eBay, not to mention she practically made me sound like a felon in the making for trying to have my credit card company eat the bill.

"Call them back." Ally clutches at her chest with a look of sheer panic. "Tell them you found it at the bottom of your purse. You can do all kinds of time for Internet fraud and credit card theft—*extortion*—and who knows how many other laws you're breaking."

Shit! Fraud and extortion are the kinds of things Wall Street swindlers go to prison for, not coeds who are trying to marry their Gender Relations professor.

I take a deep breath and try to put it all in context, considering the source. Ally is probably just overreacting because she's scared spitless when it comes to any kind of legal drama. Her once-upon-a-boyfriend almost dragged her into an attempted murder plot way back when, and she's been allergic to the color orange ever since.

"She's right." Lauren shakes her head. "You're going to land yourself in the big house just in time for your wedding day. *Although*—conjugal visits might be a little more exciting than what you're experiencing now."

Crap. I dial my credit card company without hesitating and report the happy news that I have been reunited with my credit card.

"They said they're already sending out a new one. There's that," I say, tossing my card onto the table. Maybe I'll conveniently leave it and lose it for real this time.

"That's one problem down." Lauren narrows her gaze. "Now how do we solve the problem of your terminal love life?"

"I've got just the thing." Ally gets a wicked gleam in her eye that both excites and worries me. "I think we should pay a visit to the Carrington Shopping Mall."

"Great." Lauren is on board to save the subscription sales of *The Naughty Professor* in any manner possible—including retail therapy. "That's right next to the Cake Chief's bakeshop. My appointment's set for later this afternoon. We can head over right after."

I hate to break it to Ally, but the Carrington mall might as well be made up of dollar signs. I doubt anything new in my sex life will come by way of some simple lingerie.

Nope, I'll just have to think outside the box. And the chapel. And the wedding dress.

Cruise

I lure Cal into coming over—told him I want to turn the entire damn living room into a weight room and to bring all his expensive catalogs. I watch as he navigates his truck through the bevy of pickups and expensive SUVs, most of which belong to students at Garrison.

"Holy smokes." He waves the other vehicles off as he gets out of his car. "You've got one hell of a parking problem, buddy." He starts making his way to the porch, and I block him.

"Correction. You've got one hell of a problem." I spin him around by the shoulders and lead him over to the B and B. "Prepare yourself. You're about to have a family reunion like no other."

We make our way up the steps, and I give a few unsettled fist pumps on the door. A short blonde with an ear-to-ear grin opens up. She's wearing microshorts that qualify more as a belt and a crop top with *Garrison* written across the front in sparkly letters.

"Can I help you?"

"We're here to see the Skin." Words I thought would never fly from my lips.

"Skinny girl!" She whoops it out before sauntering off, leaving the door wide open.

Inside, much as I suspected, there are wall-to-wall bodies. It's turning into a genuine frat house in here. I let a few expletives fly as we walk over the threshold.

Cal's cousin Lisa comes barreling down with her hair dyed black-and-blue, like a bruise. Her face contorts in twelve different stages of agony once she sees me, but the second she lays eyes on Cal her features smooth out, and she looks innocent as a schoolgirl.

"Cally?" She jumps on top of him and they engage in a rather long, quasi-incestuous hugging session. "Look at you." She slaps him over the arm. "You're a freak of nature!"

They both are, but I keep the commentary to myself.

"Yeah, well, you know what they say. It takes one to know one." He playfully socks her in the stomach. "What's cooking, good lookin'?"

"Just stuck in stupid Carrington. I tried to liven things up." She motions at the newly upholstered walls, and my gut drops to my knees. My mother's Victorian flocked wallpaper has been replaced with cheap plastic stickers of seagulls flying across the expanse of the living room.

Cal looks around, bobbing his head approvingly. "Like what you've done with the place."

He can't be serious.

"I didn't have much to work with." She frowns while digging her fingers through her hair.

"You'll have less to work with in a few hours." It belts out of me. I had planned on keeping my trap shut, but I can't stand what they've turned my family's pride and joy into—especially now that seagulls are flocking around the living room. Things just got serious as shit. "I suggest you back those moving vans to the entrance and get the hell out. *And* I want all my stuff back and put exactly where it belongs without a single scratch." Like I'll ever see it again. Something tells me that at the end of this nightmare, the Plague will be the new owners of the B and B and I'll be the one backing a moving van up to the cabin because I can't seem to catch a fucking break.

"Oh." She moans dramatically, clutching at her temples as if I just threatened to plant a hatchet in her skull. "I think I'm getting a headache. I'd better lie down."

"Are you still getting the spells?" Cal helps her to the couch.

"Are you still buying her bullshit?" I'm beside myself. Bringing Cal here was useless.

"She's been getting the spells since we were kids, dude. She had to spend weeks home from school."

The Skin moans into him as a thank-you for proliferating her brain baloney.

"Sounds like she's been a manipulation mastermind from the time she exited the womb. I'm going to take a wild guess that she didn't want to go to school, just like she doesn't want to leave the bed-and-breakfast."

Lisa looks up and gasps with a look of genuine rage because, obviously, I'm the first person in her life to see right through her lackluster performance.

"You sound just like my father!" she snaps.

"Your father sounds like a wise man."

"He never believed a thing I said." She bares her fangs at me as if I've morphed into the DNA dispenser himself.

"Again, he sounds like a wise man."

Cal holds a hand out to me, pleading for mercy. "Dude, her father ran out on her when she was thirteen."

"That's probably because he got sick of her damn lies." Okay, that was probably a low blow.

The Skin starts in on a violent sob, and for the first time she looks like a vulnerable, lost, albeit pathetic, little girl.

"Look, I'm sorry." And I usually am after I reduce a girl to tears. "My dad sort of did the same thing to me when I was a kid. We're not that close."

Her watery eyes look up at me. Her mascara drips into two large half-moons just above her cheeks and she looks scarier than shit.

"Look"—I say it again, as tenderly as possible—"you've got to get your crap together and get the hell out. I can't have you living here another damn second because if you do, I'm going to lose the place. And I can't lose this place. It's all my family has. You see, I sort of have a no-squatters policy, and you happen to be breaking it."

Her lips contort into all kinds of criminally insane shapes. She jumps to her feet and gives a few good solid barks right in my face before bolting upstairs.

"Now look what you did." Cal smacks me on the arm. "When little Lisa barks, that means the spell is settling in for a few solid weeks. And believe you me, no one gets a good night's rest when she's pissed."

"Little Lisa?" I say through gritted teeth. "Spells?" I shake my head at him. "I'm going to have a fucking *spell* when I have to pay an attorney to file an eviction."

Cal glances up the steps momentarily. "I've got something that might take your mind off the situation. Are you free for the next hour or so?"

Cal drives us to a bakery in the next town over. It's teeming with people, and a long line snakes out of the facility and straight up the street.

"What's going on? They giving away beer-battered donuts? Let me guess, it's frosting wrestling night?" Something tells me this is a little more than your average doughnut run, considering we bypassed a dozen other shops to get here.

"Nope." Cal parks and leans over the wheel to get a better look at the chaos. "No discounts here. Trust me, there's not a thing under ten bucks in that place. Every one of those poor bastards is paying top dollar for anything those people are willing to sell them."

"Looks like I'm in the wrong business."

He slaps me on the back. "We both are." We get out and Cal walks us straight to the front, bypassing the line and generating jeers from the crowd.

It's clean inside, warmly scented with fresh baked brownies and coffee. It makes me want to stay a while and dive into the rows of confections they've got lining the refrigerated display cases.

"I'm here to see Vito," Cal barks at a lady behind the counter, and she motions us to the back.

Vito? Maybe Cal's solution to all my troubles is a loan shark, and right about now, I'm not too sure I'd protest the idea.

"What, are you like a celebrity here?" I ask as we make our way down a long hall that opens into an enormous kitchen, and much to my delight, I spot the sweetest treat of all—Kenny.

"Cruise!" She hops over and wraps her arms around my waist. I hang on for dear life and land my lips over hers.

"Looks like you're next!" A stocky man with dark hair and a bulbous nose whacks me on the back. He's dressed in white from head to toe and flips a chef's hat on, thus completing his baker's attire. He looks official in every way and, oddly, slightly familiar. I turn to find Lauren and Ally standing there as Cal takes his place by his future bride.

"So what can we do for you guys?" The happy baker mock shoots Lauren and Cal. It's only then that I spot an entire film crew cueing up their equipment, and suddenly the picture comes into focus. This isn't just any bakery and that's not just any baker—it's the Cake Chief. I've seen enough of Molly's food porn to identify the celebrity chef.

"Isn't this great?" Kenny whispers. "We're going to be on television." She bounces on the balls of her feet as if she's waited her whole life for her close-up.

Morgan struts in with his hair slicked back, his dimples etched into his face, looking every bit the made-for-TV stud. He nods hello before wrapping an arm around Ally.

"What the hell is this?" I whisper to Kenny. I'm almost certain I'm about to get ambushed with some piece of shit news because that's just how my day seems to be rolling.

"Lauren and Cal are picking out their wedding cake."

"And what are we doing here?" I wouldn't mind if she said the same. Now *that* would most definitely brighten my day.

"We're here for moral support." She touches her finger to the tip of my nose, and I lean in and bite it playfully. I'd much rather be offering Kenny some moral support in the bedroom. God knows with her brother, the coital cop, hovering, this entire facility is off limits.

One of the crew shines a spotlight on us, and before we know it the camera is on and panning the room in our direction.

Chef Vito introduces himself to Lauren and Cal, and they briefly rattle off their wedding plans.

"And how about you?" The happy baker turns to Ally and Morgan, and their faces bleach as white as flour. I give a little smirk, glad to be front and center to witness Morgan having to face a pressing question about his relationship, and on national television no less. I bet his balls are sweating right about now.

"I don't know." Surprisingly, Morgan doesn't look rattled at all by being put on the spot. "I think we'll make our own cake." He bears into the overgrown baker, ready for a standoff.

Vito turns toward Kenny and me, and the camera follows suit. Crap. The ultrabright light blinds us—making *my* balls break out in a sweat.

"How about you two?" I can hardly make out Vito's face in the shadows. "Any wedding bells going off in the near future?"

Kenny opens her mouth to say something, then quickly closes it. Great. Poor thing is ashamed to admit it because nothing seems to be going right for us in that arena. Well, I'm about to turn this ship around.

"Yes," I say it loud and clear. "In fact, we're getting married Christmas Eve in an intimate yet beautiful ceremony." I reach for Kenny's hand and look directly into her sweet eyes. "And every gentleman on the planet can eat their heart out because someway, somehow I've convinced this gorgeous woman to spend the rest of her life with me."

Kenny grazes her milk-white teeth over her lips and my balls rattle around in my boxers, begging me to find the walk-in refrigerator where we can be alone for a few minutes. The old Cruise Elton wants to come out and play, screw Morgan Jordan and the sterile routine he's implemented in my life. Not that sleeping with Kenny has been sterile. It's been anything but. And I'd be lying if I said I don't miss the naughty meet-and-greets our erogenous zones shared just about everywhere but our bedroom.

"Christmas Eve?" His eyes squint with delight. "Let's get a cake rolling for you!"

"Let's do it," I hear myself say.

"Really?" Kenny's entire person glows at the idea. Maybe a cake is just what we need to get going in the right direction.

"Yes, really." I rub my arm over her shoulders. "We're already here. Why don't we pick out our perfect wedding cake?"

Lauren and Ally both high-five Kenny as we begin our confection-filled journey.

The girls start walking through aisles and miles of display cakes until Lauren whips out a sketch from her purse.

"I was thinking something edgy, yet timeless," she pants. "Something no one's ever done before. Something that can never be replicated and yet will spawn a thousand oh-so-close knockoffs."

Vito stares down at Lauren's design. "I have just the thing. I've never seen it done, and I predict once this show goes live, every bride worldwide will be clamoring for one of these."

"My God, what is it?" Lauren pulls him in by the apron, and it takes some muscle before Cal can gently pluck her away.

"A seven-layer goji berry and gold fleck filling—with a sprinkling of confectioners' sugar." He closes his eyes and kisses the tips of his fingers.

"*Gold?* I want!" It speeds out of her. "God, I want that!"

I pull Kenny in a little tighter in the event Lauren decides to start wielding her stilettos at the poor unsuspecting crew. I've been around Lauren long enough to know she pretty much gets what she wants. That cake was hers the minute precious metals were brought into the cake mix.

"And for you?" Vito bows toward Kenny, and his chef's hat tumbles right off, exposing the tiny bald spot on top of his head.

"Just something simple." Kenny shakes her head at me like I shouldn't refute the idea.

"No, no." I wag my finger. "We only get one wedding cake. I want you to get whatever your heart desires. If you want real butterflies cascading up and down twelve tiers, then by God that's what I want, too." I press a kiss over her lips. I meant every word.

"Okay." She touches her chest and her face turns a bright shade of pink. "Actually, I sort of like this one." She points to a pale-blue cake covered in a smooth layer of fondant, with tiny white flowers dotting their way to the top in a lacy pattern.

"It's beautiful," I say. "It reminds me of your eyes." No joke, and suddenly I've got tears in mine too. The camera is pointed right at me, ensuring that I'll look like a pussy on national TV, and right about now, I really don't give a rat's ass.

"Then that's the one." Vito turns to the camera. "And in a few short weeks we'll join these two couples on their special day when the Cake Chief takes their wedding to . . ."—Lauren jumps in beside him and they both shout—"the next *level*!"

The spotlight goes out and my balls finally stop sweating. A member of the crew whips out a clipboard and has us sign legal waivers to appear on the show.

"All right." Vito whips off his apron. "Let's get to the office and jot down all the fun details."

By fun details I'm guessing he means dollars and decimal points.

Lauren steps in. "We've already squared up. We'll wait for you guys up front. You want anything? Chocolate cake to go? A box of doughnuts?"

Kenny shakes her head and so do I. Right about now I doubt we can afford either.

We follow Vito to his office, where he dons a pair of thick-framed glasses and suddenly morphs into the chief of finance while whacking the keys on his overgrown calculator. It burps and grinds until it spits out a receipt, which he hands over to me with a shit-eating grin on his face.

"Now"—he starts sharply—"I take all your major credit cards. I need the balance paid in full. You won't believe how many fools we get who try to fake a wedding just to get on TV. After a while, we do a little digging and come to find out they don't even have a venue reserved."

I swallow hard as I take the receipt from him. About a dozen rows of numbers flow down to a series of numerals that I don't even know how to read. Fuck.

"Four hundred and fifty?" Aw, hell, it's probably a bargain. I reach back to get my wallet and my pocket is noticeably bare. Shit. I glance over at Kenny. "I didn't drive." I mouth the words every man dreads to form: *I forgot my wallet.*

"Oh, it's no big deal." She whips out her credit card and hands it to the master cake chief himself. "And four hundred and fifty is a bargain-basement price," she assures me. "This is going to be fantastic!"

The Cake Chief clears his throat. Why does this suddenly feel like a mafia-inspired shakedown? "It's forty-five *hundred*." Vito takes Kenny's card and swipes it before we can process the horror. "Declined." He frowns into his machine. "You got another?"

I've never been so relieved by a rejection in my life.

"No, actually." Kenny shakes her head while her face glows beet red. "That's the only one I have with me."

Crap. Now I feel like a sack of shit.

"I'll try again." He swipes the card and shakes his head. "It's coming up stolen." He plucks out a pair of oversized scissors and proceeds to cut the damn card right in half—and I'm only a little sorry he did it.

"Oh no, wait!" Kenny puts her precious fingers in peril while wagging them before the scissor-wielding maniac, and I gently pull her back. "But it was a misunderstanding! They're sending out a new one."

"It's my fiduciary duty as a business owner to destroy stolen plastic. It saves the next hardworking mom-and-pop from getting stiffed."

"But that was my card." Kenny sags into her seat, defeated.

He leans in and points behind him. "It makes good TV."

We glance up, and to our horror a tiny camera points down at us from high up on a bookshelf.

"You can't use this footage." I pull Kenny in close, reassuring her I won't let it happen. But with my luck I'll have no fucking control over this, either.

"I can and I will," he refutes my theory. "You signed waivers. It's all mine."

"You're going to humiliate us on television." Kenny can't get the words out without hyperventilating.

"No one's getting humiliated." He holds his hands out as if he's about to stop traffic. "People eat up stories like yours all the time. Young couple—down on your luck . . . What's not to love? We'll even show up on the big day with a free cupcake, because that's the kind of guy the Cake Chief is. It'll be fantastic. Just wait and see. Everyone loves a good old-fashioned tale of hardship. You're gonna be a hit."

Great.

Kenny and I are making our couple's debut as a human interest piece—a tale of fiscal failure, and on our wedding day at that.

I can't let this happen.

I've got one trick up my sleeve I haven't tapped yet, and I was sort of hoping I wouldn't have to. Guess I'll have to swallow my pride and have a chat with dear old Dad.

I glance over at Kenny and give a weak smile.

I'd swallow all the damn pride on the planet for her.

9

PUT A RING ON IT

Kendall

We say good-bye to Cruise, Morgan, and Cal in the bakery parking lot. Lauren was nice enough to buy them each their own box of confections before we drive wherever it is Ally is taking us in a last-ditch effort to save my sex life.

"Trust me," Ally says as we step into the sleek, cosmopolitan shopping mall, with its overabundance of glossy white flooring, mirrored walls, and impressive escalator systems that span three stories. "You're guaranteed to have a wild time once we stock up on a few extracurricular basics. Not that Morgan and I have ever had to resort to anything like *this*."

Resort? I don't ask what "this" might be. For one thing, I'm not even remotely interested in my brother's sex life. I'd rather run my neck through a table saw than try to imagine what Ally's bedroom antics might or might not be like. And second, I'm afraid "this" will be revealed sooner than later.

Ally walks at a decent clip, and both Lauren and I have a hard time keeping up with her. Obviously, "this" either closes soon or has an abnormally short shelf life, much like the sexual shenanigans Cruise and I once partook in.

We bypass a lingerie shop, and Lauren and I exchange looks. I would have bet both my boobs that's where we were headed.

Lauren gasps and squeals.

"What?" I jump a little at her unexpected enthusiasm.

"I know, right?" Ally hops to her side. "Am I a genius or what?"

"God"—Lauren's face brims with something just this side of ecstasy—"this is going to make chapter seven the most delicious chapter of all." They fall into a fit of cackles.

"Hello? Still clueless over here." I wave my hand over Lauren's face, trying to defuse the look of unrequited nirvana, but I can't seem to do so. "What's going to make chapter seven the most delicious chapter of all? Are we going to have cake sex?" Because, if we are, calories be damned, I'm one hundred percent on board.

"No." Lauren shoos me with her hand, trying to evict the idea from my brain. "You're going to have deviant sex with the naughty professor just the way God intended." She points over to a dark-looking cave tucked all by itself in the corner.

The store windows are covered with brown paper and the door is shielded with bars, like it might be closed. It doesn't even have a sign—all I see are three giant Xs where the store name should be.

Three Xs . . . Does that stand for poison or . . .

I suck in a breath. Triple X!

"This is perfect." I interlink arms with both Ally and Lauren as we bum-rush the tiny X-rated establishment. Of course we can't all fit through the door at once, so we sort of trip in sideways and untangle our limbs rather indelicately in the process.

Some seriously funky lounge music blares from the speakers, and the red-and-black-checkered carpet in combination with the low lighting and rows and rows of chains dangling from the ceiling gives this more of a demented dungeon appeal than it does a mall crawl.

I take a good look around at all the contraptions neatly stocked and compartmentalized for the pervert on the go. God, is it even legal to be here?

Lauren pulls me further in and we scuttle through the little shop of sexual horrors. To my surprise the aisles are all neatly marked: sex toys, vibrators, women's toys, men's toys, lubrication, adult entertainment, and last but not least—kinky pleasures.

"Women's toys." Ally yanks me to the left.

"No"—Lauren pulls me to the right—"kinky pleasures."

Lauren wins the tug-of-war and slightly dislocates my shoulder in the process. Nevertheless, I dutifully follow her down an aisle cluttered with plastic paddles, riding crops, restraints, clamps, and—dear God, get me out of here, it all looks so damn painful.

"This is exactly what we need." Lauren wheels an abandoned cart over and starts filling it with items as if they're all free.

I have to stop her and quick, or I'll need some of those whips to keep the creditors away. There's no way in hell I can afford all this corruption and debauchery.

"Actually"—my throat goes dry—"I'm just looking." Never before have I been so thrilled to have my purchasing power revoked, and on television no less.

"Consider it my treat." Lauren rips up and down the aisles like a woman carnally possessed.

"And this, for sure." Ally hands her a round rubber ring that hardly looks as if it can fit on my wrist.

"What the hell is that?" I take it from her.

"Cock ring." She snatches it back and pops it into the cart.

"No!" I try to pluck it out but Lauren slaps my hand away. "No cock rings." It comes from me weakly because deep down I know this is one cockfight I'm not going to win.

"Face it"—Lauren says as we follow Ally into the next aisle— "a cock ring might be the only thing that makes your love life worth reading about."

"Crap." I hate it when she's right.

"What are your thoughts on Ben Wa balls?" Ally asks, hovering over the sinful selection.

"What are those?" I peer over her shoulder as she holds up a pair of overgrown marbles.

Ally holds up a finger. "You put them in your—"

"No." I'm quick to cut her off. "And no to the rest of this crap." I pick up a long rectangular paddle that boasts of its *fur-lined pleasure strip*. "I'd hate for you to waste your money on any of this, Lauren." Or more to the point, her father's.

"Not to worry," she's quick to assure. "Trust me, *Penny*"— she gives a little wink—"you're well worth the expense. I've just expanded our distributors. You've got one of the fastest-growing serial novels out there. If this keeps up, I smell the Forbes list in your financial future. But not right away, so I wouldn't go maxing out your credit cards just yet. The money is sort of slow in coming. But the subscriptions are through the roof. You have no idea how big we're going with this. But everything is riding on chapter seven. If you knock this one out of the park, you'll be on the verge of superstardom. In fact, I've got you lined up to speak at three different sorority houses. Penny and Cruz are shaping up to be the country's next favorite naughty couple." Lauren pulls me in by the shirt with the look of psychotic determination igniting in her eyes. "Cruise Elton and his vanilla sexcapades will never know what hit him."

I glance into the cart and give a weak nod at the fur-lined paddle.

Something tells me *I* will.

"You went shopping." Cruise looks wild-eyed at all the bags I've managed to schlep in.

"Actually yes, just a couple things." I hesitate saying they're gifts from Lauren. God forbid he thinks Cal used any of this stuff, or all of chapter seven will go to hell. "I was thinking you might like them." I glance around for signs of his sister. "Is Molly here?"

"She's on a date." He says the word *date* like it's a four-letter word—which it is, but that's beside the point.

"With Kurt?" Speaking of which, we'd better hit the sheets so I can pump out something to give Molly's "date" to edit for me. We're on a tight production schedule, and we really don't have time for Cruise to be lounging around and scrolling on his laptop through God-knows-what. There's sex to be had and dollars to be made once I convert said escapades into a functioning storyline, and of course all roads lead to paying off my precious Vera and perhaps pitching in for a bouquet or two. Who knew my wedding was capable of bringing me to my knees—quite literally?

I crop up behind him and spot a picture of a luxury resort on the screen.

"Ooh, where's that?" There's a waterfall and a golf course and a view of the sparkling ocean off in the distance.

"The La Mer Inn." He pushes the screen out so we can both see. "I thought you might like it for the wedding."

"*Cruise.*" My heart melts. And here a part of me was convinced he wasn't the least bit interested. "That looks amazing." I glance down farther. Wedding packages starting at thirteen thousand. "God!"

"I'll set up an appointment if you like. I've already called and they have Christmas Eve available."

At thirteen thousand a pop, I bet they have a lot of dates available.

The strong arm of temptation bids me to shout a fiscally unsound *Yes!* After all, you only get married once and all that other BS I seem to be shoveling by the ton these days.

"Um, maybe later." Coward. I *so* should have said no. "Anyway . . ." I lean in close and twirl my fingers through his hair. "I've got a little treat planned for you in the bedroom. Give me about five minutes to set up."

"Set up?" His brows rise into his forehead. "I like the sound of this. And—I happen to have a little treat of my own."

"Sounds like a good time will be had by all." Something tells me his treat doesn't involve nipple clamps and anal plugs—not that mine does. I found out today exactly where I draw the demented line, and Lauren didn't dare cross it.

I rush off to the bedroom.

Chapter seven is going to rock. I can just feel it. More like rock the bed. Oh hell, the whole damn bedroom.

I pluck out all of the contraptions Lauren bought and rip through the packaging like it was Christmas morning. I lay them all over the bed and just stare at the perverted paraphernalia. If I didn't know better, I'd swear I was prepping for a lab experiment—a *sexperiment*. I pull off my clothes until I've reduced myself to a bra and G-string. Maybe I should put on heels? Should I strap myself to the bed? Wait, where's that cock ring?

The door rattles and I snap up the cuffs and paddle, then spin around to find Cruise standing there with not a stitch of clothing on—holding out a round, gloriously *huge* cake.

"For the love of all things chocolate." My mouth falls open and I don't know what to drool at first. I give a tiny smile while peeking over at the tiny black ring ready to bejewel his love muscle, and quite nicely.

He steps in and shuts the door, glancing behind me at the plethora of kinky equipment displayed, and swear to God, Cruise Elton *blushes*. He sets down the cake on the nightstand and presses his hands together like he's about to get to work.

"Now"—Cruise snatches the blackout blindfold and quickly straps it over my eyes—"about cheating on those exams." He pulls me into his bare chest and rides his lips slowly up my neck. "How far are you willing to go with this?"

He sounds out of character, so I slip the blindfold up an inch and inspect him for a moment.

"All the way." I enunciate each word as if it's its own sentence. "And the safe word is *red*."

He breaks out in one of his signature sexy-as-hell grins and my stomach pinches tight. "Oh wait." I reach over and swipe the cock bling off the mattress and hold it up. "With this ring, I thee bed."

He takes it from me and slips it over his penis.

"To bed and *red* it is." He secures the blindfold over me again, and I can feel the cold click of steel over my left wrist as he brings my other hand behind my back and secures them together. Cruise dips his warm hands into my panties, working his magic fingers over my folds until I groan into him.

"Oh wow. I've been really, *really* bad, Professor Elton." I moan even harder as he works me into a heated oblivion. "Make sure you use a belt." I work my hips into his as his hands have their delicious way with me. "I *said*, use a belt for God's sake."

A soft laugh rumbles from his chest.

He steps away for a moment, and before I know it he's lowering me down on the small wooden chair he keeps in the corner with piles of his clothes on top. Only the clothes are gone, as evidenced by the fact I just hit the wooden seat and my skin stings from the chill. Something firm makes its way around my waist, strapping me to the backrest. At last the belt comes into play, and I wholeheartedly approve. The icy feel of metal glides over my right ankle as he parts my knees ever so carefully before securing my feet together at the ankles behind the legs of the chair.

Here I am perfectly parted for him, vulnerable, unable to see a damn thing—and suddenly I'm thrilled I ixnayed the vaginal marbles. Then it hits me that the lights are still on and a fresh sting ignites over my entire body at the realization that Cruise has a bird's-eye view to, well, everything. I hold my breath for a moment as my entire body turns every hue of red.

The scent of chocolate wafts over me and I can feel the cake physically coming toward me. It's like I've got this sixth sense when it comes to chocolate.

"To please or to be pleasured?" Cruise asks, and I give a little laugh because there is no wrong answer here.

"Let's start with *to please* and end with *to be pleasured.*"

"Have it your way."

A soft jab of chocolate frosting touches against my lip and it takes a mouthwatering minute for me to figure out it's not being delivered by way of his finger but rather a long, hard appendage.

I take a lick off the tip and roll the rich, dark decadence around on my tongue. I'd let him know how much I appreciate the Cake Chief's way with confections, but I'm pretty sure you should never bring up how wonderful another man is while in restraints with the one you love.

"Looks like I get to have my cake and eat it, too." I lean and in and take the entire length of him into my mouth. Mmm . . . Cruise Elton never tasted so good.

He lets out a hard groan, and I can feel his entire body writhing with pleasure. I graze my teeth along his ridges just enough to entice him, and he digs his fingers into my hair. Cruise has an amazing body and an even more amazing male member that stretches my jaws to their maximum proportion. I glide him in and out of my mouth a solid five or six times before I suck in my cheeks in an effort to intensify the experience for him.

"Shit, Kenny," he groans while holding me down by the shoulders. He pushes deep into my mouth and for a second I think he's going to explode, so I brace myself, but he doesn't, and truth be told I'm fifty shades of relieved.

Cruise reaches down and releases my feet and hands in a single motion. He unbuckles his belt and pulls me to my feet. He whips off the blindfold and scoops a healthy amount of frosting onto his hand and I hold my breath.

"I thought you might want to watch." His left eye twitches as he holds the dark frosting next to his shoulder like we're about to have a snowball fight. "North or South?"

I reach over and run my hand through the frosting before digging in and breaking off a giant piece of what has to be the moistest pastry on the planet. It takes a hell of a lot of self-control not to shove the entire thing into my mouth.

"Well, Professor Elton"—I lick my lips looking right at him—"I say *both*."

Cruise starts at my neck and carefully moves down my body in the shape of the letter *S*—all the while never taking those glowing eyes off me.

I reach down to my left nipple and swipe through the frosting with my free hand and lick it.

"Excuse me, Ms. Jordan." Cruise steps in until my chest adheres to his. "I do believe you're cheating again." He sharpens his gaze over me while his cheek hikes up on one side. "The only person you're allowed to touch with that pretty pink tongue of yours is me." The smile slides off his face.

"Lucky for me." I glide my hand over his chest, up his neck, and through his hair. "I've had bona fide fantasies about you dripping with chocolate."

Cruise curls his lips, handing me the rest of the cake. I dig in with both hands and come up with enough frosted ammunition to cover every square inch of him. Then without hesitating, Cruise presses the remainder of the confection into my chest.

"Oh, is that how you're going to play?" I hold back a handful while Cruise tackles me onto the bed. Before I know it, we're slipping and clawing at one another as one big chocolate wrestling match ensues. His hands glide down my thighs before swimming up to the most tender part of me, and I giggle because I happen to love where he's going with this. He grips on to my knees and gives a devilish grin.

"Open," he says.

And I do.

Cruise

Kenny and cake—there is no better combo. I might have to initiate this as a weekly occurrence, and even her dopey brother might approve. After all, it does take place in the confines of my four favorite walls.

My hand slips through the creamy icing as I maneuver her leg over my shoulder. I run my tongue along her inner thigh, all the way up to the beautiful slick that waits for me, and I dive right in, burying my tongue deep inside her.

Kenny lets out a groan that I can feel clear into my throat as it echoes through her body. I lash delicate circles over her, taking in the nuances of her sweet spot, taking in the taste, the texture, and memorizing the way she feels. I pull out and move my mouth over the most sensitive part of her, sucking and grazing my teeth until she's twisting her hips into my body from sheer pleasure.

"Have I ever told you how much I love the way you taste?"

Kenny's entire body curls when I say it. I happen to know she loves it when I talk dirty to her, because she has a visceral reaction each and every time I do.

Kenny hikes up on her elbows, her face brightened strawberry red while her teeth tug over her bottom lip.

"That's because you've impaled me with chocolate."

I give a slow lick that spans from the bottom to the top, and she moves beneath me approvingly.

"Not true," I refute her calorie-laden theory. "This happens to be a chocolate-free zone." I run my tongue over her again, harder this time, and a quiet cry escapes her throat.

"*Cruise*." She runs her fingers through my hair and clutches on. "Do something with a belt."

Did she say *belt*? I try to look up but she redirects my head right to where it was to begin with, so I continue on with my lingual efforts. Kenny is soft, and sweet, and I'd never want to taint this part of her perfect body with anything that diverts from her own natural sweetness.

That cock ring I stupidly put on slips a notch, but my hands are too busy pinning her knees back to the bed to bother with it.

"Yes, Cruise, *yes!*" She shouts it out so loud, the walls vibrate, and any second now I except Molly to join in on our lovefest while hammering her fist to the wall, but she doesn't. It remains perfectly silent, with nothing but the sound of Kenny's wild panting and my own breathing picking up steam. My hard-on rockets to life as never before, and a sharp pinch ensues at the base of it. I try to flick Kenny's hand off, only to find she's nowhere near my lower region. I try to ignore the strangulating feeling building around my dick and focus on the fact Kenny is about to lose it under the supervision of my tongue.

"Yes, Cruise, yes! Faster, *harder*." She pins me down, and it amps my testosterone past the point of no return while the rest of my anatomy begs to get in on the action. A squeezing pain ignites deep in my penis and shoots through my balls like a firecracker just exploded through them.

"*Fuck!*" It roars from my lungs and Kenny screams right along with me.

"What?" She jumps up near the headboard and takes cover as if there's an infestation of rats.

"Holy shit!" I stare down at my dick in mindboggling pain. It's swelled to twice its size—and it's purple as a welt.

"Oh my God!" Kendall hops off the mattress and spins in a spastic circle. "What the hell are we going to do?"

"Shit, shit, *shit*!" I burst through the door and make a beeline for the kitchen to look for a fucking knife, of all things. I violently open doors and drawers, howling nonstop like a lunatic from the brilliant pain of it all.

Molly and some dude turn up to see what the commotion is about.

Molly's face turns an instant flaming red as she screams at the sight of me. Her date for the evening looks down at my dick in horror, and somewhere in the back of my mind it registers this is the idiot who teaches her creative writing class.

Kenny bops up and down in front of me, her boobs bouncing like chocolate-covered melons as she wields sharpened blades in my face—scissors.

"Yes." I snatch the kitchen shears from her and pause as I stare down at my newly deformed dick.

"I'm calling 911!" Molly's date howls as he takes off into the living room. Molly's gone, and most likely for good now that I've scarred her emotionally. Some father/brother combo I've turned out to be.

Then the painful throbbing subsides a bit. It turns out thinking about Molly makes my dick wish it could melt right off my body, so I force myself to think of Mom—and sure enough, it gives a painful jerk backward as it tries to evict the ring of fire I've attached.

Kenny gets on her knees and digs a finger between me and the contraption, and Molly comes back in with a giant towel, only to scream at the sight as if she's being mauled.

Kenny gives a firm tug, and I let out a roar powerful enough to blow the roof off every damn house in Carrington. She holds up the black rubber circle victoriously as Molly throws the towel on my back and runs like hell out the front door.

It's over.

A siren wails its way closer, and I shake my head.

Just fuck.

———

Once the ambulance leaves, I take my bruised ego and my bruised dick back to the bedroom, where Kenny has already stripped the bed of its chocolate mayhem.

"Have they left?" She looks up at me, still naked, still very much drenched in my favorite confection, and gives a dirty grin.

"They have. And so has Molly. Permanently, I'm assuming." I head over and scoop Kenny up in my arms, dotting kisses across her neck. "I think we could both use a shower."

"Yes!" She gives a little bounce. "I think hot, steamy shower sex is just what we need to round out this scene—I mean *night*."

"It's been quite a scene, that's for sure." I give a wry smile at the mess. "Next time I think we might want to invest in a tarp."

"*Yes*. And a tarp practically calls for all kinds of delicious things, like Jell-O and honey"—her fingers drip down my chest—"and ice cream and fudge." A wild look ignites in her eyes as she gazes past me at some pornographic horizon.

I lean in and kiss her like I'm dousing a fire. I don't care what Morgan says—I sure as hell appreciate Kenny's wild side.

"Are you sure you're up to this?" She glances south of the border as I get us to the bathroom and twist on the faucet.

"We're about to find out."

Once the water hits a comfortable temperature, we step in and Kenny lovingly lathers me up. I don't know that I've ever been so proficiently cared for. I take the soap from her and return the favor as a chocolate puddle forms at our feet.

"You know, we never did eat that cake." She rakes her fingers gently over my chest, leaving a series of lines in their wake.

"We ate the best parts." I land a tender kiss just shy of her temple. "Besides, we'll have another cake from the Chief in a few short weeks and we'll eat all we want." I squeeze the shampoo in my hands and gently work it through her hair. I can feel my dick struggling to rouse from unconsciousness.

"No, we won't," she corrects. "My credit card was declined and dismembered." She takes the shampoo and does the same to me, and I can't help but smile down at her.

"I'm heading back and taking care of everything. Don't you worry—we'll have our cake and eat it, too."

"Really, you don't have to do that. It was far too expensive. We can get another one."

"I want to." It's true. "I'd do anything to make you happy."

"I swear to you a forty-five-hundred-dollar cake won't make me happy. It'll just put me a little more miserably in debt."

"Don't worry, I've got a backup plan up my sleeve. But right now, I just want to focus on you." I help rinse her hair out and run my hands over her arms until she's shiny and clean, just the way God intended. My hard-on blinks to life and I wince.

"Hello there." Kendall looks down with a smile tugging on her lips. "Are you okay, big guy?"

"He's fine. A little stiff but that's to be expected." I dip down and let it slip between her legs for a moment. "There—he's better now."

"I think we should let him go home." She guides my hand to her sweet spot, and I give a soft groan in her ear. "A special part of me is just dying to give him a hug."

Kenny flicks the tiny metal handle at the base of the tub and reroutes the water flow. She squeezes just enough shampoo under the current to create a bubble bath.

"That's why I like you," I say, pulling her carefully down over my body. "You're always thinking. You're a crafty one."

"If you only knew the half of it." She settles her head over my shoulder as if she could fall asleep this way as we stretch out over the length of the tub. She takes a hard sniff and her chest hiccups as if she's ready to have a good cry.

"Hey, sweetie." I sit up a little and pull her with me. "What's got you down?"

"Nothing." She shakes her head but the tears glittering in her eyes send a different message.

"Is it because I bolted just as you were about to—"

"No." She brings her fingers to my lips and I kiss them. "It's not that, I promise." She shifts in my arms to get a better look at me. "It's just this whole wedding thing. It's silly. *I'm* silly. All I need is you, Cruise, and yet a very psychotic part of me demands I have the perfect chapel—the perfect dress, which by the way I don't. Long story—not going there."

"Got it." I comb my fingers through her hair, and my dick pokes up from the bubbles to see if the game is still on. "It's not silly and *you're* definitely not silly. The reason you feel so strongly is because deep down those are things you've always wanted. Those are your heart's desires and they're powerful. Trust me, we can and we will have both of those things. Go to the shop and pick out any dress, Kenny. I want you to have the one you've got your heart set on."

"No, really, it's okay. After that cake we won't be able to afford it. Besides, I'll feel terrible spending another dime." She cinches up an inch to land a kiss on my lips. "I have a pair of white sweats I can throw on. They're from Garrison, so it's sort of a double bonus."

"I wouldn't mind if you were naked. On second thought—save that for the wedding night. Besides, I'll feel terrible if you miss out on the dress of your dreams. I promise you, we'll be fine. Go and pick out your dress tomorrow and I'll run by once you give me the all-clear and pay for it—sight unseen. I promise I won't take a peek."

"Nice try, Elton, but it's not happening. We're starving college students. I get that."

"Correction, *you're* a college student. I'm just starving." Suddenly I feel like shit. Maybe I should have waited to ask Kenny to marry me. But then, if the point was to wait for my finances to perk up, I have a feeling I would've been dead and buried by then. I should have realized Kenny had dreams of her wedding day, and now I feel like an ass for deflating them all.

"You're enough, Cruise Elton." She pulls her lips roughly over mine and my dick grinds for attention. "Come here." She reaches down tenderly and guides me in.

I let out a guttural groan that stretches out far longer than I want it to. "Oh, that feels so damn good." I should have figured the only thing in the world that could heal me was Kenny herself.

And now that I've set a bruise on her dreams, I want to return the favor and heal those, too.

Kenny moves her hips over mine, easy and gentle. I run my hand down over her back, grazing lower until it touches down over her special spot and I bring her right there with me in the erotic exchange.

I bite my lip and push my head back into the tub just before I'm about to lose it. I wait until Kenny quivers over me with a loud guttural cry, then push in deep inside her. We ride that wave together, with Kenny wrapped around me tight as a coil. I don't think I can name one thing that has ever made me as happy as Kenny has. She deserves the world, and I want to be the one to give it to her.

"Well done, Professor Elton," she pants hotly in my ear.

I give a little chuckle. "I could get used to that title."

Too bad it won't be true.

10

WITCHES AND BITCHES

Kendall

Halloween.

Bleh. After I turned thirteen and the candy haul trickled to nothing, it wasn't much more than a party holiday. Then again, I didn't do much partying back in high school, so I'm actually looking forward to getting dressed up and having fun tonight.

Cruise and I meander into the kitchen after a long night of chocolate wars. Poor guy. He's limping a little, and who could blame him? He practically had his penis throttled by that measly bit of rubber. That satanic device should have come with a warning. But then again, it might have. Who reads warning labels, anyway? I should have known Cruise was too big for that thing. That was one of the first things Ally and Lauren told me when I met them, that Cruise Elton had a very special part of him that was the size of a telephone pole. And that sounds just about right. Although they both happened to hear it secondhand. It would be beyond weird if my best friends had slept with my future husband. It's weird enough that one of them is sleeping with my brother. But it's a good weird.

Cruise heads over to the coffeemaker and I join him to start breakfast. We both stop cold and turn to look at the man sitting at the table, reading from his laptop.

It's Professor Curl-Your-Toes.

Crap! Did he spend the night? Did he curl Molly's toes? Oh God, I have a feeling the entire day is about to go to shit.

"Morning." He glances at us briefly before turning his attention back to the screen. His hair is sticking up in the back, and, as if his bedhead isn't incriminating enough, he's wearing nothing but a rumpled T-shirt and boxers. He slides his glasses up the bridge of his nose, pretending things are status quo, and he continues to leer at his computer screen.

Molly comes strutting down the hall wrapped in a robe, with her hair slicked back, fresh from the shower, and I'll be damned if she's not downright glowing.

"I see you two are up," she snarks at Cruise and me before heading over and wrapping her arms around her creative writing professor.

Holy smokes. Cruise is going to commit a homicide in less than three seconds.

Cruise gags. His face turns an ashen shade of purple. He staggers over to the opposite end of the table, and for a second I think he's going to tip the whole thing over on the unsuspecting soul hiding behind gold-rimmed glasses.

Kurt jumps to his feet. "I think he's having another episode," he tells Molly. "Do you need me to call an ambulance?" He directs his words to Cruise, nice and slow, like there are some serious mental issues to contend with.

"Oh"—Cruise nods with a touch of a psychotic laugh—"we'll be needing an ambulance all right, but it won't be for me."

Molly lets out a scream as she throws herself over her own version of the naughty professor.

God. This is going to end in tragedy, and now I'll never get him to edit my stuff again.

"It's against school policy to sleep with a student," Cruise barks while rounding the table, inching his way to a felony.

"That didn't stop *you!*" Molly snipes.

She's got him there. But then again, he did get fired for it.

Kurt holds out a hand while unwisely removing himself from Molly's protective shelter. "Look, it's technically not against academic policy and procedures for a student and—"

Cruise blindsides him with a left hook that sends poor Kurt and his questionable policies backward and onto the floor.

"No!" Molly screeches as if she just witnessed the slaughter of a baby seal. "You can't do this to me." Molly cradles Kurt's head in her lap while wailing up at her brother. "Do you see me hitting *Kenny?*"

"That's different." Cruise knocks a chair down just for the hell of it.

"How is it different?" She screams it at the top of her lungs, and I think for once we're generating more noise before 7:00 a.m. than the Plague.

"It just is!" Cruise roars back.

Molly lets out an ear-piercing cry of frustration. "I'm lucky he came back after watching the two of you run around last night covered in *feces*, and you with your broken dick leash!"

I suck in a breath.

"God! We weren't—it wasn't a leash—and it was *chocolate*." I sputter it out so fast Molly doesn't even blink in my direction.

"I don't care what it was," she barks. "You're both sick! The two of you think you're better than everybody else and you're not."

She glowers at Cruise with a strangulating stare. "And I'm sick and tired of being treated like a kid. Come on, Kurt." She pulls him up. "Let's go somewhere we're wanted."

"No, wait." Cruise shakes his head. He lets out a heated breath while squeezing his eyes shut tight. "I'm sorry. I'm sorry I hit you." He flails his hand toward the poor soul. "And I'm sorry I treated you like a little girl." He takes a step toward Molly. "I just don't want to see you get hurt."

"Well, I'm *not* a little girl, and the only one hurting me around here is *you*! I'm getting my stuff and moving in with Kurt." She gets right in Cruise's face. "Just try and stop me!"

She speeds off to her bedroom and slams the door.

"Molly, wait!" Kurt maneuvers around Cruise with his hands out in the event he has to spontaneously fend him off. "I'm pretty sure there's a policy against professors and students living together." He bolts down the hall and bravely entombs himself in the room with Molly.

"Crap." Cruise winces. "I just can't seem to do anything right lately."

"I'm still here." I go over and wrap my arms around his waist.

"You're the only thing I've ever done right, Kenny." He sags into me with those powder-blue eyes that I can't get enough of. "You sure you want to paddle yourself with a loser like me?"

"Are you kidding?" I brush my lips over his ear. "You're a far cry from a loser and just to prove it, I'm going to saddle you right now."

I drag him off to the bedroom.

On to chapter eight.

After a rather luxurious yet sort of aching lovemaking session with Cruise—who swore he was fine yet winced his way through it—I head to school, sans Molly. I decide to skip my first two classes and instead take up residency outside the student café, clicking away at my keyboard with all the delicious details about last night's confectionary delight. Not even the throngs of people in various levels of costume can distract me. Well, except for the zombie who's running loose and threatening to eat unsuspecting people. Judging by that lewd grin on his face, he means it. Maybe he distracts me a little, but nonetheless, details pour out of me and onto my parched keyboard like a shower in springtime.

My phone goes off and it's a text from Lauren. **Where are you?**

I'm just about to text her back when my phone buzzes again, and this time it's a text from Ally. **Have you seen it?**

Have I seen it? I glance around. **Have I seen what? ~K**

I text Lauren back and tell her I'm at the café.

The students in the café seem to be their usual, less than enthusiastic selves. I look for clues of whatever "it" might be, but all I see are clusters of girls reading the school newspaper, and every now and again they break into the requisite cackles. Usually, whenever someone's got their nose buried in that glorified dishrag, there's a sex-driven article in it.

I take in a quick breath.

"Oh no." Wait—my book is strictly by subscription only. My heart starts beating again. Thank God. For a second—

"This!" Ally pops up, rattling a newspaper in my face, and before I can snatch it, Lauren materializes and plucks it right back.

Lauren's face is covered with green pancake makeup. It takes a moment to register she's in full costume, and the pointed hat that just landed at my feet belongs to none other than the Wicked Witch herself.

"What?" I jump up and wrestle Lauren for the paper, ignoring the fact she's decked out in her Elphaba garb. We tumble to the floor, and I victoriously snatch the paper, tearing it in two in the process.

I pull my half forward, but all I see is the partial word *essor*, and *own* below that in a giant block font.

"Let me see this." I pluck the other half from Lauren's green fingers.

"Could the Naughty Professor be one of Garrison's own?" I take in a sharp breath, and then another and another until I think I might pass out.

"Breathe." Ally smacks me on the back.

"This is terrible." I plunge my face in the crinkled paper and sniff into the ink.

"Cut the drama—it's not so terrible." Lauren plucks me up until we're all seated around my laptop, with the latest chapter in all its kinky glory winking back at me. I snap the laptop shut because suddenly it all feels devious, like I'm trying to pull a fast one on Cruise.

"Honestly, it's nothing, Kendall." Ally sags in her seat, sorry for me because we both know it's *something*.

"I'm over it." Lauren tosses the paper behind us. "Let's change the subject."

"How did it go last night?" Ally leans in close.

I do my best to shake it off. Maybe Ally's right and it's not a big deal. "Your dick ring nearly cost me a lifetime of pleasure," I tell her. "And by the way"—I turn to Lauren—"thank you for the chocolate cake. Cruise never tasted so good." We let out a wild cackle, and suddenly I feel strangely connected to the girls seated with me. "You know"—I reach out and pick up their hands—"I've never felt so close to anybody before. Well, of the female persuasion." I'm not even sure I ever felt this close to my own mother.

"Aww!" Lauren and Ally sing in unison, and the three of us engage in a rather awkward group hug.

"So"—I take a deep breath—"I suppose it's time I come clean to Cruise. And then of course he'll hate me and we'll cancel the wedding, though ironically, there isn't one thing I actually have to cancel." I sag in my seat. "No chapel, no dress, no cake, and no reception. I guess it was sort of a joke to think I could ever have those things to begin with."

"What about the dress from Patagonia?" Ally looks genuinely worried about the Vera I have trekking all those long miles to get to me.

"It's not scheduled to arrive until next year. So there's that."

"Would you stop with the pity party?" Lauren's eyes glow like hot coals. I hate to say it but green skin becomes her, and that wart she glued to her upper lip has an odd touch of glamour to it. "Would you look at yourself? *Quitting?* Feeling sorry for yourself? Is this who Kendall Jordan is? I think *not*. You and Cruise are the happiest couple I know. And yes, I'm demoting Cal and me." She glances over at Ally. "Sorry, but you and Morgan, too." Lauren makes a face. "You and Cruise are what other couples wish they could be. You're fearless, both in and out of the bedroom. You're willing to risk it all for love and if you lose it all—well, you still have each other."

My face heats up at the thought of all the ways Cruise and I have been fearless. More like reckless.

I shake my head. I'm too emotionally choked up to correct her.

"Okay." She plants her palms on the table. "Name three things you need to make your wedding day perfect."

"Cruise." A part of me wants to repeat his name two more times, but a very selfish part of me overrides the urge. "A beautiful dress, and the chapel at Garrison." There, I said it. It feels like a giant boulder just rolled off my chest.

"Okay." Lauren gives one of those circular nods that exudes absolutely zero confidence in whatever she's agreeing to. "You'll have Cruise. You'll wear a beautiful dress." She closes her eyes for a moment as if she's trying to call out an incantation. "And you'll have it at Garrison."

"Just like that?" I'm partially intrigued by her willingness to believe it.

"Just like that."

I wish I could believe it, too.

———

Later that night, Cruise and I pull up to Alpha Sigma Phi and both sigh with contentment.

"This is where it all began," I say, hugging the witch's hat on my lap. That's pretty much the extent of my costume, unless you count my little black dress.

Outside, a ton of people mill around the mini Greek mansion in costume—mostly girls in slut versions of just about every character known to man.

"See?" I point over at a group of vampire jocks. "*Now* don't you regret not wearing a costume?"

Cruise pinches at his five-o'clock shadow, and my panties melt just looking at him.

"I am in costume." He tweaks my knee and glances out the window. "I'm your broom."

I reach for the door handle and pause. "You mean my *groom*?"

"No, I mean your *broom*." He gives a little wink, opening his door. "I'll let you ride me around the bedroom once we get home."

"Very funny." We head up the walk together. "But of course I'll take you up on it." I squash the pointed hat that I picked up at the student store this afternoon onto my head. "Hey, you know what?" I pull him in by the waist as we make our way up the steps. "I'm sort of in the mood to fly around Alpha Sigma Phi." I run my hand down the back of his jeans and give his bottom a squeeze. "Are you up to taking me to the moon in a few minutes?"

"Hell yes." He leans in and gives me a generous kiss. "Let me check in with Pen, and we'll head back to the cabin."

"*No*, not the cabin. *Here.* I want you to fly me around right here in the very place we met. It'll be special. Bathroom or closet?" I give a coy smile. I barely got the latest installment to Kurt this afternoon, which reminds me—I should probably let Cruise know that Molly wasn't in class. Although something tells me I should wait until I've had a chance to test out my new broom.

Cruise glances around—probably looking for Pen, whom I spot toward the back, by the refreshments table.

"Come, come." I pull Cruise along through the dimly lit room teeming with bodies. Oddly, there's no music, but then again, the crowd is so loud I wouldn't be surprised if it was drowned out.

Pen steps away from his harem for a moment. He's bare-chested and he's got on a huge chain necklace with a gaudy dollar sign attached. It's only when he high-fives Cruise that I notice he's wearing a purple velvet cape, and I'm afraid to ask.

"So you finally channeled your inner douche." Cruise socks his half brother on the arm. "I'm liking it."

"Takes one to know one," Pen counters. "I'm a pimp, by the way. And these are my midnight ladies."

The ready-and-willing harlots ogle Cruise like he might be their next victim, and I'm quick to step next to my future broom.

"We were just about to take off." Cruise slaps him on the back. "We'll get together later this week and hang out, man."

"Oh no, we weren't." The Penny in me gives Professor Belton a stern look. "You were just about to walk me to the bathroom." I tilt into him until my cleavage quivers as if it's begging. I know for a fact the bra I'm wearing is like Kryptonite to both the real and imagined naughty professor.

A perky blonde in a cheerleading uniform pops over and lands in front of Cruise. "Oh my God, it's you!" She bounces in her ruby slippers like they're on springs. "You probably don't remember me." She zigzags her finger over his chest, and I waste no time in smacking her away. "Thanksgiving Day." She wrinkles her nose. "I guess technically it was *night*." A stream of high-pitched laughter bubbles from her. I'm well aware Cruise once bedded his way through Garrison, so it doesn't surprise me that we've run into one of his former mattress-mates. He was pretty prolific before we got together. But for this bimbo to bring it up in front of me really rubs me the wrong way. "Anyway, so which one of you is responsible for the book?" She looks from him to me. "By the way, I think it's genius. I've never laughed so hard in my life—and the sex!"

"Oh!" Crap! "It was nice seeing you, Pen!" I yank Cruise along until we're all the way to the opposite end of the room, and lucky for me I spot a long hallway that, hopefully, will lead to indoor plumbing.

"Do you know what she was talking about?"

"The little lush back there?" I wave her off. "She was so toasted I can still smell the vodka on me just from standing next to her." I shove a fistful of hair up my nose and whimper.

"I thought she said something about a book." He shakes his head.

"No, she said *look*. She asked which one of is responsible for this look." I roll my eyes dramatically. "She was mocking us for our noncostumes. And rudely, so soon after reminding you about your Thanksgiving feast." I shudder as the words leave my lips.

Cruise tightens his arms around my waist and gives a little smile. I can tell he enjoys the hell out of my jealous side.

"I promise, I have no memory of it." He dots my lips with a kiss. "You've wiped every other experience I might have had right off the map. There's only you, Kenny Jordan. For the rest of my life, my body worships at one altar and it's right here." He runs his hands down my back until he rounds them over my bottom.

My insides burn with heat to have him.

"Well, it's your lucky night." I nibble on his earlobe, and he gives a soft shudder. "Because I'm not wearing any underwear."

"Shit." He pulls me deeper down the hall, past the long line of bodies waiting to use the facilities, and stops abruptly.

I jump to his side, only to find Morgan with his hand buried in Cruise's chest as if he's blocking his path.

"Where you kids off to?" He gives a disapproving smirk, and I can see his dimples digging in, even in the dark.

"None of your business," I say, removing his hand from my future broom's chest. "Notice how we weren't asking where *you* went."

"That's because it's pretty obvious I was in the bathroom." He glares at Cruise. "And it's pretty obvious where you're going, too." He butts into Cruise's shoulder violently before stalking back to the party.

"Ignore him. He's clearly wasted." I try to pull Cruise farther down the hall, but he's immovable as stone. "Come on." I nod toward a row of closed doors. "I want you to *come*—with *me*." I tweak my brows, proud of my play on words.

"Mmm . . ." Cruise's entire body vibrates with that moan, but he doesn't budge.

I lean in close to his lips. "I'm not wearing underwear." I hiss the reminder like a threat of vaginal proportions.

Cruise touches his hand to his forehead for a moment. "And we're out of here." He pivots in the other direction and speeds us to the exit.

"What the hell?" I say, just as a live band starts up in the common room, nearly blowing my eardrums and the roof off simultaneously. Gah! I recognize that horrid screeching as the same violent guitar strumming that rips through the neighborhood every single night at the B and B.

"It's them." Cruise looks like he's ready to break more than a pair of drumsticks. His gaze shifts away from the band momentarily. "I'll be right back."

"Forget them. The last thing I want is you in jail on Halloween."

He shakes his head, never taking his eyes off the band. "Look, I'll meet you out front in five minutes. I promise, no one gets hurt tonight."

"Fine." We part ways and I walk out onto the porch, bumping into a pair of familiar-looking witches—Lauren and Ally.

"Here's the rest of my coven." I snatch off my hat and run my fingers through my hair. Ally's face is covered in a light-blue glow, and she too has opted for a little black dress. Lauren is in full theatrical regalia—wart and all.

I spot Cal and Morgan on the lawn, knocking back a couple of beers.

"The next installment runs tomorrow." Lauren gives a devious smile. "I have a feeling 'The Naughty Professor Does Chocolate' will get *delicious* reviews."

Ally twitches in her heels. "Lauren let me sneak a peek. You guys really *are* wild."

"*Were*." I make a face as I glance over my shoulder and spot Cruise with someone dressed as Cruella de Vil. Whoever the skank is, she's conveniently draped herself over his shoulder.

Who's that girl he's talking to? Probably another past conquest taking him down memory lane. I bet she's propositioning him into making a few new memories right this minute. God, what if she's talking about the book? And here I haven't told him anything yet, and deep down I'm pretty sure I don't want to. She wraps her arms around him tight before he pulls away and wisely maneuvers around her. Ha! Nice try, hussy, but I win. "Anyway"—I turn back to the girls—"I tried to seduce him and incite some frat house she-nanigans, but he's insistent we drive home."

"He won't do you at the Greek, huh?" Ally teases. "I suggest you invoke a serious punishment for turning you down. I think a paddling is in order."

"I doubt that's necessary. Life seems to be doing enough of its own punishing lately."

Ally cuts a look to Lauren. "What do you think?" She kicks Lauren in the shoe. "It looks like she can use a pick-me-up."

Lauren shakes her head a little and grits out a smile in my direction.

"What is it?" This isn't the first time Lauren's acted strange. "You've been keeping something from me, haven't you?" Oh God, Lauren isn't the type to keep secrets. This must be huge.

She glares at Ally like she's ready to slit her throat, before turning to me. *"The Naughty Professor* is doing *well."*

I glance around for Cruise. Suddenly it sounds as though we're exchanging international secrets.

"How well?"

Lauren presses her dark-crimson lips together. "I may have neglected to mention that I've been selling outside of Sorority Net."

"Oh? Like Fraternity Net?" I groan. "Am I going to have every pervert on the planet after me? Wait . . ." I shake the thought away. "Guys never read that stuff the same way. Girls read it with heart and emotion, and guys see it as filth and perversion. Oh God! I've been writing porn!" I bring my hands over my head and stomp in a circle.

"No, you haven't." Lauren administers a much-needed smackdown. "You're writing a love story—*your* love story. Remember? It just so happens to include a few . . . okay, *many* open-door scenes."

"That's right. We were all made with open-door scenes." I breathe my way through the trauma.

Ally steps in and cradles my cheeks in her hands. "Kendall, you and Cruise are epic. Word on the street is girls want to *be* you. Well, *Penny Whoredon."* She gives an impish grin.

"So that's the big news?" I look to Lauren. "You unleashed me on the male population as well?"

"No, that's not even true, is it?" Ally jabs the green witch next to her.

"All right." Lauren shakes her wand at Ally. "I wasn't going to say anything because I didn't want to add any pressure to the situation"—it comes out like a scolding—"but . . ." She turns her gaze to me and grins, causing the layers of green make-up around her eyes to crack in a thousand tendrils. "No, there is no Fraternity Net. God knows if there is, there's no book board—picture-book board, maybe." She shakes the thought loose. "I've put you on traditional sites. Your sexy stories are chart toppers, *and* another hit or two could . . ." She presses those blood-red lips together again, and I'm tempted to whack her over the head with her wand.

"Could what?" I shake her by the shoulders.

"Could land you a spot in *USA Today*."

"The newspaper?" I'm confused. "Why is the media involved? This isn't a federal issue, is it?"

"No, it's a book issue. I'm talking bestseller list."

I suck in a lungful of cool night air and accidentally inhale something the size of a moth, but I really don't care because . . . Oh. My. God. *USA Today!*

"*No.*" I shake her by the shoulders.

"*Yes.*" She grabs hold of me and throttles me right back. "Here he comes." Lauren straightens and pretends to smooth my dress. "Use the paddle with the spikes."

"I have a paddle with spikes?"

"What's spiked?" Cruise rubs his cheek against mine, and I almost have a Cruisegasm as his stubble rakes across my skin. Nothing feels better than that sexy slow burn.

"The punch Pen's serving." I give a little wink to Lauren and Ally.

Cruise buries a kiss next to my ear and whispers, "There's something I'd like to spike." His hand drift up my thigh and his fingers quickly brush over my bare bottom. Cruise wraps an arm around my waist and says a quick good night to Lauren and Ally.

I turn back to say good-bye and note Cruella has emerged with a douche bag attached to her side, whom I recognize as Rutger. I do a double take at the skank covered in the dalmatian-print coat, and the devil herself bleeds a black smile right in my direction—Blair Lancaster.

Just what the hell was she doing touching my Cruise?

Cruise

The bed-and-breakfast is hopping. Cars line the periphery as if they're serving free food and booze inside, and they probably are. I know the Plague has momentarily left the building, because they're at the frat house we just left.

I've given up trying to talk sense into Lisa, aka the-one-who-got-under-my-skin, and have also given up on procuring legal counsel in an effort to boot them the hell out. I'm going to have to do it myself, but not before I enlist the help of Cal, the *pal* who got me into this mess to begin with. But that good time's not happening tonight. Tonight is about Kenny and me. She almost had me falling to my knees right there at Sigma Phi, but Morgan the moron catapulted out of the woodwork and employed his cock-blocking skills. Who am I kidding? He's right. I need to grow up and stop treating Kenny like a sorority house discard. She's going to be my wife—she's already my life. I need to start treating her with a little respect.

I come around to Kenny's side and settle my arm around her waist as we walk up to the porch.

She leans into me and purrs. "You ready to have the time of your life, Professor Elton?"

Kenny licks her pretty pink lips, and my hard-on and I both say, *"Yes."*

I hardly have time to unlock the door before her hands are plucking off my shirt.

"What should we do tonight?" She stares off with a blank look in her eyes, and for a second I wonder if she's even talking to me.

I wave my hand over her face and pull her in. "What do mean, what should we do?" I swipe a kiss over her neck. "We should do *each other.*"

"Oh, right." She brushes it off, casual as swatting a fly. "I was thinking action—role-playing. *Gah!* I almost forgot." She runs to the bedroom with her hands in the air, and instinctually I scan the vicinity for vermin.

"What?" I follow her over, only to find her digging through the menagerie of shopping bags that have amassed at the foot of our bed.

"This." She holds up something long and wooden with studs poking from the back. "And *this.*" She then holds up a smaller, svelte version lined with fur.

"Are we playing racquetball?" Not that they look like paddles, they sort of . . . Oh fuck, they do.

"Not unless you're volunteering the balls." She glances down at my crotch and I'm suddenly fearing for the boys.

"Whoa." I hold up my hands for a moment. It's almost as if, now that I've confined our satisfaction to the bedroom, Kenny is about to sexually combust from the pressure. It's as if all of my irresponsible screwing has hardwired her to crave the *twisted*, the *perverted.* I've inadvertently created a kinky Kenny. "What's with the weaponry?" Truthfully, I'm afraid to ask.

She lets out a dark laugh and her hair falls over one eye, giving her that vexingly sexy look that reduces me to a drooling dildo. If

Kenny Jordan wants to paddle my balls across the room a couple of times, then by God I'm going to let her.

"Where do you think we should play this game?" She slinks over with her hips swiveling, her full lips parted and waiting.

"Right here, baby." I unbuckle my belt and slip it off. I'm just about to toss it to the side when she grips my wrist.

"You might want to hang on to that. I have a feeling we'll be needing it." She glances around with a disapproving look. "This won't do. I don't think Molly will be back tonight, so we could try the living room." She struts right out the door and I follow.

Crap. "You never know. And with my luck she'll be hauling the rest of her professors with her, and I damn well better like it."

Kenny shakes her head and points a finger out the door. "I'll grab a blanket in the event we want to lie down." She snatches the afghan my grandmother made right off the couch. "Do we still have those chains?" She tilts into me without the slightest hint that she's teasing because, dear God, she's not.

"Are we going camping or to bed?"

"Oh please." She glances at the ceiling as she speeds past me to the fridge. "You sound like you're eighty. This is *us*, Cruise." She holds up a can of whipped cream. "That should do." She hitches her finger in my belt loop and pulls me toward the door. "Now let's find a really romantic spot."

"Kenny." I pull her back, hardly able to control my laughter. "It's freezing out. Even the trick-or-treaters have abandoned the effort." I cup her face with my hands and gently pull her in. "I promise you, we can have just as much fun, warm, between the sheets."

Her eyes enlarge into the shape of full moons, and I'm pretty sure I just said the very words that have the ability to push her over the edge. Kenny seems to be allergic to the sheets as of late.

She opens the door, letting in a cool tail of wind that whips right through the tiny cabin, evidence that I'm right.

"Out." She holds up the thorny paddle, and I'm quick to comply.

"I'm not wearing a shirt," I tease as she gently pats my ass with the studded device.

"You'll be wearing less than that in just a few minutes."

"Did you just do a costume change? Because I'm liking this dominatrix side of you."

"You're the alpha male and don't you forget it." We head out into the dark night. The bed-and-breakfast glows like a pumpkin, and appropriately so on this All Hallows' Eve. Groups of girls take turns breaking into cackles. They're probably laughing at what an idiot Cruise Elton turned out to be. I'd laugh, too, if I didn't want to cry like a pussy first. Kenny pulls me along until we're tucked behind the B and B, with a tall row of pines buffering us from it. A stream meanders near us, bisecting the property all the way past the old mill, where it takes a turn before hitting the highway.

"You rescued me, you know that?" I stop short of the edge of the property. Kenny bites her lip while offering that shy, sweet smile, and a fire rakes through my bones. I want her right now—to hell with her sexually oppressive brother.

"How in the world did I rescue you?"

I run my hands up her legs and warm them between her thighs. "You helped me find my way back to who I was. When you came into town a year ago I was lost, meandering in a sea of faceless girls." I press a kiss against her lips and swallow hard. "You released me from that bondage. Not one of them had anything I needed. It was you I was looking for all along. When you walked in that room, it was like a light went on and I knew I was supposed to be with you."

"That was beautiful." Kenny's lips quiver as she blinks back tears. "Thank you for that. You know"—she glances down for a moment—"you're the first person who really showed me what love is. I mean, of course Morgan loves me, and my mother. But with Mom it was always work and men first. And with Morgan, well, he was too busy looking out for me to understand that I didn't need his protection as much as I just needed *him*. But it's all better now." She wipes the tears away quickly. "I'm standing with the right person—the love of my life." Kenny wraps her arms around me and buries her face in my chest.

"So"—she pulls in and takes a deep breath—"did I hear you say *bondage?*" That wicked gleam returns to her eye. Kenny plucks the belt from my hand and leans against the tree. "Go ahead—tie me up." She thrusts it back into my hand, and I reluctantly wrap the belt around both the trunk and Kenny.

"Tell me why we're doing this, again?" I whisper in the event I lit a fuse, and I think I may have.

"Cruise." She takes a breath and a plume of foggy air escapes her mouth. "This isn't about us. It's bigger than us. Just get with the program already and spank me."

I tuck my head back a notch. "If it isn't about us, who is it about?" I'm almost amused, but equally frightened at what we've become.

"It's about *us*, the 'bedroom' us. Professor Elton . . . you know . . . Now tell me how naughty I've been." Her shoulders wiggle, giddy with the idea.

"You *have* been naughty." I gently bite her lower lip, then pull it out as far as it can go. "So very, very naughty." I run my hand up her heated thigh and land in that sweet spot between her legs. My eyes close for a moment in appreciation of the fact she's gone commando for the occasion. I blink back to life, pull my hand free, and unbuckle her from the tree.

"Wait!" Kenny struggles to secure the belt again. "What are you doing? We were off to a great start."

"You're not wearing underwear." I shake my head. "You probably should."

"What?" Her voice rises to an unnatural level.

"You're doing all these wild things because I've led you to believe they're normal. And instead you should wear underwear and let me love you in the privacy of our bedroom." I wrap my arms around her and she bats me away as if my shirt's on fire.

"What the hell has gotten into you?" Kenny's dimples go off with disapproval as she retrieves both paddles from the ground and holds them out like she's about to deliver a double beating.

I take a step back and withhold the laugh already rattling around in my chest.

"This is not funny. Get back here," she demands.

"Oh yeah?" I take another slow step away. "What are you going to do if I don't?"

Her mouth opens wide, evidence she's stunned by what she's just heard.

"You are going to get back here, and you are going to tie me to this damned tree, Professor Elton—then you're going to spank me until I cry out with pleasure with *this*." She holds up the demon paddle with teeth. Kenny shakes her head and holds out the other one instead. "I mean *this*."

"Is that so?"

"Yes, that's so." She takes a step forward. "Now get back here right this minute. This is going to get really ugly if you don't."

A smile tugs on my lips. "Then I'm afraid it's going to get really ugly. In fact"—I bend my knees and hold out my hands as if prepping for a full frontal assault—"you're going to have to catch me first."

"*Cruise.*"

"Kenny." My chest rumbles with a laugh as the chase ensues. I trail around the pines and in and out of the shadows, taunting her to catch me. As soon as she gets within reach, I pull back and jump out of her way.

"This isn't funny." She snatches at my elbow as I lure her all the way to the cabin.

"All right." I step to the door and turn the knob. "If you catch me, I'll let you have your way. But first you're going to have to paddle me for noncompliance." I'm damn well going to let her catch me as soon as we get into that bedroom. And she can bet I plan on doing a little paddling of my own.

A fire rises in her as she chases me through the doorway. I let her get in a good whack to my ass in the middle of the living room before wrestling her wrists together and settling a wet kiss on her lips. I dart my tongue in and out of her mouth, increasing my ache to have her that much more.

I scoop Kenny into my arms and take her back to the bedroom, then put some smooth jazz on "Repeat," so loud I can't hear myself think—and won't hear Molly bang on the wall.

Kenny holds up a paddle, her face rife with disillusionment.

I reach over and pluck off her dress before taking the fur-lined paddle from her and gliding it up along her leg, the inside of her thigh, stopping shy of that special spot reserved just for me.

I'm going to spend the rest of the night making sure she understands exactly how much I love her, how much she deserves to be loved in every gentle and sane way. I hope she understands. I hope she sees we can have it all, right here, in the privacy of our bedroom.

Molly thumps on the wall and shouts at me to turn down the music, so I do.

I'm damned if I don't, and damned if I do. I only hope it's not that way with Kenny. I hope she's on board with the new us, and that I haven't destroyed anything we worked so hard to build.

11

HURTS SO GOOD

Kendall

A week drifts by as fall slowly morphs into an all-too-cruel winter with nonstop rain, sleet, and the prospect of blizzardlike conditions on the ever-gloomy horizon.

Lauren asked Ally and me to drive to the bridal shop for her final fitting. We head over and step up to the glitzy establishment that shines like a jewel pressed against the cold, gray expanse of the world. A dress catches my eye just as I'm about to open the door, and I pause. It's my Vera, beautifully draped on the flattering form of some headless mannequin, and I wish more than anything that the headless mannequin were me.

"You can do this." Ally comes up from behind me and rubs my back as though she's prepping me for a boxing match.

"I know," I whisper. "I'm really happy for Lauren." I take in a lungful of fresh air and enter the salon. It's warm inside, sweetly perfumed with cinnamon and spice and everything nice—and yet oh so seemingly out of reach. A row of white candles are lit across the front counter, giving the space that sacred ambiance every wedding deserves—except for mine. I'm sure the courthouse downtown will have the harsh fluorescents on overhead. Of course a few will be out due to a lack of city funds—one will be blinking on and off, trying to induce both Cruise and me into a seizure.

Don't even get me started on the bevy of "Wanted" posters that will undoubtedly be lining all four walls of the fine establishment. God knows, nothing says romance like a band of armed fugitives and the government.

"Morgan mentioned that your mom is finally coming back tonight." Ally does her best to cheer me up. "Are you excited?"

"Yes." I feign enthusiasm as we head to the grand room where several pedestals are set out for brides to show off their wares while jealous best friends sit and nod disapprovingly. "I do miss my mom. I spoke with her a few days ago, and she said she had a fantastic time touring Europe. I'm sure she has a ton of great stories. Will you be there tonight?"

Cruise and I are meeting at his father's house, where his ex-stepmother, my Aunt Jackie, lives. Cruise let his father know the bed-and-breakfast is filled to capacity, so they can't stay there. I'm not sure if Aunt Jackie will be around tonight, but if she is, it's guaranteed to be highly entertaining. She has a weakness for younger men and vodka, and has copious amounts of both in the mix whenever possible—thus the divorce.

"I wouldn't miss it." Ally waves over at Lauren, who's standing by a display of overgrown Victorian gowns. "Oh my God! Are these the dresses?"

Ally plucks a blush-pink dress off the rack and holds it to her body. It's poufed out like a hot-air balloon at the bottom, and the girth of it is covered in heavy brocade, with gold embossing throughout. "Oh, these are gorgeous."

"I'll say," I whisper, picking up a sky-blue gown with gold-lace impressions. "What are these for?"

"They're for you. They're sort of my bridal party gift to you. I'm having Cal's sisters and my cousins come in this weekend, but I wanted to give you your dresses today. Do you like them?"

"No." Ally's mouth falls open as she again holds the dress against her body. "I *love* it. When can we take them home?"

"Tonight, if they fit. I gave them your sizes, but the seamstress may want to adjust them to perfection." She motions toward the fitting room. "Shall we?"

The three of us head back to change in a palatial dressing room that's about the size of the cabin. The bridal shop has a small army of attendants helping us ease into the gowns, and I imagine this is what being a model would be like. Only we're not getting ready for some runway show—we're getting ready for the rest of our lives. Lauren's life, to be exact.

"It fits like a dream." Ally spins, looking every bit a princess. The gold flecks and pink hues complement her pale skin, her vanilla-colored hair. I can't help but be a little envious. Ally looks ready for a wedding of her own in that dress.

The gal helping me pulls the zipper taut, and my dress sags.

"Pretty," I say, even though my boobs look like they're hanging down to my knees. It figures.

"We'll get it adjusted." Lauren wrinkles her nose at me.

The attendants help her into her gown, and I gasp at the sight of her. Lauren was beautiful in the dress a few weeks ago, when we first saw it, but now—without the sign of a single clothespin holding the back together—she looks like an angel that just flew down from heaven.

"Stunning," I say. Really, it's the only word that fits.

"Lauren!" Ally bursts into tears, and I give a hard sniff because it's taking everything I've got not to lose it. "Lauren, it's perfect. *You're* perfect." Ally and I close in on her as all three of us huddle together with our arms wrapped around one another.

"It's hard to believe that in a few short weeks I'll be married and all this will be over." The attendant hands us each a tissue, and

Lauren gives a loud and aggressive blow. "Which reminds me, I have an entire itinerary to give you both for the following weeks. I've already scheduled our nail and hair appointments—spa days have already been factored in, starting next Tuesday, then every week after that right up until the wedding. I need you both relaxed and calm"—she fans the tears from her eyes—"placid and serene. Ally, no chocolate for you until after the ceremony—we both know you have a tendency to break out." Her steely eyes dart over to me, serious as shit. "Kendall, I'll need the final chapter in two weeks, so think up some grand conclusion, a real nail-biter of a climax if you know what I mean. Then I'll have my formatter piece the entire thing together and you'll have a genuine book on your hands. I also need—"

"I can't do it." I smooth my hands over my dress to keep the residual tears away. "Nothing exciting has happened for weeks. Face it—it's true. Cruise is losing interest in me."

"What?" Lauren plucks at my shoulder. "I'm calling bullshit." She barks it out while in her wedding dress, and it looks hysterically wrong. "You just get back on that pony and you *ride* him. You ride him all around campus if you have to and then you can set your hair on fire for all I care, but you're going to bring this puppy home. Speaking of which, please, no more boring bedroom sex. The women reading these are already having boring bedroom sex, and they're counting on you and Cruise to keep their deviant dreams alive."

"There's not a lot I can do," I say, slipping out of the bloated gown. "I've tried just about every trick in the book. The bottom line is, that special glow has left our relationship. We've crossed that dreaded threshold, and now we're boring, just like everyone else."

"*Kendall.*" Ally swoops over and hugs me while I stand there in my boy shorts and push-up bra. "Cruise loves you. Have you talked to him about this?"

"Well"—I consider the question for a moment—"not really. I guess that's the next step. But just thinking about having that kind of conversation with Cruise makes my stomach turn. It feels one step closer to"—my chest heaves as I hold back tears—"saying good-bye." The attendant shoves the box of tissues in my face and I pluck a few out, pressing them into my eyes as a rush of tears hits me unexpectedly.

"Oh, honey." Lauren gently rubs my back. "I promise, once you get that amazing, creative, perhaps a little dangerous yet extremely *inventive* climax for the final chapter, your happily-ever-after will come right on its heels."

"You think so?" I blubber through the waterfall streaming down my face.

"I *know* so." She presses a quick kiss to my cheek. "And so will *USA Today.*"

<hr />

Later, through a miraculously clear night, Cruise and I drive to see his father, Andrew, and my mom at his dad's gorgeous, rambling estate. It'll always hold a special place in my heart, since that is where Cruise proposed to me. Actually, it was out in the field after we went horseback riding. He got down on one knee and we made love right there in the snow. But that was when our love was new and everything was just the way it was supposed to be. I wonder if we can ever get back to that. Maybe a visit to the barn is in order. I glance around at the black-velvet night, and I somehow doubt we'll venture much farther than the house tonight.

I spot Morgan's truck parked out front, and I perk up a little at the sight.

"Looks like your brother's here." Cruise frowns when he says it, and my mouth falls open at his quasi insult.

"You say it like it's a bad thing." We get out of the car, and he comes to me and wraps an arm around my waist. "I happen to know he thinks of you as the brother he never had." My father's errant children scuttle through my mind, and I'm quick to shoo them away.

"And I think of him as a brother, too." It comes out with an edge of sarcasm. "Besides, I always have a great time when your big bro is around. Trust me." His lips pull back, giving him a slight look of regret.

"You're not funny. Morgy really does love you."

"I can feel the love, all right." His brows lurch as if he doesn't believe a word.

I leave it alone for now. I'm not ready to get into it with him. Morgan does try around Cruise. And fists haven't been exchanged for months, which has to be a good sign.

A pair of oversized wreaths adorn the double entry, with oak leaves in every shade of cranberry. I used to love fall, and yet now it feels like I'm surrounded with death and dying everywhere I look, starting with my relationship with Cruise.

The door swings open wide, and both Andrew and Mom are there to greet us. They look tan and healthy, and they have that special glow that only people in love seem to have.

"God, Kendall"—Mom holds me by the shoulders—"you're so pale and thin. Have you been eating?"

Morgan comes up from behind her. "I think she needs some sun." He reaches over and tousles my hair.

My gaze drops to the polished marble floor as I try not to cry. "Yes, I've been eating." Leave it to my mother to prove a point without knowing it.

"Well, have you been hiding under a rock?" She pinches my cheeks hard, and I gently deflect her efforts. "Cruise, you need to take better care of this girl."

"I'm fine." I glance over at Cruise. "He does take care of me, and quite nicely."

"Nice to see you, Karen." Cruise leans in and hugs Mom. "I've been on my best behavior around Kenny, I promise."

Best behavior? What the hell is that supposed to mean?

"Aww." Mom clasps her hands together. "I love it when he calls you that."

Andrew is quick to usher us into the great room, where, to my surprise, I see Aunt Jackie juicing it up with Pen and Ally.

"Look who's here!" Aunt Jackie bounces over in her silver heels, her all-too-tight jeans, and an ill-paired sequined crop top. "Kendall-poo and my Cruisy boy!" She embraces us both at the same time and accidentally spills her wine down my back, where it flows along like an icy river.

I let out a cry as the white wine cascades all the way to my jeans and onto the floor.

"Oh, hon"— Aunt Jackie waves a hand at me—"don't you be embarrassed. Happens to the best of us. Ain't that right, Karen?" She slaps Mom on the back and breaks out in a cackle. "Remember that time you pissed yourself while we were on our way to the Sigma Nu mixer?"

"No, actually that was you," Mom corrects, and it only encourages Aunt Jackie to break out in one of those hacking laughs with nothing but air coming out for a minute straight. Aunt Jackie vibrates as her dark hair sprays around her head like a jagged rainbow.

"I actually didn't have an accident. This is wine," I say, glancing down at the puddle.

Ally already has a dish towel at the ready, and she helps mop it up.

"I've got some sweats you can throw on upstairs," Mom says. "First room on the right. They'll be baggy, but you'll be dry."

"Cruise?" I try to entice him by making big eyes at him. "Would you mind helping me? I really don't know my way around, and the house is so big." Technically, it doesn't even qualify as a house. It's more like a museum—or a *mausoleum*. I lick my lips to make sure he gets the message, loud and clear.

"Oh." He glances at my brother and his brows furrow. "Actually, Ally, why don't you help her out? I'm sure you're better at girl things."

My mouth falls open.

"No, Ally, that's okay." I press a hand into her chest, and she steps back. "I'm fine with just Cruise." I take his hand, but he slips his fingers away.

"Ally, it's the first door on the right. You can't miss it." He turns to Morgan like they're suddenly best friends. "So what do you think of those Gladiators?"

I pluck at Cruise's shoulder and forcibly take his hand again.

"Excuse us," I say crisply as I pull him along the length of the expansive room to the base of the stairs. "Why am I having to drag you with me?" My eyes practically cross—I'm that angry.

His jaw clenches and my stomach melts. Traitor. I'm supposed to be royally pissed, but Cruise's vexing sexiness doesn't help the situation.

"Because I happen to know for a fact you're going to want to land parts of my body in yours," Cruise says. He kisses my hand sweetly, and his five-o'clock shadow grazes my skin, sending a sizzle all the way down my thighs. "I promise, I want that, too."

"Great!" I sense a spectacular climax coming in more ways than one, and God knows I want them all. I'm that greedy tonight, and to prove it I pull Cruise up the stairs with me.

"Not great." He reels me back in. Cruise sighs into me. His entire person sags as if he's gearing up for some disturbing speech he knows deep down I don't want to hear. "I'll wait outside the room. We can leave early if you like."

I glance up the stairwell. The hallway leading to the right isn't at all visible from down here. I smile coyly up at Cruise. We're about to have hot hallway sex, and he doesn't even know it. He leads me by the hand, and I dutifully ditch into Mom and Andrew's room. God, this place is huge! The bed is the size of a city. Well, a small cherry-stained city with large white clouds on top, but nevertheless . . . Fresh flowers sit in a cut-crystal vase in one corner. There's a bay window, and a round tufted couch is perched in the center of the room for no good reason—and holy crap, there's just miles of empty space in here. I open the door to get Cruise.

"You need to see this." I motion him inside, but he's quick to shake his head. "Have it your way." Honestly, I don't have a clue what's gotten into him. I strip down to nothing and hop back into my heels. If Cruise Elton refuses to have sex with a naked woman in kitten heels, then I'll know for sure something's wrong—especially when the naked woman in question happens to be *me*. I fluff out my hair and it covers my boobs, leaving my nipples poking out as if they don't want to miss any of the action. I crack the door and stick a leg out, and he gives a whistle. My lips press in, holding back the smile that wants to let loose because that little vocal gesture just so happens to have me swimming with relief. I bolt out the door and do the big reveal, and his eyes ride up and down my body with a lewd grin perking on his lips. There's the Cruise Elton I know and love.

"Okay." His features dim as he takes me in, but that lusty look in his eyes is proving impossible to extinguish, not that I want to. "Go ahead and get your clothes on. They're waiting for us downstairs."

And there goes the Cruise Elton I know and love.

"Who cares?" I strut forward, parting my legs just enough to pique his interest.

"Hot damn." Cruise bites down a smile and lands his hand on my bare bottom. He presses into me and takes in a breath through his teeth. "Fuck, *Kenny.*"

"Yes, fuck Kenny." I nod into the idea. Technically, it's *Penny* I'm channeling, and I'm desperately trying to bring out the *Cruz* in him.

"Mmm." He shakes his head. "I am dust."

I can feel the hard protrusion through his jeans growing at a promising rate, so I press my thigh into it, acknowledging the fact.

A burst of laughter emits from downstairs, with Morgan's being the most obnoxious, and it causes that lewd grin to slide right off Cruise's face.

"On second thought." His hands ride up to my shoulders, and he gently puts us at arm's length. "We'd better not."

"No, it's fine. They're all having a great time. They'll hardly even notice we're missing."

"Oh, they'll notice." He nods like it's a fact. "I'll just wait for you at the bottom of the steps."

"No." I try to hold on to him by digging my heels into the floor but he keeps moving, and I end up sliding along with him like a naked three-year-old who refuses to leave a toy store.

"Kenny." He tries to gently peel me off.

"Cruise." I'm quick to unbuckle his belt and undo his jeans, like I'm trying to rescue his penis from a denim blaze he's currently engulfed in.

"Don't do that," he says with a dull laugh, as if he's resigned to the fact, and yet he's still dragging us down the hall toward the stairwell.

"You mean don't do this?" I pull his spare appendage free and hold it up as if the two of us are proclaiming victory, only in this case Cruise himself is sort of the villain working against us.

"Careful there." That cute grin breaks out on his face as he tries to put his dick back inside his boxers, but I won't let go and there's no way in hell he's going to shake me off.

"Face it," I whisper as he tries to pry me off like a snake. "We're going to have hot mansion sex right here whether you like it or not." I leap onto his waist and Cruise bounces off-kilter. "You used to be into this, remember?"

"Maybe I'm not into that stuff anymore." His lips cinch at the tips. "I think—" Cruise trips and staggers to regain his balance.

"Whoa." I grip his hair and pull his head into my chest as he stumbles into the thick stone railing.

To my chagrin I spot Morgan at the bottom of the stairwell. Then it's all a blur. Cruise tumbling down the first few steps. My naked body sliding off him rather ingloriously, with his face then touching down in an area my brother should never bear witness to. We tumble in opposite directions, with Cruise trying to snatch me back by the hair, and then the unthinkable happens—I tumble right into my brother's arms. Morgan catches me awkwardly, his hand settling square over one boob. I let out a scream worthy of a good horror story, which is exactly what this night is shaping up to be. Then Morgan screams as he gingerly sets me down on the landing. A fire pumps through his eyes as he openly glares at Cruise.

"*You!*" Morgan wastes no time in lunging for him, and poor Cruise hardly has time to put away his boy toy. Before he has a chance to properly get dressed, he tries to deflect Morgan, and his unnaturally large man-parts are sort of flapping with the girth of his hard-on still semi-erect.

"Stop!" I try to pluck Morgan off Cruise before they break one another's necks, just as Aunt Jackie runs to the base of the stairs.

"What the hell?" she shrieks. "They're all naked!"

"Oh, *they're* not naked," Mom counters from the other room. "*You're* three sheets to the wind!" She clip-clops over just as I scamper up the stairs. "Oh hell!" Mom barks. "They *are* naked!"

Andrew, Pen, and Ally rush to the foot of the stairs just as I peer from behind the hall.

"Cruise!" Aunt Jackie hollers. "My God, you have a third *arm*! You didn't get that from your father, you know!"

Mom swats her. It's nice to see they haven't let a little thing like marrying the same man get in the way of their friendship—although, technically, Jackie wanted the divorce.

Andrew and Pen run up the stairs and wrangle the boys apart, leaving Cruise with his spare parts dangling awkwardly for all to see.

Aunt Jackie bursts into applause, and I'm pretty sure it's Cruise's penis she's cheering. I'd join her, but right about now the only thing I feel like bursting into is tears, so I do.

Loud, whimpering, harrowing cries come from deep within me, and a sense of silence settles over the house—followed by the sound of Cruise's zipper as he safely tucks away the very thing he doesn't seem to want to give me.

"Hey, come here." He tries to pull me in but I jerk my arm back.

"No, it's okay." I run into the bedroom, totally humiliated. Eventually, Ally and Mom come in to see what's the matter.

"It's complicated." I sniff into a tissue while Aunt Jackie appears with a purple quilted robe, then I slip it on. "I'll talk to you about it some other time." I hiccup as I offer my mother a hug.

"Ally? Do you think I can get a ride home with you guys?"

"Absolutely." Ally nods.

"Thank you."

Little does she know the home I mean is *hers*.

It looks like the final chapter of *The Naughty Professor* will be a total work of fiction, and nothing could depress me more.

Cruise

head downstairs, barrel out the front door to cool off, and Morgan follows me, looking for trouble.

"Hey." He gets in my face, so I give him a good shove that sends him flying.

"What the hell do you want now?"

"Relax." He sticks his oversized mitt in my chest. "I came out to let you know Kendall is coming home with me. She says she's embarrassed—she needs some time to think."

I pause for a second, just staring at him wild-eyed because I couldn't have heard him right.

"What do you mean she's going home with you? I'll take her home." My heart thumps in my chest. That altercation we just had was pretty huge. She's got to be confused as to why I rejected her like that. I glare at her moron of a brother because he very well knows why. I bet he's been orchestrating a breakup from the start.

Before I can accuse him of anything, Ally speeds Kenny out. Kenny's body is wrapped in a robe, and her face is slicked with tears. She turns her head away as the two of them pass me.

"Kenny, wait." I try to move past Morgan but he holds me back.

"She doesn't want to talk to you," he rumbles. "Give us a few minutes before you take off. She wants to run by the cabin and pick up her things."

"What? *Kenny!*" I shout as Ally entombs her in the truck. "Shit." I glare at Kenny's useless brother. "This is all your fucking fault. You know that?"

Morgan inches his head back. "You're the asswipe who doesn't know how to keep it in his pants. Get the message, douche bag, girls don't want to be treated that way."

"Yeah? Well, Kenny *does.*"

He pulls back and lands his fist on my jaw, and I crash into the bushes.

"You stay the hell away from my sister, asshole. Or I'm going to rip your pretty little head off next time." He stomps over to his truck.

"No, wait." I try to move, but I'm effectively pinned by the branches. It's as if the entire universe is against Kenny and me. "I didn't mean it that way."

Just what *did* I mean? I'm an asshole all right—for not giving in to Kenny's insatiable needs and for giving in to Morgan's instead.

———

A few days tremble by, and Kenny refuses my phone calls and visits. I've intercepted Ally a few times, and she insists Kenny just needs a little time to clear her head and cool down.

I sit in the kitchen as the sun comes up, thinking the entire world took a shit on my shoulders. My head feels stiff and my brain vibrates from lack of sleep. Overall, it's like I just stepped out of the microwave.

Every day without Kenny has been a nightmare. Morgan threatened to get a restraining order if I so much as made one more drive-by in the middle of the night. I can't help it, though. Everything's fallen to crap without her. I miss her beautiful face in the morning, the sweet smell of her hair, her soft body crushing up against mine. I even rifled through the bags at the foot of our bed and took a look at all the things Kenny had bought for the two of us to enjoy together. Every bracket and racket you would want to pleasure your partner with was in those bags, and now every last part of me wishes she were here to do those things with me. Hell, I'd let her have her way with me on the roof in broad daylight if she wanted. Or in downtown Carrington—in front of the entire student population at Garrison. And even in front of her cock-blocking brother. I'd do anything she wanted, anywhere, anytime, and anyhow, so long as she'd have me back. I had paradise in my arms, but now she's left me and there's nothing to embrace but the stale air in the cabin.

The door rattles from down the hall, and Molly staggers out wearing nothing but a T-shirt that barely covers her bottom. Sadly, that, too, reminds me of Kenny. A skimpy T-shirt just so happens to be what she throws on in the morning after a long night of sleeping naked in my arms. That's my favorite part about us— sleeping intertwined, her warm body pressed against mine.

"Get dressed," I gruff. "I don't want to see you like that."

"As if I'd listen to you." Molly reaches into the fridge and starts plucking out the ingredients for a buffet breakfast.

"You should listen to what I say. You're my sister. Trust me— you don't want to go around dressed that way."

"You can't tell me what to wear. This was all Kendall wore when her brother was here, and you didn't hear him complaining." She shakes her head. "Some guys understand their sisters have to grow up, but not *you* . . ." Molly rambles on and on, but her blabber quickly turns into white noise—and all I hear is indiscernible mumbling, albeit irate and directed at me.

Wait a minute. Morgan is definitely *not* some hero. And for sure he didn't appreciate Kenny walking around here with nothing on but a T-shirt. It's all coming into focus. I should have taken what he said in context. The dude is her brother. Of course he doesn't want to think about Kenny and me having a good time outside our bedroom. Hell, he doesn't want to think of Kenny and me having a good time *inside* our bedroom. And for sure he didn't want to see it with his own two eyes. No wonder he's gone batshit. I gave him a front-row seat to our sexual shenanigans when we took up residence in his closet for the night. That's exactly why he lectured the holy crap out of me. I stunned the living shit out of him when he found my hard-on pointed at his sister.

I wipe my face down with my hand for a moment. Crap. And now he has Kenny safe and sound—fuck-free, might I add, sleeping on his sofa.

I snap my laptop shut and take in a breath. "I think I'm going to head to Garrison today."

Molly shakes her head. "It won't work. She doesn't want to see you. Face it—the two of you are ancient history."

The bathroom door opens and Professor I-Can't-Control-My-Hose struts out.

Crap.

I grunt out a hello and watch as he wraps his hairy arms around my sister. His bedhead stands erect an inch above his head like I'm betting his dick did last night.

"That was quite a good morning you gave me." Molly pulls him into a kiss by way of his overgrown ears.

Okay, so that incher of his reprised itself this morning. My palms flatten out over the table and my legs pump a mile a minute. It's taking everything in me to keep from sticking his face in that sizzling frying pan.

A light knock lands on the door and I fly to it, hoping to see the most beautiful brunette in the world, but it's not Kenny.

"Mom." I pull her into a brief hug and help her inside with her suitcase. "Boy, have we missed you. Isn't that right, Moll?" I give a shit-eating grin toward the lovebirds in the kitchen. I happen to know for a fact nothing kills a boner faster than having someone's mother show up.

"What's going on with the B and B?" She pulls me in. "You've really got that thing packed to the hilt. I'm proud of you, son."

I don't bother telling her I'm getting ready to initiate third world assault tactics to get them out. And if that doesn't work, I'll turn the whole damn thing into a bonfire if I have to, right after I make sure we have fire insurance.

"Thanks." I give her a gentle pat on the back.

She fills us in on how Grandma's doing—which is fine, apparently. They're back to not getting along, which is the status quo, so in that sense I guess it's good news. "If you'll excuse me, I'm going to take a quick shower." I hold a hand out at the moron standing in nothing but his boxers next to my half-naked sister. "Feel free to engage in a parent-teacher conference if you like."

I head off to grab a clean towel. It's time to get ready for Kenny. There's no way I'm letting another day slip by without her.

And I don't care what her brother has to say about that.

———

Garrison University is covered in a robe of gray clouds. The trees are dusted with fog, and even the crows that streak across the bleak sky sound as if they're crying out in pain. It's as though the entire world is reflecting how I feel—how absolutely miserable I am without Kenny in my life. She took the light, and all the oxygen I need to breathe, right along with her.

I walk past the tall, Gothic-like building that once housed my office and cringe. Maybe Morgan's not that moronic. After all, it was my reckless behavior that put my entire future on the line. A dull smile plays on my lips. Then again, I don't regret a moment of that reckless behavior since it involved the love of my life. I walk past the brick building with a heavy feeling—without Kenny in my life it's as though I've hoisted the whole damn school onto my back.

"Mr. Elton?" A familiar male voice booms from behind me. I turn to find Dr. Barney and with him is—son of a gun. "Professor Bradshaw?" I go over and offer a heartfelt hug. "Damn, you look good." I don't think I've ever said that to anyone of the same gender, but here he is—looking fit and pleasantly plump, his old self.

"Why, thank you." He socks me in the arm as we part. "I'm feeling fine these days. Doctor says I'm healthy as a horse and stubborn as a mule."

"That's what I like to hear." Last I heard his cancer was in remission, but looking at him, you'd think he never went through hell in the first place. He was skin over bones last year, and now he's right back to where he started.

"I heard a few things myself." He crimps his lips with disappointment. "A woman—these sacred halls—very little clothing." He shakes his head. "Sounds like a gender relations nightmare—or success story." He gives a little chuckle. "I guess that depends on how you view it." He belts out a hearty laugh and Dr. Barney joins in.

"It was definitely a success." Until a week ago, but I omit that tiny detail.

"So what brings you to campus?" Dr. Barney looks suddenly suspicious, as he should, since my motives are anything but chaste. That is, if Kenny will give me a second glance.

"I was just meeting up with a friend."

"Listen, Cruise"—Professor Bradshaw leans in and pokes his finger in my chest—"I'm willing to go out on a limb for you. If you still want it, I'll find a way to get you reinstated into the graduate program. Just keep your nose clean from now on. I've got your number. I'll contact you as soon as I get confirmation. Does that sound good to you?"

My stomach cycles like I'm going to be sick in a good fucking way. "Hell yes, that sounds good to me." An entire flood of relief pours through my veins. Then the bed-and-breakfast rushes through my head, and I sort of miss the place even though I haven't set foot in it for months. I like the thought of running it, but there's no reason I can't do both. "I look forward to hearing from you."

We say good-bye, and I spin toward the student café, where Kenny hangs out when she doesn't have class.

My heart races. My blood pumps a million miles an hour, and I can feel the adrenaline rocketing through me. It's turning out to be my lucky day, and I have a good feeling it's about to get even luckier. If I'm smart I'll ride the coattails of this new wave of fortune and kick the Plague out on their nonpaying rears before the week is through. And if things really go my way, I might have enough luck to put the B and B back together and rent it out in time for the holidays. There's nothing like Christmas in Carrington. My heart sinks at the thought because if I don't have Kenny in my life this Christmas, it's going to break me in ways that I've never imagined.

Just thinking about losing her—losing our precious *wedding* day—makes my heart ache.

I step over to the café, scanning the place for my lovely bride, and a frown takes over. No sign of my favorite brunette. But buried in the back, texting into her phone with the force of a Cat 5 hurricane is my least favorite blonde—Blair. And to think that at one time I thought she was going to be Mrs. Cruise Elton. That's one disaster I'm glad I escaped.

I head over and her face brightens when she sees me.

"Well, look who it is!" She leaps up and embraces me with her wandering hands, and I carefully extract her from my person. "I've been looking forward to spending time with you ever since you begged for a little alone time on Halloween." Her voice hits that annoying upper register, and I try not to groan audibly as I take a seat across from her.

"That's funny, I don't remember begging." I try not to smirk. After all, I want something from her.

"Isn't that funny?" Her features soften as she twirls a cup of coffee in her hands. "Everyone has their own version of how things happen." She presses her lips together for a moment.

"It's like my grandfather used to say: every pancake has two sides."

"He was a wise man." She tucks her hair behind her ear and her eyes glitter up for a moment. "I remember your grandpa. I remember a lot of things about you—about *us*."

Here we go. Not sure I want to walk down memory lane today and for sure not with Blair.

She shakes her head, and her lips shrivel up for a moment. "I thought I'd be the one marrying you one day. I spent my whole life pining for you and then when we finally got together I was so happy." That last word fades to nothing. It's becoming clear Blair is close to genuine tears.

Shit.

"I really screwed things up royally, didn't I?" she sniffs.

"I think we both sort of wiped out together," I offer. "Our relationship wasn't near what it was toward the end as it was in the beginning." I'm not sure I should have gone there, but nevertheless it's true. We started off with stars in our eyes and ended in a pit of quicksand. Ironic, because that seems to be the trajectory Kenny and I have followed, and now the unappealing reality has me scared shitless.

"Yeah, I felt you cooling things off," she whispers. "I'm not blaming you for what I did. I'm just saying I noticed the kisses were decreasing—you weren't holding me in public the way you used to, and I just wanted to feel special again." She cradles her coffee and gives a hard sniff. "Rutger gave me that."

I press into my seat and sag. "I remember the day I found out you were with him. I was pretty ticked." More than ticked. "I got shitfaced and wanted to beat the crap out of everyone in sight. Then you took off with that douche from Dartmouth." My chest bumps with a laugh. "But I guess I knew it was over before any of that ever happened. I think we were together for so long we didn't know how to get off the train."

"We could still try." Desperation grows in her eyes. "I still feel something for you, Cruise. Neither of us is married. We could start out as friends and see where things go?" She clasps me by the wrist and instinctually I glance over my shoulder because this is usually when the universe tries to inject Kenny in the scene, but, thankfully, there's no sign of her.

"Look"—I gently slip out of her grasp—"I get it. I'm sorry you still feel so strongly, but I'm not there anymore. And the fact you deliberately got me fired, almost cost Morgan his scholarship—that you *hit* Kendall . . . It's not cool. I can't be okay with any of that."

"I know." She gives a hard sniff. "I wish there was some way to make it up to all of you." Tears flow from her freely and her lips quiver. "I love you so much that it makes me insane to see you with anybody else. I wish you'd put yourself in my shoes for once. Imagine how much pain you'd be in if you made one stupid mistake and you lost *Kenny*. If you hurt this much you wouldn't mind taking down a job—a scholarship or two. You'd want to lay this bruise over the entire planet so the whole damn world could feel your pain. I fucked up, and now I'll have the rest of my life to pay for it."

My heart breaks for Blair, and I don't want it to. I want to set her up as the villain, the enemy, like she's been for so long, but I can't do it anymore. I can feel the walls crumbling, so I reach over and pull her into a quick hug. She sniffs into my neck. Her chest rattles as she breaks down and cries right here in the student-run coffee shop.

"I'm sorry you feel so much pain," I whisper. "I hope you're happy now with Rutger. I want that for you."

I'd die if Kenny met someone else and flaunted her happiness in my face.

A cold shower splashes over our heads, and both Blair and I jump to our feet, sopping wet.

Kenny seethes at the two of us, and my heart stops. Looks like the universe was right on time. Her lips quiver. She never takes those cobalt-blue eyes off me. Her dimples wink in and out in rhythm to her anger and she looks cuter than hell, but my heart breaks for her because I wish to God she hadn't just witnessed a damn thing between Blair and me.

"I wish I never met you," Kenny hisses, looking right at me.

Ally pulls her in. "Let's get out of here." She bears her fangs at both Blair and me before hustling Kenny to the door.

I try to go after her, but Lauren appears from nowhere and gets in my face. "Nice work, dickwad," she barks.

"Stop." Blair pushes her back. "We were just saying good-bye." She looks up at me with a hint of relief in her dark eyes. "We needed to say some things to each other. We needed to finally let go."

"Well, good." Lauren sharpens her eyes at the two of us. "Now maybe you can *both* give Kendall some peace. Leave her the hell alone—that goes for you, too, Cruise." She stalks off after Kenny and Ally.

"I take it things aren't going so well between the two of you." Blair seems to be back to her gloating self.

"Yeah, well, no one's perfect." I say, brushing the excess water off my arms.

"Sorry to hear it."

"We'll be on track again soon. And when we are, we'd really like to get married on Christmas Eve at the chapel. Any chance you'd gift that date to me?" I give a bleak smile.

"You know, I really believed *we'd* be getting on track again soon, and we didn't." She shakes her head. "Things don't always turn out the way we hope, and your dream wedding at the chapel is one of them." She takes a quick breath. "Sorry"—she shrugs—"there's not a snowball's chance in hell." She picks up her book bag and walks right out the door.

I shake my head. Same old Blair. Not that I'd give Kenny and some douche my wedding date, either. But then again, all I want is for Kenny to be happy. Hell, I'd give her the wedding date and even show up with bells on as a guest if she'd let me. That's how much I love Kenny.

I glance down at my watch. It's almost time for Kenny's last class of the day Creative Writing. Maybe I'll sit in the back and hang out until after. Maybe then I'll fall to my knees and beg forgiveness for every stupid thing I've done these past few months. I only hope she can find it in her heart to forgive me.

Then again, I'm not so sure I would.

12

THE NAUGHTY PROFESSOR

Kendall

I'm shaking."

I'm physically shaking with rage as Ally and Lauren offer to sit in on my last class of the day, Creative Writing. And to think I was ready to cave and speak with Cruise. I had finally shaken off my embarrassment and was fully prepared to plead mea culpa about the entire situation—then *this* happened. And why is Blair always at the epicenter of every damn earthquake in our lives? God, I wish she would just disappear.

Lauren goes up and talks to Kurt for a moment, probably asking permission to stay, but he's so spaced out half the time he wouldn't notice if the entire football team took up residence in the classroom. And it's so damn dark, save for a tiny spotlight above each desk, I'm not sure he really knows who is and who isn't supposed to be here. Besides, he'll be too busy chewing granola on the desk with his holey socks while making googly eyes at Molly.

Lauren swoops back and takes the seat next to me. "It's all settled."

Molly speeds over, and her eyes widen with horror once she gets a good look at me. "What's wrong?"

"Your brother," I hiss without hesitating. I cried like a fool once Ally dragged me out of that coffee shop. I'm sure my mascara has granted me that Alice Cooper effect no girl strives for, and my face is red and blotchy, but I really don't care. It's the modern version of dust and ashes, and if Cruise Elton would rather be with Blair Lancaster, then I'm done caring about the way I look—I'm done caring about just about everything.

Molly's mouth opens for a moment as she glances over my shoulder, but she reconsiders speaking and settles silently in her seat like a good teacher's pet.

"Good afternoon." Kurt looks right at Molly as he says it. Now that it's been firmly established they are in l-o-v-e, I want to puke on his shoes, only Kurt's not wearing any because he systematically takes them off just before he sits on his desk and makes it clear he's down to one pair of argyle socks.

Kurt assumes his position on the desk and shifts side to side while getting comfortable, cross-legged, and swear to God, Lauren wretches at the sight.

"Be glad you have Cal," I whisper. Unlike me, who has nobody.

"All right, class." Kurt has an ironic way of talking down to us and at the same time trying to appeal to us as contemporaries. "Only one session left after Thanksgiving, then it's finals. And as I told you at the beginning of the semester, the only thing you'll need to do is email me your story by the fifteenth of December. I should have grades posted by the twenty-fourth."

I whimper a little because that used to be my wedding date. I slink down in my seat and Ally hoists me back up.

"Breathe," she instructs. "I predict you'll be happy sooner than you ever imagined."

"I can imagine a lot of things, and that's not one of them."

"I have an announcement to make." Kurt tosses his bag of granola to the side, so this must be serious as shit. Maybe he's about to propose to Molly, and she'll get married on Christmas Eve? Nothing can surprise me anymore.

Kurt stands, and that act alone garners my attention. "Though I haven't had the privilege of reading all of your work yet, I have had the privilege of reading a handful of stories—and from what I can gather, we've got some very talented people in our midst. I've no doubt some of you will go on to do great things." He presses out a devilish grin at Molly, and I roll my eyes. I'm sure visions of her doing *him* are clouding his perverted mind. "Now, one of you in particular has shown herself to be quite the scribe and extremely prolific, might I add. In fact, I guess you could call her a sexual scribe, if you will."

The class breaks out in titters and for a moment I wonder if he's talking about Molly again, but I have a feeling I'm the sexual scribbler in question. Just great. The day is already in the crapper, so it makes perfect sense for me to be outed in front of my peers. "Ms. Ashby." He beckons and Lauren gets up and heads to the front of the class with a black paper bag in hand—a cute bag with handles and a little pink bow on the side. Wait . . . she's not in this class. Why did Kurt call her up?

I whisper to Ally, "Is she giving him a gift?" What the hell is going on?

Kurt clears his throat. "The student I was referring to is Ms. Jordan."

I suck in a quick breath.

He holds his hand out to me. "Kendall, would you be so kind to join Ms. Ashby and me up here?"

Oh God. My entire body ignites, and it feels like I'm about to explode from embarrassment in one bionic blast and take the entire class with me.

It takes every ounce of energy to evict myself from my seat and head on over. I look out at the class and give a brief, painful smile. It's dark out there. I can hardly make out Molly or Ally, let alone anyone beyond the second row.

"Well"—Lauren clears her throat—"when my friend here began this crazy writing journey earlier this semester, I wanted to support her any way I could. Both my friend Ally and I did." She motions toward Ally, and she happily trots up to stand beside me. "Kendall's writing was far too delicious to keep within the confines of her laptop, so I went ahead and made Kendall's work available as a subscription on Sorority Net." Lauren takes a deep breath as if she's gearing up for the kicker. "What Kendall didn't know was that after a few successful weeks, I began selling her stories through other venues as well, and she became a smash hit for those, too." Lauren tears up, and so do I, because I couldn't have moved an inch without her and Ally by my side. Cruise, too, but I suppose he's beside the point right about now. "The surprise, Kendall"—Lauren picks up the cute black bag and dips her hand into it—"is that once you handed me the final chapter of *The Naughty Professor* . . ." She pulls a paperback out of the bag with the picture of a woman's hands tied behind her back on the cover. "I had it printed just for you," Lauren says, carefully handing me the book.

"Lauren!" I hug her tightly and pull Ally in, too. The class breaks out in mild applause. "I can't thank you both enough for being there for me."

Lauren and Ally pull back.

"There's one more thing." Lauren glances down at the book in my hand. "Something special happened yesterday that sent me to the printers with a quick change for the cover."

I glance down. "*The Naughty Professor* by Kenny Spanx. A *USA Today* Bestseller," I read aloud, taking in a never-ending breath.

"And this . . ." Lauren hands me a slip of paper, and not until I scan it does it register that it's a check in the amount of $3,000. "There's more on the way. This is just the initial payment."

My heart stops in my chest. It's all too much for me to comprehend.

"Congratulations, Ms. Jordan." Kurt carries on his applause and the class breaks out in a spontaneous roar. "Penny Whoredon and Cruz Belton are quite the erotic powerhouse." He turns to face the class. "Feel free to join us for refreshments provided by Ms. Ashby in honor of this rare success."

The side doors open and a fleet of carts are wheeled in by what appears to be an entire catering staff. Each cart is laden with mugs and carafes and stacks and stacks of . . .

Lauren frames her mouth with her hands. "Cupcakes from the Cake Chief!"

"And Starbucks coffee!" Ally shouts with a laugh caught in her throat as the class begins to mill around, and a partylike atmosphere breaks out.

Ally runs over and swipes cupcakes for the three of us. They're a beautiful pale blue, just like the cake Cruise and I wanted for our wedding, and my heart breaks a little as I look at them.

Lauren holds up the tiny frosted confection as if she's about to make a toast, so Ally and I do the same.

"To the Naughty Professor!" Lauren chants.

"To the Naughty Professor," Ally and I say in unison, albeit much less enthusiastically on my part. After all, unlike Penny, I didn't get the professor in the end.

"Can anyone join this party?" a male voice asks sweetly from behind, and I spin on my heels because it sounded just like—Cruise.

He gives a shy smile and his dimple implodes on one side of his mouth. His pale-blue eyes are the exact color the rain wishes it could be, and I press my lips together to keep from crying at the sight of him.

Lauren and Ally both shoot daggers at Cruise, and I hold up a hand as if calling them off. Lauren gives a slight nod, and Ally socks Cruise in the arm before my two best friends amble down to where Molly and Kurt are mingling with the masses.

"Why didn't you tell me?" His forehead wrinkles and his eyes hold a world of pain, as though he's genuinely hurt.

"Because I was too ashamed." There. It feels as if a lead coat has just slipped from my body.

"I'm proud of you." A smile slides up his cheek as he picks up the book and reads over the description. "Penny Whoredon and Cruz Belton." His chin dips a notch and he gives me that lewd grin I miss so damn much. "You didn't even bother to hide our names."

"My name's not Penny." I bite down over my lip.

"My name *is* Cruise—though you got creative with the spelling." He comes in and wraps his arms around my waist, and I melt into him with both body and soul. His warm cologne greets me right along with that bulge I miss so much scraping against my belly.

"Nobody reads that stuff anyway." I glance down and swallow hard.

"Apparently a lot of people read that stuff." He dots a kiss on my forehead. "And they should, because Penny and Cruz are warriors both in and out of the bedroom. I know this because we're living it."

"I'm sorry I broadcasted our personal affairs." I shrink a little in his arms.

"Are you kidding?" His chest rumbles with a soft laugh. "I'm more than ready and willing to give you fresh material."

"Really?" I'm genuinely confused. "I thought you weren't into that kind of stuff anymore."

"About that." He looks past me and nods. "*That's* exactly what happened."

I turn to find Morgan headed in our direction.

"Having a party without me?" My sweet, yet often overprotective, brother wraps his arms around me and swings me side to side before landing a quick kiss on the top of my head. "I'm so damn proud of you, Kendall."

"You are?" I bite down on my lip. "You didn't read it, did you?" God, I'll die if he says yes. I'll never be able to look at Morgan again.

"Nope." His dimples dig in. "And there's no way in hell you're going to get me to. Ally tells me you wield a mean pen, and I'll take her word for it. Speaking of which, I'd better find her. I hear there's a cupcake somewhere around here with my name on it." Morgan dissolves into the crowd, and Cruise wraps his arms around me again.

"So what did Morgan have to do with it?" I'm deathly curious now.

Cruise touches his nose to mine for a moment before pulling back. His jaw redefines itself and he hesitates, like he's reconsidering what he's about to say.

"He caught up to me one day in the gym and told me to start treating you right. That if I really cared about you, I wouldn't be having a good time with you anywhere but our bedroom."

"I'm going to kill him." I start to head off, but Cruise reels me in like a fish.

"Don't." He gives a kind smile, and my heart melts. "I think I finally figured out that he was just doing what any big brother would do. And I'm sorry I bought into it—but not entirely. Kenny, if you ever think I'm going too far, don't hesitate to say so. You'll never hurt my feelings. My only concern is what makes you happy."

"So you're reinstating our out-of-the-bedroom relationship again?" A burst of heated adrenaline spirals through me, right down to that sweet spot between my thighs.

"Ready and willing. Name the time and place, or better yet, surprise me. I'll be there—aiming to please."

"Perfect." God knows I'm amped up and ready to go. "Right now, me and you—the tower. I want to make love to you right here at Garrison."

Cruise

I swallow hard. Kenny wants to reinstate our out-of-the-bedroom relations posthaste right here at Garrison, when less than a couple of hours ago I promised Professor Bradshaw I'd keep my nose clean—and, essentially, my pants on.

Kenny says a quick good-bye to Lauren and Ally before pulling me out into the cool, crisp air. She zips us through campus as if she has a fire to put out, and seeing how enthused she is to get this private party started, I'd say she does. We walk up to the tower and take the elevator to the top, with my arms wrapped around her the entire way. Kenny and I step out, greeted by a harsh wind that needles us with its icy fingers.

The tower is the tallest structure on campus, and from this vantage point the world looks small as a thimble. All of Garrison glitters at our feet. The gray day bleeds to evening while the students scuttle below us like a small army of ants.

I wrap my arms around her again, and clasp her left hand.

"You're still wearing it." I kiss my grandmother's ring on her finger.

"I never want to take it off."

"And I never want you to." I pull her in tight, and Kenny starts in with my zipper. "About that." I tip my head back in frustration.

"I thought you said—"

"I did, and I meant it." I tell her about my encounter with Professor Bradshaw.

"Cruise!" She jumps up onto my hips; her legs wrap around me, and I spin her in a circle. The world below sways for a moment as I start to lose my balance.

"Um, maybe we should get off the roof," she whispers while slipping off my body. "I don't want to jeopardize your chances in any way."

"Sounds good. But only after I do this." I lean in and crash my lips to hers. Selfishly, I want to kiss Kenny right here, on top of Garrison—on top of the world, because that's exactly how I'm feeling . . . on top of the entire freaking universe.

Kenny and I are back, and this time it's forever.

———

A week slips by and it's the Wednesday before Thanksgiving. The kitchen has been overrun by the women in my life, and the cabin is lit up like a pumpkin pie factory. I had to come clean with both Mom and my dad regarding the eternal Plague that has taken over the B and B. It wasn't easy, but they both seemed to understand how things went to shit so quickly once I mentioned Cal was involved.

Kenny and Molly break out in a fit of giggles, and my entire being fills with a warmth I have never known. It's nice to see them getting along, Mom and Karen, too, for that matter. Kenny feels every bit like family, and something about this preholiday madness makes the cabin feel a lot more like home than it ever has before.

"My boys!" Dad slaps both Pen and me on the back before landing on the sofa next to us. "Tomorrow is going to be one of the best Thanksgivings we've had in a long time. It's been ages since we've spent it together."

Ages is right. In fact, outside of Christmas, I had a habit of not seeing my father much during the year. A lot has changed in my life over the course of twelve months.

"Tomorrow is all about the food." Pen plucks at his Levis as if he's putting his waistline on notice.

"Tomorrow is all about family." Dad leans forward and touches his hand to my knee, his bright-blue eyes settling on mine. "I can never apologize enough for not being there for you, son." He presses out a bleak smile. "I want you to feel free to come to me with anything. I'm your father, and I plan on overcompensating in any way I can for letting other people get in the way of that role. I guess I had a lot of growing of my own to do. I hope you can forgive me."

Kenny gazes over at me with heavy eyes before returning her attention to the mixing bowl. She looks back up and nods, urging me to accept his apology.

"There's nothing to forgive." I lean over and pull him into a half hug. "It's water under the bridge. I know you're there for me." My stomach pinches because it's been on my mind just how much I might need from him by way of currency since I got the first letter of default from the bank two days ago. Not that I intend on following through with that groveling session. I'm pretty sure I would eat my shoes for dinner before I took our relationship to that level.

The door bursts open as Morgan and Ally stride in.

"I knocked, I swear." He holds up a hand. Kenny runs over to him and offers him a big hug, assuring him he never has to knock. I wouldn't go that far, but for the most part, she's right.

"All right. Jordan's here." I motion for Dad and Pen to get up. "I've got a little project I need your help with."

I rally the menfolk outside, and Morgan is reluctant to follow. The bed-and-breakfast is rocking and rolling with the windows vibrating in sync with the electric guitar. A smattering of cars have parked haphazard in the lot, and already there's a steady stream of people from Garrison meandering in and out.

"What's up?" Morgan growls, no doubt distressed because we've drifted from the food.

I pull back the blue tarp on the far end of the porch, revealing the pet project I've been working on the past two days.

"Boys"—I kick at the small arsenal—"we're about to serve an eviction notice."

A silver Range Rover pulls up to the cabin, and Cal and Lauren get out.

"What the hell?" Lauren balks at the mass of rifles, magazines, paint tanks, the rounds and rounds of colorful ammunition.

"You saw nothing," I say.

"This night better not end in a police detention center." Before heading into the house, she shoots Cal a look that says, *I'll have your balls on a spit if it does.*

Cal steps forward. "This night better not end with felony assault charges, Elton."

"Man up," I say, passing out paintball rifles like candy at Halloween. "It's time we teach some squatters a lesson. I need every room cleared. Every last person removed from the premises."

"Then what?" Morgan is the last to gleefully embrace his weapon of quasi destruction.

"Then I change the locks." I hold up a small bag of tools I've put together to do just that.

Pen glances back at the B and B and shakes his head. "Dude, you know if just one of those pussies says you hurt 'em, they're going to own the freaking thing and you'll be the one being evicted."

"With real guns," Morgan is quick to chime in. "By the feds."

A piercing guitar solo that sounds like it could be heard on Jupiter cuts through the evening air and grates on every one of my last fucking nerves.

"Who's in?" I ask, taking up my weaponry and tool bag.

Dad follows right alongside me. "I'm with you every step of the way, son."

"Sorry in advance if we get arrested," I say as we traverse the minefield of expensive vehicles laid out in front.

"Don't worry." He wraps an arm around my shoulders. "I've got an entire legal team ready to pull us out of just about any kind of jam. Try not to maim anyone, would you?"

"Got it."

We hit the porch and to my surprise we're joined from behind by Pen, Morgan, and Cal.

Cal kicks his way inside and shouts, "Everybody out! This is a raid!"

The entire place lights up with the sound of girls screaming. Cal's got his shirt off and his muscles are bulging in the menacing way that only they know how to do, and he fucking looks like Rambo, like a nut off the sidewalk who's ready and willing to shoot the place up.

"Out!" Morgan shouts as he and Pen head upstairs.

Dad and I bust into the living room, where the band comes screeching to a halt, and we fire off round after round, dotting every member of the Plague with bright-pink splotches. The bodies in the room refuse to clear out and the squatters' elation only seems to grow, what with the fist pumping, the incessant laughter, the outright cheering. The band stops playing and decides to go old-school by way of destroying everything in the vicinity while wielding their guitars like baseball bats.

Holy shit. My grandfather's bookshelf splinters right before my eyes. Bodies are flying into one another as the entire downstairs spontaneously turns into a mosh pit, and jetting from the ceiling an oversized tube starts pumping out . . . snow?

"What the hell?" Dad goes over and sticks his hand under it, then brings it up to his nose. "It's foam."

By the time I trek over, the room is brimming with suds.

The band starts up again. "It's time for the big finish, everyone!" the lead moron shouts into the microphone. He and the drummer proceed to carry out a racket so loud my ears mercifully begin to bleed just to tone down the crap they're trying to shove down my throat.

Morgan and Pen stumble into the room, covered with soapy residue from head to foot.

"They've got the fucking place rigged." Morgan looks shocked by the carnage.

I shake my head in defeat and cast down my weapon.

It's done. I wish I could say that I was shocked that the bed-and-breakfast is morphing into one giant spin cycle, that it surprised the fuck out of me that the one thing entrusted to me was going down the drain by way of laundry detergent, but it didn't.

"It's a foam party, dude!" Pen belts out a hoot as if he's simply one of the revelers. "This is exactly how the Plague ends each of their concerts! This is fucking *epic*."

"It's not epic. It's over." I push the nose of Pen's gun to the floor. "We lost this one."

The doors to the entry burst open and Kenny charges in with a look of fire in her eyes. She doesn't even blink at the bodies covered in white slime—she simply lets out a roar and makes a beeline for the lead singer.

I jump back as she passes me by and jumps on the makeshift stage. Kenny doesn't think twice before snatching the microphone right out of his hand.

Ally and Lauren are quick to join her onstage.

"That's it!" Kenny screams so loudly that half the foam-covered bodies slap their hands over their ears. "The party is *over*! Do you hear me? Everybody out right fucking now!"

The foam continues to rise, and at this point it looks like the place has been overrun by a bunch of abominable snowmen, disgruntled ones at that because, by God, they're all headed for the door.

"Hey"—Morgan jabs me in the ribs with the tip of his weapon—"why didn't you think of that?"

I rattle his assault rifle just as the foam rises to our waists. "Because my way was a lot more fun. And for your information, I'll be running my relationship by my rules, too. I get that you're her brother, but you need to back off when it comes to Kenny and me. I got this, dude."

He frowns a little as the room clears, mostly from the fear of drowning.

"I got it." He offers me a knuckle bump and I'm slow to comply, but I do. "Be good to her, man. I'm watching you."

"I know you are."

Kenny comes over, and I help her and everyone else out of the room as the entire crowd drains to the front of the property.

We watch helplessly from the front lawn as white billows of foam ooze out of every orifice of the bed-and-breakfast.

"And there she goes," I sigh, pulling Kenny in tightly by the waist.

A siren wails in our direction as Lauren leans into Cal. "Is this the part where we all get arrested?"

"We can only hope someone gets arrested." Cal shakes his head.

"And with my luck"—I blow out a slow breath—"it's bound to be me." Hell, I'm probably looking at life for giving the whole damn place "the spells." Maybe a prison term isn't such a bad thing. Maybe that's exactly what will ensure Kenny will have a long and prosperous future—me in an eight-by-ten cell far, far away from her.

"That was fantabulous!" A short blonde runs over, and it takes a minute for it to register that the fresh-scrubbed petite girl is in fact the Skin.

"Little Lisa!" Cal swings her around like he hasn't seen her in decades. "You look fantabulous yourself. Have the spells cleared?"

"Nicely." She nods. "I just wanted to thank you." She steps over toward me. Without her requisite sky-high heels, she looks all of twelve. "The Plague says it hasn't had this kind of a send-off in years. It's really impressed with the amount of work you put into it. Shooting up the place in their signature color was beyond their wildest expectations." She lands her hand over her chest and presses her lips together. "We're all very touched."

"What the hell are you talking about?" I'm not up for one more ounce of bullshit tonight.

Her mouth opens wide. "You didn't know? It's our last night in town. I stopped by last week to let your wife know we'd be out by Thursday night."

"I don't have a wife," I deadpan. Not to mention that Kenny wasn't anywhere near the cabin last week—she was at Ally's.

"Then who is that?" She points behind me, and I follow her finger right over to Molly.

"Oh!" Molly touches her hand to her mouth for a moment. "I totally forgot to tell you! She said they were taking off sometime this week and she wanted to meet with you." She bounces a little when she says it, and only then do I see what might have distracted her—that nutty professor of hers glued to her side.

Crap.

"That's great that you're leaving. But who in the hell is supposed to clean up this mess? You and your stupid band just cost me the business my grandfather broke his back trying to build."

The Skin's mouth falls open and her eyes fill with tears. "That's the most beautiful thing I've ever heard, man." She gives a hard sniff.

"Save it, sister," Lauren snips. "You and me are going to have one long talk." She pulls her off into the sea of bodies.

"Looks like Lauren is going to wield a little prelaw her way." Kenny lays her head over my chest.

Kenny and I both know this is too big for Lauren, for an entire legal team, to tackle. Something tells me God himself wouldn't be interested in cleaning up this mess.

Nope.

The bed-and-breakfast is a total loss.

I'm about to marry the love of my life with nothing more than the shirt on my back.

"Don't worry," Kenny purrs into my ear. "Maybe we'll get a Christmas miracle just when we need it."

I dot her lips with a simple kiss.

I hate to break it to Kenny, but it's going to take more than one miracle to pull us out of this mess.

A shooting star glides across the sky right over the bed-and-breakfast, and the crowd gasps while pointing skyward.

Kenny jumps into my arms. "It looks as if our miracle is on its way."

Maybe it is.

13

WITH THIS BLING

Kendall

Christmas Eve

Cruise and I slept all night knotted up in one another's arms. Yesterday the cleanup crew officially finished its month-long dry-down of the bed-and-breakfast.

Lauren got the Plague to foot the bill for the clean up, and, thankfully, outside of some destruction to one of the downstairs bookshelves, there wasn't a whole lot of damage to the place.

"Morning, princess." Cruise strokes my back with his warm fingers, and I curl into him, just happy to be spending yet another day in his arms. But we both know it's not just another day. It's our wedding day.

His body twitches to life, long and hard against my thigh, and I give a little giggle while backing away.

"Watch it there, Mister. I've invoked a vow of celibacy until much later tonight, so you and your *hail to the chief* are all out of luck."

"It's hail to the queen." He presses his soft lips to mine and every last part of me wants to cave. "And I'd wait a thousand years if you asked me to." He gently pulls my chin up until I'm looking into his watery-blue eyes. "You're the pot of gold at the end of the rainbow, Kenny."

I mold my body to his until the rhythm of our hearts echoes through to one another's bones. It feels safe like this with Cruise. It feels like home.

"Cruise Elton, I love you."

A loud clatter erupts from outside, followed by a bang against the front door.

I throw on my robe while Cruise jumps into a pair of sweats, and we hightail it to the door.

Cruise whips it open and an icy breeze knifes its way in, cutting right through the flimsy silk robe I'm wearing.

"What's this?" Cruise reaches down and pulls in a rather large box wrapped in brown paper. "From Patagonia."

"Oh my God!" I scream, dragging the parcel to the kitchen, where I snatch a knife from the butcher block.

Cruise holds out a hand as if he's about to deflect my efforts.

"Stand back," I snipe. "That's my Vera in there." I slit the package open before he can say another word, and I yank and pull until I see the first glimmer of scrumptious fabric. It's the color of calorie-laden whipped cream, and suddenly I'm craving a latte.

My hands dig in through the surplus of packing popcorn and my fingers clutch onto the scrump—*scratchy* fabric . . . I pull it out, hesitantly, and inch by inch my biggest nightmare is revealed.

"Crap," I whimper.

"What's the matter?" Cruise whispers as if he's afraid to ask.

I pull out the dress and just stare at the cheap Halloween-grade fabric, the misaligned seams of the sweetheart neckline, the wide-toothed plastic zipper that runs up the back—all details affirming that the only occasion this dress is meant to be worn is a bad costume party.

Molly comes up from behind me. "Holy shit."

"Not now, Molly." Cruise is quick with the reprimand.

"No, it's okay," I pull it in closer, hoping somehow it'll morph into the dress I want it to be.

"Look at that." Molly points to the tag. "It's a *Verra*. Everybody knows *Vera* is spelled with one *r*."

I close my eyes for a moment. "I thought it was a typo," I say below a breath.

"Hey, it's okay." Cruise pulls me in and holds me. "You weren't planning on wearing that thing today anyway."

"You're right." I tighten my grip around his waist. Mom is letting me borrow one of her sequined gowns. It's silver and a size too big, but I suppose that's as close to a wedding dress as I'll ever get. "You're all I need, Cruise Elton."

And at the end of the day, there is no bigger truth.

———

Now that I've effectively evicted Cruise from the cabin, Lauren and Ally have come by to help me get ready. I took the money from my book sales and bought each of them and Molly a bridesmaid's dress in a pale blue, the exact color of the cake Cruise and I tried to purchase from the Cake Chief. It really is my favorite color.

Ally gives us something hot from Starbucks to warm our bones, while Molly curls my hair to perfection. I did my own makeup, mostly because I didn't want Molly turning me into a circus clown. She offered plenty of times to do it for me, but she's in the midst of an experimental phase with blue frosted eye shadow, so I couldn't take the risk. Besides, I'm pretty big on the natural look.

"I think I'll step out for some air." Lauren jets from the cabin for the hundredth time.

"You think she's sick?" I look to Ally. Lauren has been acting strange from the moment she arrived.

"She's not sick." Ally rolls her eyes at the idea.

"Then maybe she's allergic to my courthouse wedding." She took one look at my fake Vera and nearly barfed up a lung.

"That might be true, but who the hell cares?" Ally rubs my back like she's prepping me for the boxing match of a lifetime. "In just a few short hours, you are going to be Mrs. Cruise Elton, the envy of every girl on the planet." She wrinkles her nose. "Well, except me. I'm pretty damn happy with Morgan." She gets a dreamy look in her eyes.

"You can count me out, too." Molly chirps. "Personally, I'm glad you're the one who's going to end up with my brother." She gives a quick squirt of hairspray to the loose curls she's crowned me with. "I've always wanted a big sister, and I couldn't think of anyone better than you, Kendall." She lowers her gaze to the floor for a moment. "I mean it. I'd really love to see our relationship grow. I want to talk to you about boys, and go shopping, and get our nails done, and stay up late watching chick flicks."

"Really?" I touch my hand to my chest. In all honesty, I never thought Molly cared for me that much.

"Yes, really. Now get up and give me a hug before I take it all back."

I spring to my feet and pull her into a nice, long embrace. Molly is gorgeous and deep down inside she's just as beautiful. She's Cruise's sister, and now she's mine, too.

"I love you, Molly. You're every bit the sister I've always wanted."

The front door flies opens, and Mom waltzes in with a giant grin on her face, but her arms are noticeably empty.

"Where's the dress?" I spit out in a panic. Good God, I really am going to wear my white Garrison sweats today. "Breathe," I say to myself just below a whisper.

"Did someone say *dress?*" Cruise's mother, Sam, saunters in carrying a giant garment bag with Aunt Jackie trailing in after her, holding up the back end.

"What's this?" I speed over. Mom never mentioned that her silver sequined gown was the size of a peach tree. Just perfect. I'm going to look like a giant disco ball on my wedding day.

"This, my love"—Sam carefully lays the gown over the couch as if it's a body and unzips the oversized bag—"is your wedding dress."

I suck in a sharp breath.

"But that's—" I can't finish the sentence. If there's one thing I've learned in life it's that if it seems too good to be true, it usually is. "Yeah, right." I take a fistful of fabric into my hand, fully expecting to feel the cheap polyester of my Patagonian costume store discard, but I don't.

"Watch it there, missy." Aunt Jackie smacks my hand away. "We need you to love her gently, if you know what I mean." She strokes away the wrinkles I've caused as if she's petting a kitten.

"What is this?" I straighten. It suddenly feels like I'm in a dream. My Vera is right here in the cabin. There has to be a catch. I look to Sam. "Did you borrow this from the bridal shop?" I swear to God if the three of them conducted some bridal shop heist just to get me to the altar in style, I'll slap them all silly. Well, shortly after the wedding. No use in pulling on my Garrison sweats when there's a perfectly good Vera in the living room.

"No, hon." Sam steps forward with tears in her eyes and pulls me in by the cheeks. "This dress is one hundred percent yours, baby girl." She plants a kiss on my cheek before pulling away.

"Aunt Jackie?" I take a stab at my next potential fairy god-mother. Aunt Jackie has been nothing but kind to me ever since I came out here with essentially nothing more than my suitcase. She's lent me her car for a year straight, for Pete's sake. It's like I'm the daughter she never had.

"Wasn't me, kiddo." She sniffs hard into her tissue.

"Mom?" Of course it was my mother. She married Cruise's father, who happens to be sitting on a pile of money. "I should have guessed right from the start. Thank you." I wrap my arms around my mother and hold her for a very long time. My mother has had panache when it comes to wedding gowns for as long as I can remember, so this shouldn't surprise me.

"I'll take the hug from my little girl, but it wasn't me, either." She reaches into her purse and pulls out an envelope.

I carefully pluck out the letter.

> Kenny,
> I hope this is the right one. I brought Lauren and Ally with me and they assured me it was. Please wear it with joy knowing I never once laid eyes on it. When I see it for the first time, I want it to be on you. I can't wait to make the most beautiful woman in the universe my bride.
> See you at the altar.
>
> Love,
> Cruise

Tears flood my vision, and it's all I can do not to break down into a full-blown sob. My sweet, wonderful Cruise just made the most romantic gesture known to man. He hocked his livelihood to buy this dress, and I can't help but feel guilty for even hinting at something so extravagant.

Lauren steps back into the room, and her eyes widen at the sight of me.

"Don't even think of ruining your mascara!" She barks like a drill sergeant. "We've got a wedding to get to."

And with that, the next hour is spent primping and crimping, pulling and tugging, as I squeeze into the wedding dress, a perfect size eight. Sam has the seamstress from the bridal shop on call in the event there's an emergency altering session that needs to take place, but the zipper glides up with ease, and the dress molds to my body as if it's a long-lost second satin skin.

"Holy crap." Ally staggers backward. "I've never seen anyone look so beautiful." Tears spring to her bright-green eyes, and she's quick to blink them away.

"It's time." Lauren gives me a solemn nod. "Let's go find your groom."

I pull Lauren and Ally in for one final hug as a single woman.

"Let's."

———

Molly, Mom, Sam, and Aunt Jackie all file out of the cabin while Ally holds my train from behind.

"Okay." Lauren holds up a finger. "So there might be one thing I forgot to mention."

My stomach flips. "Knew it." I spew the words out. "This was all too good to be true." But wait, I'm wearing my Vera with one *r*, and I'm about to make the world's most perfect man my husband, so whatever piece of crap news Lauren is about to crack over my head won't really matter. "Give it to me."

"Remember when I said I'd take care of all the details at the courthouse for you?"

"Yes," I say slowly because I can smell a mishap of gargantuan proportions coming a mile away.

"I did." She pumps out a quick smile.

"Oh, thank God." I heave into her. "For a second I thought you were going to say it was booked three years in advance."

"Well, it's not, but I have a feeling you're not going to want it after what I have to tell you—and if you *do*, I totally respect that. After all, it's your day and if standing courtside in front of a judge and an entire bevy of people waiting to get into traffic court is your thing, then so be it."

I give an incredulous huff. "This better be good, Ashby, because you just ground your Louboutin stiletto right through the heart of both the government and my humble nuptials. And I'll tell you right now, I'm a hell of a lot scarier than Uncle Sam."

"I promise it's good." Lauren digs her pinkies into her eyes to wipe away the tears that are coming. I don't think I've ever seen her cry before and suddenly my heart melts. "In fact, I think you're going to love it."

She leads me out by the hand, and I suck in a never-ending breath at what I see.

"Oh my God." I try to take it all in. "What's this?"

Nestled in the courtyard of the bed-and-breakfast is an entire winter wonderland, complete with pale birch trees laden with twinkle lights, and a flowered archway filled with waterfalls of wisteria. Rose petals line a genuine aisle, leading all the way to the miniature version of the Garden of Eden. And standing at the end of the makeshift altar is sweet, gorgeous Cruise in a crisp black tux, his hair slicked back to perfection. He's speaking with

Morgan, and I can hear his voice carry all the way over. It warms me from head to toe.

"I hope you don't mind." Lauren bites down over a devious smile.

"Why in the world would I mind? This is too fantastic for words."

Ally comes up from behind us. "It is, isn't it?"

"What's going on? There's no way Cruise could have ever pulled all this off. The flowers alone cost more than the car I'm driving." Considering it's an imported luxury ride, that says a lot.

"Cruise bought the dress." Lauren takes up both my hands. "But the rest of the stuff was donated by vendors."

"Isn't this great!" Ally squeals like I just won the lottery, but I think everyone here knows I'm not that lucky.

I suck in a breath. "Oh God! Cruise has some fatal disease and he's using his final wish on me." A horrible feeling coats me from the inside out, and now all I want to do is run over to him and tell him we'll make our way through whatever physical terror is racking his body.

"Would you stop?" Lauren smacks me. "It's bad juju to curse your groom with a fatal illness before you make it down the aisle. Nobody is dying. The vendors donated everything so that their products and services could be featured on the Cake Chief."

"Oh. That makes total sense. *Not.* Speak English, Ashby. I'm spending way too much time trying to decode my wedding day and far too little time cozying up to the groom." Who by the way looks more than a little comely, and I mean that in a ridiculously erotic manner.

"I gave you my show." She shrugs a little. "The wedding edition of the Cake Chief is all yours. You'll have one hour of television to forever commemorate your special day. And as soon I presented the opportunity to the vendors, they were more than happy to gift you their services. So"—she throws up her hands—"enjoy your wedding day! The only thing you have to do is make some memories."

"Lauren." I pull her in. "You know I'll never be able to thank you for all this."

"You can thank me by being my maid of honor, right alongside Ally."

"Really? I'm humbled."

"Yes, really."

"Well, I won't do it unless the two of you stand up for me. I don't think Molly will mind sharing her duty."

"Deal." Lauren helps me out onto the porch just as a slick black limo pulls up to the cabin.

The driver gets out and opens the back door while my mind is reeling at what trick Lauren or Cruise might have up their sleeve next, but what crawls out assures me it's not Lauren or Cruise's doing by a long shot. It's Blair Just-in-Time-to-Ruin-Your-Wedding-Day Lancaster.

She saunters over in her signature red wool coat, and just the sight of her boils my blood. I don't care if Cruise says they parted ways for good the other day, she's still got him buried in her cold black heart. Cruise Elton isn't someone you just get over. He's the type of perfection you mourn the loss of for years. God knows I would.

"What the hell do you want?" Ally steps into her face as if she's about to start a fistfight.

"I wanted to wish the bride well and give her something I know for a fact she wants." Her beady eyes narrow in on me as her thin lips stretch out in a line.

Ally snorts. "If you're going to hang yourself from the balcony, I suggest you wait until the reception."

"Wait until after cake," Lauren snips. "That's traditionally when gifts are given."

"Shush, both of you." Blair closes her eyes for a moment. "I came to let Kendall know I'm not going to need the chapel. I called off the wedding."

Nobody moves.

"You mean *Rutger* came to his senses and called off the wedding?" Ally nods, suspecting this to be true.

"No, it was me." Blair glances over at the bed-and-breakfast in all its wedding day glory. "Anyway, it's yours if you want it." She takes in a deep breath and holds it for a moment. "It's not happening for me today. But I'm sort of hoping someday someone special will come into town and sweep me off my feet." She washes her gaze over me and gives a dull smile. "You're a beautiful bride. You scored the man of a lifetime. Don't let him go." She presses her lips together so hard all color bleeds out. "He may never come back." Blair runs to the limo and it quickly speeds right off the property.

"There's that." Ally pulls me in as we watch the dust rise in the horizon from Blair's wicked wake. "It's up to you, Kendall. If you want the ceremony at the chapel, here's your chance. It looks like all your dreams are about to come true today."

I glance over at Cruise in the distance as he patiently waits for me. "Damn straight they're coming true. And I don't need the chapel. Everything I've wanted was right under my nose, all along. I couldn't think of a better place to get married than right here at the B and B."

Lauren motions toward the crowd and a band strikes up the wedding march.

Is that . . . a rock band?

"Hey . . ." I recognize the signature sound of that electric guitar, the way it quivers and wails, making the song its own. "Is that . . . ?"

"The Plague." Lauren gives a depleted smile. "I couldn't find a band and they offered to play. They have a gift they want to personally give to you and Cruise after the ceremony."

"I bet they do. It's probably some revenge foam send-off to our honeymoon. Never mind. Let's get me hitched."

Morgan waits for me at the start of the aisle, and I link my arm with his.

"You look beautiful, sis." He leans in and plants a gentle kiss on my cheek. "You sure you want to do this?"

"I've never wanted anything so badly."

"That's the right answer." He pats my hand and we begin our long descent toward Cruise.

Cruise gives a brimming smile and his eyes glitter with tears. He's so breathtakingly gorgeous, my knees go weak and my thighs tremble at the sight of him.

This is all really happening.

I'm about to marry the love of my life.

I'm about to become Mrs. Cruise Elton.

Cruise

'm not sure how I got so damn lucky but there she is, the most stunning woman in the world walking my way with a beautiful smile on her face and it's all for me. Kendall Jordan is a vision in white—a real live angel, and she's about to become my wife. No matter how hard I try, I can't wrap my head around it. It's too good to be true, but I'm not questioning fate or destiny or any of the other relationship higher-ups because something magical is about to happen and only a fool questions this kind of luck.

Morgan nods toward me as he escorts Kenny those final few steps.

"Take care of her, bro," he whispers. Morgan was never a bad guy, never someone who wanted to break up Kenny and me. He was simply a good brother trying to look out for his little sister.

"I will." My smile expands as I look over at my lovely bride and all the butterflies I was feeling dissipate with that soulful look her eyes are giving mine. "You look stunning."

"So do you," she says with serious intent, her eyes moistening with tears.

The preacher starts in on the ceremony and finally we're asked to give our vows.

I clear my throat. "Kenny, I am so humbled and honored that you would choose me as your partner in life. I can't wait to live out each and every day with you by my side." I swallow hard because I'm about to lose it. "I want you to know my life's goal is to make you happy. There's not one day that will drift by without me telling you how much I love you, how damn lucky I am to have you." A wave of laughter circles through the crowd. "You're everything to me, and I want you to hear it, to feel it, each and every day. You deserve all those things and more. I plan on loving you until the day I die, and then after that, right into eternity."

She gives a hard sniff as the preacher signals her to go ahead.

"Cruise"—she presses her lips together—"when I came into town, you were the first person to greet me. You were friendly. Perhaps a little too friendly." Another light titter circulates. "But I knew there was a spark, and I wanted to explore it, to see if there was anything truly there between us, and there was. Cruise, what we have has exceeded all of my preconceived notions of love. This is something otherworldly, something so huge and spectacular it can't be classified by one simple word. This is everything good and right all rolled into one, and I get to have it forever with you. I want to thank you for that. I want to thank you for loving me so fiercely and for letting me love you back. Thank you for giving me your heart—you had mine that first night. I look forward to a future filled with you right by my side. I wouldn't want it any other way—not with anyone else. What we have is perfect love, Cruise, and I don't plan on missing a moment of it."

Tears roll freely down my face. I'm losing it, and I really don't care who sees it.

The preacher goes on and we exchange rings. Kenny slips the simple platinum band we picked a few weeks back over my finger, and I admire it for a second. I've never been one to wear any type of jewelry, but this is one piece I don't plan on taking off anytime soon—or ever.

Morgan hands me Kenny's ring and I slip it over her finger.

"That's not the ring," she whispers from the side of her mouth.

"I know. I thought my grandmother's ring was a perfect engagement ring, but I want you to have something all your own. If you don't like it, we can go back and pick something else out. It was more of a gesture—I swear I want you to be happy with it."

"Cruise, I love it." She chokes up. "It's perfect."

The preacher nods and says those special words I've longed to hear all day.

"Congratulations, Mr. and Mrs. Elton. I now pronounce you man and wife. You may now kiss the bride."

"Kenny," I whisper as I cradle her face in my hands, "I love you."

"I love you, too." She inches in. "Now kiss me."

And I do.

———

The night sky above Carrington glows a soft lavender as the heat lamps do their best to take the chill out of the air. Lauren thought of everything, and I'll have to think of a way to thank her and Cal for all the time and effort they put into this. Dinner was a five-star meal, enough to warrant a thank-you all its own.

The Plague starts in on a love ballad, and I clasp the hand of my beautiful bride.

"May I?"

"By all means."

Kenny and I walk down to the makeshift dance floor, and I hold her in my arms as we sway to the rhythm of our love.

"We did it." I touch my nose to hers.

"We sure did," she whispers. "With a little help from our friends—and the Plague."

"Who would've imagined."

"Not me, for sure, but tonight has cast its own special brand of magic on the world. Who knows what miracles lie ahead?" She bats her lashes up at me.

"You do realize that about a dozen lewd thoughts just sailed through my brain."

She belts out a laugh and her teeth shine like a row of shooting stars. "I wouldn't have it any other way."

I hold her tightly until the song ends, and the microphone lets off some feedback.

We glance over and through the main gate a familiar chef's hat bobs its way over. The Cake Chief himself wheels in a cart that has a giant white box with a bow on top. Kenny and I head over.

"Kendall and Cruise"—the Cake Chief breaks into spontaneous applause—"you did the unthinkable!"

Please, God, don't let him say a word about the credit card debacle we had a few weeks back. True to my word, I revisited his office and anted up for the cake Kenny and I picked out, so that better be what lies in the overgrown box.

"You kids tied the knot in style!" He belches out a laugh and not a whole hell of a lot of people follow suit. Zero to be exact. "So here's a gift from me to you."

One of his henchmen removes the box and there's the powder-blue cake, just as I suspected. The crowd lets out a collective *ooh* and Kenny beams just looking at it.

"In addition to this beautiful confection"—the Cake Chief rolls his neck with his signature attitude the camera has grown to love—"I'm offering you a free cake from our bakery every month for the entire next year as a way to extend the celebration."

Kenny squeals and jumps up and down, and we both thank him. I'll have to see about getting that tarp sooner rather than later.

"Good job, guys." The Cake Chief offers us each a quick embrace before he cuts his finger across his throat and the cameras stop rolling. "Swing by once a month, and we'll take care of you guys. It was good doing business with you." He slaps me over the shoulder. "Treat the little lady right and maybe she'll return the favor." He gives a quick wink, and with that he and his crew are off.

"So where's the honeymoon?" We turn to find Lisa, aka the Skin, dressed in a reasonably sane manner for the evening. I'm sure she's keeping busy trying to mismanage the band.

"Nowhere, thanks to you," I'm quick to point out. That's not entirely true. Kenny and I plan on driving up north to a resort Morgan said he took Ally to last summer. There will be a bed and a view of the ocean, but all I'll really need is a bed and a view of Kenny.

"Really?" She dips her chin with a disapproving smirk. "Well then, I hope this changes everything." She hands me an envelope, and I pull out the contents.

"A check," I muse, staring at it for a moment. The numbers sink in and my hand starts to shake because—holy *shit*—I've never held this much money before. "A hundred thousand US dollars?"

"Yes," she growls. "And I wouldn't consider the fact it's in US currency as a boast. There are a few other countries where the numbers translate a little bit better."

"What's this about?" Kenny sounds equally skeptical.

"The Plague felt horrible about the misunderstanding." Lisa makes a face. "The Plague wanted you to have it as a goodwill offering. Consider it a wedding gift."

Kenny shakes her head. "Oh, I don't know, that's an awful lot of—"

"We accept." I slip the check into my pocket before Kenny can carry out her polite protest.

"Good. Congratulations." She stalks off in Cal's direction, and I don't stop her.

"Cruise." Kenny looks up at me through her lashes. She knows it drives me wild when she does that. "I don't know. It's all too surreal. The dress, the ring." She holds up her finger and the diamond reflects its sparkle right through her eyes. "Are you sure today really happened?"

"I swear to you, it really did." I wrap my arms around her waist.

"Can I ask how we possibly could have afforded this beautiful rock?" She glances back down at her ring and a tiny smile breaks free.

"I have something to tell you." I pull back and let the moonlight kiss her features thoroughly and sweetly, just the way I'm dying to. "I already have the B and B booked through April."

"What?" She jumps, fueled by excitement, and I'll be damned if I'm not about to jump with her, I'm still that fucking psyched.

"It turns out the live band is a big crowd-pleaser. I've had an entire slew of college sweethearts calling in, dying for a weekend getaway that's as hip and cool as ours." I rock her in my arms when I say that last part because from now on everything will officially be *ours.*

"Cruise, that's fantastic, but isn't the Plague heading off on tour?"

"Thankfully, yes. But Morgan has been helping me round up some local bands and we've got a long line of musicians just waiting to play the Elton Lounge."

"Mmm . . ." She purrs with a look of contentment I haven't seen in her eyes in a while. "You know who else is just waiting to play with an Elton?"

"I like where this is going."

Ally and Morgan come up and say good night.

"Do you have to leave so soon?" Kenny laments as she reaches out to both of them.

"We're off to see Ruby tomorrow." Ally wraps an arm around Kenny's shoulder.

"Ally and I got her a puppy, and we need to deliver the little guy in just a few short hours." Morgan brushes his finger against Kenny's cheek. "You did good. He's a keeper."

"So you finally approve?" Kenny tightens her grip around my waist.

"I finally approve. We'll see you two in a week. Have fun." He offers me a knuckle bump before they take off.

"We will have fun," I say it mostly to Kenny. I want to add *wherever the hell we want*, but keep the Morgan-based commentary to myself.

Lauren and Cal approach and we engage in a rather strangulating group hug.

"Be back in time for my big day," Lauren says as she pulls away. "It wouldn't be the same without you guys."

"We wouldn't miss it," Kenny assures her. "We'll be back in plenty of time. Don't go batty trying to drill down every last detail. Sometimes life has a way of surprising you." She gives Lauren a quick wink.

"Will do," Lauren says with a wave. "Don't be afraid to try new things! *The Naughty Professor* is just begging for a sequel. Think bigger, think daring—think acrobatics!" She wails as Cal pulls her off into the night.

"Why haven't we done acrobatics before?" she whispers.

"Because we weren't writing a book."

"We should write a damn book."

I chuckle into Kenny as the crowd begins to melt away. "You ready to start rocking the sequel?"

"Paddle or belt?" She gets that wicked gleam in her eye, and I damn well approve.

"Neither." I pull her in and dot a searing kiss over her lips. "How about we let tonight write a sweet story all for us? And then, after that, we'll set book two on fire."

"Sounds like a plan."

"Penny and Cruz will never know what hit them."

Kenny looks up at me lovingly. "Sort of like me, the first night we met."

"You never did answer my question, Coke or Pepsi?"

"That's because I didn't want either. I only wanted you." Kenny rests her head against my chest and we watch as couples dance around us at our wedding. Molly gives a wave from over her professor's shoulder and I groan. Which reminds me, I plan on having a serious talk with him about how to treat my sister.

"Let's get out of here." Kenny takes my hand and pulls me away from the crowd. "I want you all to myself. It's time to start our happily-ever-after."

"I completely agree." I wrap my arm around her waist as we take off onto the rolling green lawn of the B and B. "I think our happily-ever-after began one year ago at Alpha Sigma Phi."

"Then what starts tonight?" She gives a coy grin like she already knows.

"I think forever starts tonight."

"Forever," she sighs as she pulls me in. I smile down at the most beautiful girl in all of Carrington, Garrison, the country, the world—my wife. Our lips find one another's under the blue velvet night and we indulge in a kiss that could stretch out from here to eternity. Kenny has branded herself on my soul in the best way possible. And tonight promises to sear over our hearts as one beautiful, lasting memory. When someone is meant for you, sometimes you know it at a glance, and that's all it took for me when Kenny walked into my life. I knew that she was the woman I was destined to spend the rest of my life with—that I had finally found someone for me.

We start out on the road before us toward the unknowable future, but one thing is for sure: Kenny and I will be there to cross the threshold of each new day together. It doesn't get any better than this.

Kenny gets a lusty gleam in her eye. "Quickie in the cabin? Or wait until we get to the hotel?"

"Both."

And we do.

EPILOGUE

Kendall

New Year's Eve

Ally and I stand in front of Lauren's wedding cake and try to make heads or tails of it.

"Well if it isn't my two best friends!" Lauren comes up from behind us and pulls Ally and me into an awkward hug. She's gorgeous in her smooth satin gown, her hair pulled back in what Ally dubbed "the bridal helmet." Of course she's slightly shitfaced, too, but it's her party—she can drink vodka if she wants to. And apparently she very much wants to.

"You look amazing and everything is perfect." I motion at the setting. Lauren has transformed the Carrington Country Club into a bona fide medieval castle, and the masquerade ball theme gives the impression we've truly stepped back in time.

"Thanks." She eyes the cake with a sleepy look on her face. "So what do you think?"

Ally and I exchange a look before returning our attention to the multitiered goji berry with gold flake filling disaster. It's just a cake. No frosting, no fondant, no nothing. If there was powdered sugar on it, it's long since blown way. The edges of the cake are raw and crumbly, and there are dark spots all over it. I'm assuming the blotches are the berries, but they just make the cake look as if it's been sitting out too long and is getting moldy.

Ally sags in her pale-pink gown. She looks like a princess, and judging by the way Morgan keeps trying to sneak her off to the back, I'm guessing he thinks so, too.

"It looks great." Ally nudges me as if I should affirm her theory, so I offer a vigorous nod.

"No, it doesn't." Lauren frowns into the severely played-down confection. "It's an unfinished cake with disgustingly gross spots." She pulls me and Ally in by our waists, and we all look down at it with mournful expressions. "If we're going to do this life thing together, I fully give you guys permission to tell me when the decisions I make suck."

"Deal," I say. "But you both need to do the same for me."

"Hear, hear!" Ally holds out her fist and we engage in a three-way knuckle bump. "So what's next for us?"

"Finish school, start businesses, have babies." Lauren tightens her grip over us. "And we'll do it all together."

"Can we play?" Cal pops up from behind us with Morgan and Cruise. The three of them look dapper in their tuxedos, their half-moon masks adhered to their faces.

Morgan steps in and presses his hand into the small of my back. "I heard you got a pretty special phone call."

"I did." I tilt into him. My father called to congratulate me on my wedding, and I was able to speak with each of my half siblings for the very first time. My little sisters were bursting at the seams with questions, and as much as the old me doesn't want to admit it, there seems to be room in my heart for more siblings. "Cruise and I are planning a trip out West this summer to meet them."

"Maybe Ally and I can join you. It could be our first family road trip." He socks Cruise on the arm.

Cruise curls his lips. "We'd like that." He carefully pulls me from my brother.

"May I?" He takes me by the hand and nods toward the dance floor.

"Of course." I press a quick peck on his lips as we make our way forward and begin swaying to the music. "So what do you think? Impressive, right? Too bad it cost her father a kidney on the black market. Did you see the gold leaf chocolate medallions? For a second I thought I was sucking on a coin."

"You were. Trust me, there's more precious metal on that treat than there is in any US change in circulation."

"Too bad it costs a mint to get married. Soon a decent ceremony and a reception will be luxuries very few can afford. Thank God for Lauren's quick thinking and the B and B."

His brows rise an inch. "Hey, you just gave me a great idea."

"Minting our food with precious alloys?"

"No, hosting affordable weddings at the B and B."

"Cruise!" I step back and take him in. "That's perfect!"

"It could be another business venture we share, Mrs. Elton. Plus any venture that lets me spend more time with you is a venture I approve of."

"I love the sound of that, especially the Mrs. Elton part." I touch my finger to his chin. "And now that you'll be back at Garrison, we'll get to spend our nights *and* days together."

"Speaking of which, I'm rewriting my thesis."

"You are?" Cruise's thesis was his labor of love.

He gives a quick nod. "I've gone from highlighting the heresy of love to focusing on the thrill ride of love at first sight. It does exist, and my love for you only seems to multiply."

"You just melted me." I pull him in, never taking my eyes off his.

"Good." He lands his lips on mine. "Because I want to keep melting you, and kissing you, and loving you for the rest of our lives."

"Well, you're off to a damn good start."

"That's because you make it easy." He leans in with a quick kiss. "And thank you for my gift."

"What's that?"

"For giving me the perfect someone to love."

I examine him like this, with that sexier-than-hell smile of his breaking loose, that sparkle he gets in his eye whenever we're together. I hope I always have the ability to put it there.

"Thank *you*, for giving *me* the perfect someone to love."

Cruise draws me to him, and our lips crash as we engage in a kiss that encompasses our past, our present, and our future together.

Whatever the future holds I'm okay with it because with friends like Lauren and Ally, a brother like Morgan, and a husband like Cruise by my side, I know we can get through it together.

Sometimes that's enough in life—good friends, family, and someone to love.

Thank you for reading *Someone for Me*. If you enjoyed this book, please consider leaving a review at your point of purchase.

ACKNOWLEDGMENTS

To my awesome, awesome readers! I hope you've had just as much fun with the Someone to Love series as I have. Thank you for your tremendous and kind support through the years, and I hope to share many more wonderful stories with you in the future. You're amazing, and I really do love you like family.

To my husband and four wonderful children: You're so much better at laundry and doing the dishes now than ever before. I couldn't have written a single word without your backbreaking help. And my favorite thing to hear is still "I can't believe you used to do all this by yourself." It's nice to know you've got my back. I will always have yours.

To the outstanding team over at Skyscape—Marilyn Brigham, Courtney Miller, Jenna Free, Robin Cruise, and all those in marketing and sales and everyone else who put an effort into making the Someone to Love series sparkle and shine—I thank you profusely from the bottom of my heart.

A special thank-you to my literary agent, Rachelle Gardner, my rock through all this madness. Thank you for your unwavering support and wealth of great advice. I'm so thankful that you've put up with all of my crazy shenanigans, and for that I'm forever indebted. Ready for more shenanigans?

To Him who holds the world in the palm of His hands, thank you—I owe you everything.

ABOUT THE AUTHOR

ADDISON SIEGEL

Addison Moore is a *New York Times*, *USA Today*, and *Wall Street Journal* bestselling author who writes contemporary and paranormal romance. Her work has been featured in *Cosmopolitan* magazine. Previously she worked for nearly a decade as a therapist on a locked psychiatric unit. She resides with her husband, four wonderful children, and two dogs on the West Coast, where she eats too much chocolate and stays up way too late. When she's not writing, she's reading.

Feel free to visit her blog at:
http://addisonmoorewrites.blogspot.com

Facebook: https://www.facebook.com/pages/Addison-Moore/140192649382294

Twitter: https://twitter.com/AddisonMoore